Now And Forever

Michele Brouder

This is a work of fiction. Names, characters, places and incidents are either a product of the author's imagination or are used fictitiously, and any resemblance to actual persons, living or dead, events, or locales is entirely coincidental.

Editing by Jessica Peirce

Book Cover Design by Rebecca Ruger

Now and Forever

Copyright © 2023 Michele Brouder

All Rights Reserved. No part of this book may be reproduced or transmitted in any form or by any means, electronic or mechanical, including photocopying, recording, or by any information storage and retrieval system, without permission in writing from the author.

Chapter One

Della

Della Rossi smiled at the retreating figure of the town's doctor, Sam Morrison, as he left her olive oil shop. She liked the look of him, most especially his self-assurance and the way he carried himself. It helped, of course, that he had beautiful thick brown hair that she longed to touch and run her fingers through. Sam had just dropped off some fresh zucchini and tomatoes for her, which he grew in his backyard garden, just like Della's late father used to do. It wasn't an extravagant gift, but a gesture she found touching just the same. She watched him against the backdrop of the colorful awnings of the shops along Main Street in Hideaway Bay, until he disappeared completely.

Next to her, Sue Ann Marchek, her able assistant and best friend, raised her eyebrows.

"What?" Della asked, feigning innocence.

"Dr. Morrison is already halfway down Main Street and you're still smiling. *And* there's a twinkle in your eye."

Sam was a frequent topic of conversation between Della and Sue Ann, one that Della never tired of. Sue Ann insisted that Della had a crush on the doctor and that Sam was equally as smitten with Della.

Della laughed and protested feebly, "There's nothing going on there."

"Isn't there?" Sue Ann said with one eyebrow slightly arched, not fully convinced.

"Of course not." She scoffed at the idea that she was flirting with one of her customers. Especially the town's doctor. Not that she was one of his patients. She'd been going to a Dr. Beverly Acker in Lavender Bay, the next town over, and she was happy there even if it meant a bit of a drive.

"I may not know much, but I know Dr. Morrison goes through a lot of olive oil," Sue Ann pointed out. "He must be bathing in the stuff."

Della snorted; she couldn't help it. It was true that Sam was in the shop several times a week. His favorite balsamic vinegar was a toss-up between the black cherry–flavored one and the tangerine, and he'd recently purchased a stainless steel olive oil can. And it was remarkable how many boxes of assorted olive oils he'd bought as gifts for friends, family, and staff.

Before Sue Ann could comment further, Isabelle Monroe approached the counter with a basket full of items. Isabelle was one of those enviable women who were naturally beautiful. Tall and lithe, and toned from all the swimming she did, she had an abundance of long, dark, curly hair that was currently held back with a scarf. Her face was smooth and tanned, and she wore no cosmetics. Meanwhile, Della didn't venture out of the house unless she'd done her hair and put on her "face."

"Hey, Isabelle, how's everything?" Della asked.

"Fine." The oldest Monroe sister unloaded two bottles of olive oil, one small bottle of espresso sugar, and two different kinds of popcorn toppings onto the counter.

"How's Alice?" Sue Ann asked.

Alice Monroe was the youngest of the three sisters, and her wedding to Jack 'The Colonel' Stirling was scheduled for September. According to the gossip, the guest list was ever-burgeoning, with practically the whole town being invited. Della was looking forward to it. It had been a while since there'd been a proper wedding on the beach. There'd been the occasional impromptu matrimonial ceremony but nothing in the recent past of this size or scale. A beach wedding was the most romantic thing, Della thought, especially in the evening with the sun setting over Lake Erie.

"She's nervous, as you can imagine," Isabelle said. "It's all Lily and I can do to keep her calm. As much as I'm looking forward to the event, I'll be glad when it's over, for Alice's sake."

"Where are they going for their honeymoon?" Sue Ann asked.

"They haven't decided yet."

"And how are Joe and the kids?" Della asked. Isabelle had been seeing Joe Koch, a widower with three children, for more than a year. It seemed serious enough.

Isabelle broke into a huge smile. "They're fine. Joe's actually out of town right now for a teachers' conference."

"The shoe is on the other foot," Sue Ann said with a nod. "It's usually you flying off to different parts of the country, writing your magazine articles."

Isabelle laughed. "It is."

"Are Joe's parents watching the kids?" Della asked.

Isabelle shook her head and smiled. "No, they're on an Alaskan cruise. I'm staying at Joe's with the kids for the week."

Della gave Isabelle a lot of credit; she had no children of her own, and being with Joe meant taking on his three kids of various ages and personalities. Certainly not for the faint of heart. But then Isabelle seemed formidable in her own right.

"What will you do with them?"

"The same things we usually do," Isabelle said. "If the weather holds, I may take them camping over the weekend."

"How's it going so far?"

"Fine. They're good kids. It's the dog, Luther, that's the biggest problem."

"Ankle biter?" Della asked with a wince.

"Trash picker?" came from Sue Ann.

Isabelle laughed. "No, none of that, thank goodness. Joe is his person, and the dog is out of sorts without him there. He sits in the middle of the living room and stares at Joe's chair." She paused for effect before adding, "All day long."

"A cat would be better," Sue Ann chirped in. "They're fiercely independent." It was known throughout town that Sue Ann had adopted a rather large stray cat she'd named Ivan. The tom now sported a collar with a tiny bell and slept indoors at night. He was living his best life.

"I'm so used to Charlie," Isabelle said, referring to her sister Lily's Great Dane.

"I think smaller dogs tend to be more hyper," Della said with a grimace as thoughts of her grandmother's Pekingese came to mind. He was both a biter and a barker. On reflection, she thought, he really had no redeeming features. Della herself had no pets; she didn't want to be tied down. And her mother, whom she lived with, had never seemed keen on animals in the house.

Another customer approached, and Isabelle pulled her bag off the counter and said, "I'll see you later."

"Don't forget the social club has an informational meeting coming up on doing genealogy research." Della pulled a flyer off the countertop and handed it to Isabelle, who narrowed her eyes and scanned it.

"You know, I was thinking about doing a story about this," Isabelle said.

"Really?"

Sue Ann stepped away from their conversation to look after the other customer.

"Yes, especially with all this DNA testing."

Della tilted her head to one side. "What do you mean?"

There's been some fascinating stories about people finding out they're not who they think they are."

"Meaning?"

"Meaning someone up higher in the family tree may have had an encounter no one knew about that resulted in some biological surprises."

"That sounds awful." Della reflected for a moment and said, "I can't see that happening here. It's a pretty staid little town." That's what she liked about Hideaway Bay. It was full of good people. There wasn't a lot of drama.

"I don't know about that," Isabelle said. "Everyone has secrets."

"Maybe."

She waved goodbye and stepped outside into the sunshine. She pulled her sunglasses off the top of her head and put them on, walking away in the direction of her home.

Her last comment gave Della food for thought, but she shrugged and walked away. Her own family tree had sturdy roots.

Chapter Two

Alice

"Ugh," Alice said as she stepped off the scale. It was up by ten pounds. At this rate, she'd never fit into her delicate Edwardian-style wedding dress come September.

When she stepped out of the bathroom, she ran into Isabelle, who wore a look of concern on her face. "Everything all right? I thought I heard you groan."

Alice exhaled a deep breath. "I've put on ten pounds in the last month. I'll never fit into my dress."

"Do you think it has anything to do with all the baking you've been doing? I've put on five pounds myself," Isabelle countered with a grin.

There was truth in Isabelle's question. Alice had been baking up a storm. It distracted her from her anxiety, and her upcoming wedding had resulted in "a case of the nerves," as their Gram used to say. It wasn't that Alice didn't love Jack or didn't want to marry him; it was that she was nervous about this big life change.

"I'm trying to keep my mind off the wedding," Alice said as she followed Isabelle down the stairs.

"Maybe baking isn't the answer," Isabelle said.

"Probably not."

"We can't eat it all fast enough."

"Even Lily has put on a little bit of weight," Alice noted. "But she needed it. She looks great now." Lily now possessed curves.

"She does," Isabelle agreed.

They ended up in the laundry room at the back of the house. It wasn't a utility room per se; it had originally been a back porch, but the washer and dryer had ended up out there. Isabelle removed the wet clothes from the washing machine.

"It's such a nice day I think I'll hang these out back," she said, lifting the laundry basket.

"I'll help." Alice picked up the plastic basket of clothesline pegs off the shelf and held the back door for Isabelle.

Outside, the sky was blue with frail, wispy clouds, and the morning sun was climbing with increasing warmth. Isabelle set the basket down on the ground between them and hung one of her bathing suits, followed by a beach towel from her swim the previous night. Those after-dark swims had become a habit for her, and Lily and Alice were relieved that Joe was usually with her, along with the dogs, Charlie and Luther.

Isabelle moved left and Alice moved right.

"Do you want to get together tonight? You and Jack with Joe and me?" Isabelle asked, looking down the clothesline at her younger sister.

Alice shook her head. "I can't. I'm going to Della Rossi's social club."

"Oh? What's on tonight?"

Alice did an inward giggle. FOMO—fear of missing out—was the only way to describe Isabelle's expression.

"Della is heading up a genealogy project."

Isabelle dropped her arms to her sides, a clothes-peg in one hand, a wet item of clothing in the other. "Right, she mentioned that. You want to research our ancestors? We already know we're mainly English and Irish, with some Polish coming down through Grandma Reynolds's side. Unless you want to look into the Monroe side of things?"

Alice shrugged. Their father had abandoned them when they were young, and his family had not been a particular force for good or bad in any of their lives.

"Monroe also sounds like an English name," Alice said with finality. She'd made peace with the idea that she identified as a Reynolds more than a Monroe. It had nothing to do with DNA.

"Maybe," Isabelle said. "Unless they changed it when they came into the country. That happened a lot."

"No, I'm not going there for the genealogy aspect."

The furrow in Isabelle's forehead deepened and her mouth opened slightly. "You're going to a genealogy meeting, but you have no interest in finding out about our ancestors. You'll understand when I say I'm confused."

Alice laughed and waved her hand toward the back of their home. "I'd like to find out about the previous owners of the house."

"Why?"

Alice shrugged, still smiling. "I don't know. I'd like to know about the other families that lived here." She didn't know why this should come as such a shock to Isabelle; after all, she was a writer and investigated all sorts of things.

Isabelle snorted. "They're all dead now."

"I realize that, but this is a house that's full of happy memories for us, and I wonder if it was the same for everyone who lived here. We know Val Fisher's grandmother, the chocolatier, was happy here for a short time, but we don't know about anyone before that."

Isabelle picked up another article of clothing and pegged it to the line. "You work full time, you're baking up a storm, and you have a wedding in a couple of months. Do you really have time for all this?"

Her concern was valid. It was true, Alice had a lot on her plate. She and her law partner, Ben Enright, were busier than ever, sometimes working late and taking turns working a half day on Saturdays because they didn't want to turn people away. Baking relaxed her, so there was a lot of that going on in the run-up to her wedding, and she was giving out baked goods to just about everyone in town. As for the wedding planning, there wasn't much to do at the moment. Everything was booked, and all she had to do was sit back and wait until that final week when all sorts of last-minute things would need to be done. But still, she preferred all the busyness as a distraction. She didn't want to have too much time to think and brood about leaving the house on Star Shine Drive. They'd all been so happy there, even more so in recent years when she and her sisters reconnected after a period of estrangement. The house on Star Shine Drive was a magical place for all of them.

As she'd thought about this over the past months—she was the type to reflect before and after pivotal events in her life—she wondered if it had been true for the other families that had resided in the house.

Isabelle was speaking, but Alice was lost in her thoughts.

"Huh?"

"I said, is it wise to add one more thing to your to-do list?" Isabelle asked, taking the last item of clothing—a T-shirt—and attaching it to the clothesline.

"But if it's interesting and something you want to do, does it have to go on the to-do list?" Alice challenged.

"I don't want to see you get run down or stressed out."

"Said the oldest sister to the youngest sister," Alice said with a laugh.

"Accept that that will never change. When I'm eighty years old, I'll still be looking out for you."

I hope so.

Alice lifted the empty basket, but neither one of them moved.

"Why don't you come to the social club meeting," Alice suggested. "You could look into our Monroe side."

Recently, Isabelle had tracked down their long-absent father. It hadn't gone well, but it closed a door that had been slamming open and shut for most of their lives.

Isabelle snorted. "I don't have the time!" She opened her hand and ticked off her own list with her fingers. "Between dropping kids off to baseball, football practice for Aidan, escape rooms for Kyle and Mimi, and all the birthday parties and ballet and sleepovers for Casey, I wouldn't have time to wind my watch if I had one!"

"Do you mind doing all that?" Alice asked.

Isabelle's eyes brightened. "Are you kidding? I love it!" She appeared thoughtful for a moment. "I never thought motherhood was for me. And I don't regret not having kids, but I like this, this ready-made family. Not that I'm looking to replace their mother, but I like being a positive force in their lives and introducing them to different experiences."

Alice smiled. "Who knew Isabelle Monroe had such a soft spot!"

Isabelle put her finger to her lips and said, "Shh. Don't tell anyone. I have a reputation to maintain."

Alice traced an X over her heart. "Cross my heart and all that."

Her gaze settled on the house once again. Although it wasn't the biggest house on Star Shine Drive, to her it was the loveliest. It had been a house filled with love. Had it been like that for everyone who had lived there? She found it hard to believe otherwise.

But she was determined to find out.

Chapter Three

"Mom, are you coming to the meeting tonight?" Della asked from her position at the kitchen sink, where she was rubbing an ice cube against a piece of gum on the bottom of her sandal. She'd stepped in it on her walk home from work. They were her favorite pair of summer shoes, so she rubbed vigorously as the ice slowly melted in her hand.

"No I am not," her mother said sharply.

Della smiled to herself. Her mother, Jeanne Rossi, had strong opinions on things, and had no problem verbalizing them. Jeanne currently sat at the kitchen table, which was covered in newspapers, working on her stained-glass art. When she had retired from her nursing job twenty years ago, she'd vowed she wasn't going to spend her days watching television. And she hadn't. She kept busy. She'd started with the stained glass three years ago, when she'd taken some classes and had been hooked. It was one of her longest-running hobbies aside from scrapbooking, and she liked to do jigsaw puzzles, but only on a winter night.

The ice cube had melted, but Della didn't give up. There was only a small piece left of the sticky residue. When the last piece was removed, Della, feeling victorious, wiped the bottom of the shoe with a paper towel, slipped it back onto her foot, and gave her hands a good wash as her mother had taught her many years ago.

She joined her mother at the table and leaned over her shoulder, watching the gnarled hands work the glue gun and fit the pieces in. On her left ring finger, Mrs. Rossi still wore her plain gold wedding band, even though Della's father had been dead for years.

The current project showed a black-and-white striped lighthouse on green grass against a cobalt-blue sky.

"That's pretty, Mom," Della said.

"Thanks, honey."

Della looked at her mother and tried one more time. "Aren't you interested in learning who your ancestors were?" Genealogy was a popular hobby among the retired set.

Jeanne stopped what she was doing and looked up at her daughter. "Now why would I want to find out about my dead relatives? I didn't even know them."

Point taken. "All right, Mom. I'll see you later."

Jeanne turned her head as Della headed out of the kitchen. "And don't rush home to me, I'm fine. Have a life."

"I'm fine, too, Mom," Della said with a laugh.

When she'd been working her power job in New York City all those years ago, never once did she imagine she and her mother would be roommates at any point in her life. The thought made her chuckle. Life could be so funny sometimes. When she returned to Hideaway Bay to help care for her father as his health declined, she'd moved in with her parents. After his death, she had never gotten around to moving out of the family home.

She'd adored her father and was proud of her Italian heritage, even if she did take after her mother's side in regard to her looks. She and her mother had been living together for more than a decade now, and neither interfered with the other's life. Her mother had never been that type. She'd said repeatedly that Della needed to live her own life. They got on pretty well. From time to time, she entertained the idea of moving out and getting her own place, even buying a home—she certainly had the money to support that—but those thoughts were fleeting, and things went on as they were.

It might have become awkward if she'd had a man in her life, but Della had been too busy these past few years building up her business, the Hideaway Bay Olive Oil Company, on Main Street. In a sense, it was the love of her life. Not that she wouldn't have liked to have a partner or a significant other or even the old-fashioned term of boyfriend, but at her age—late forties—it seemed almost impossible.

She headed back to the bathroom, where she applied some mascara and put on clear lip gloss. After she put her cosmetics away, she finger-scrunched her bob-length hair and headed out, excited about the possibilities of this genealogy project. She was eager to explore her own past and heritage. Her father's parents had come over from Italy over ninety years ago as a newly married couple, and she remembered her grandmother talking about the old country from time to time.

It was Della's dream to go to Italy someday, and wouldn't it be something if she could find the town her grandparents had come from. She couldn't recall her grandmother ever mentioning it, and her father, though the son of immigrants, had always been forward-looking, speaking at length of his love for America, not interested in looking back. As Della aged, her heritage had become increasingly important to her. She was sorry she hadn't asked more questions when they were alive.

The evening was warm and dry, so she decided to walk over to the parish hall from her house on Starlight Drive. The sky was beautiful shades of deep red, orange, and purple. She loved this time of year.

Most of the residents were outside enjoying the warm summer evening. They were riding bikes, pushing strollers, tending to gardens, mowing lawns or sitting on their front porches sipping lemonade and watching the daylight fade. She waved and said hello to everyone she passed. As the owner of a busy local shop, she knew just about everyone.

On the walk over, her father came to mind as he often did, and thinking about him brought a smile to her face. Because she'd been born on the Fourth of July of the bicentennial year, her father's nickname for her had been "firecracker." She'd give anything to hear him call her that one more time. With a sigh, she realized that no matter how long someone you loved was gone, you never stopped missing them. Your life did go on, you put one foot in front of the other every day, and it wasn't long before there was a lot of time between the loss and the present. Time was no healer, but it was a buffer, and it did temper that rawness of new grief.

The parking lot of the parish hall was packed with cars. The social club had been her brainchild as a way to force her to do something other than work. There'd been a need for more balance in her life; she needed to do things that were fun, things she was interested in. As a small-business owner, it was all too easy to spend every waking minute working at the shop.

As soon as she pushed through the doors, the buzz of noise increased as the sounds of conversation and the tinkle of laughter carried out to her. The place was notorious for poor acoustics. There'd been talk of tearing the hall down and rebuilding a more purpose-built function space, but some of the townspeople were nostalgic as the older generation remembered when it was built back in the '40s.

Della was pleased to see that every seat was occupied. She'd been there earlier in the day, setting up. She was glad for the turnout. There were a lot of people interested in tracing their family tree, and lots of familiar faces in the crowd.

Sue Ann and her boyfriend, Dylan Satler, a local carpenter who specialized in home improvements, were at the front of the room, organizing things. Dylan had initially resisted joining the group but then decided if Sue Ann was doing it, so was he. They were such a cute couple, Della thought.

Jackie Arnold was there with her boyfriend, Tom Anderson. His father, Ben Anderson, was also there. In the back row was Baddie Moore, holding a notebook and pencil against his thigh.

Alice Monroe was there, but her sisters were not. Conspicuously absent was Thelma Schumacher. When Della had approached her about joining them, she'd snorted and said she was too afraid to find out anything about her ancestors. "It's a tree I don't want to shake too hard!" she'd said with a guffaw.

Also absent was Martha Cotter. Coming from a well-heeled family, Martha had said with a sniff that there was no reason to trace her genealogy; she already knew it by heart. And to prove that, she had rattled off her maternal line going all the way back to the American Revolution, which to Della seemed easy to remember given that all the women in Mrs. Cotter's family had been named Martha.

Tables and chairs had been set up, and everyone present had brought their laptops as there would be a tutorial and a walk-through of how to navigate online genealogy sites like Ancestry and Family Tree Maker, and tips for finding those elusive ancestors who'd left no paper trail.

Della couldn't wait to get the meeting started.

A woman entered the hall behind her, slightly breathless. She was tall with short, stylish silvery hair. Behind a pair of fire engine red eyeglasses were two arched eyebrows and a pair of bright blue eyes. A pair of long, thin silver earrings dangled from her ears.

Della didn't recognize the woman and asked, "Can I help you?"

"Yes," the woman said. "I'm Dina Carruthers. I'm looking for"—here she paused and looked down at something written on her hand—"Della Rossi."

The genealogist. Della thought it might be fun for the group if they had a professional on hand to offer suggestions and help them navigate their searches through birth and death certificates, census records, ships' manifests, and whatever else she could suggest.

She thrust out her hand. "That's me. I'm Della Rossi."

Dina Carruthers shook it heartily. "It's nice to meet you. I'm really looking forward to tonight."

"So am I," Della said. "What can I help you with?"

Dina lifted her floral Vera Bradley bag. "I've got my laptop here. I'll just need to plug it in and get my PowerPoint presentation onto a screen."

"We've got both a screen and a whiteboard ready for you."

The meeting lasted almost two hours as Dina gave a quick talk and tutorial, and walked them through the process of getting their DNA results via testing from some of the genealogy websites. Della sat in the front row with Sue Ann and Dylan, occasionally looking up from her laptop and over her shoulder at the sea of bent heads behind her, all working on their own family trees. Caught up in the excitement, she clicked through and ordered one of the DNA kits, charging it to her credit card and paying the extra fee for it to be expedited and her results pushed to the front of the line. She opted to have it shipped to the store as she didn't want comments from her mother, whom she was sure would be dismissive.

At the end of the evening, as they were stacking the chairs against one wall and the tables against another, Della was approached by Sam Morrison. Sue Ann lifted an eyebrow and grinned, elbowing Dylan next to her, who looked up, spied Della and Sam, and smiled.

Those two, Della thought. *They need a hobby other than trying to fix me up.*

"Della, how are you?" Sam asked.

"I'm great," she answered truthfully. "You?"

He smiled. "I can't complain."

She liked Sam Morrison. A lot.

Her gaze landed on his beautiful hair, and without thinking, she blurted, "Do you do your hair, or does it lie naturally like that?"

He burst out laughing, most likely not expecting this question. "It just dries like that."

"Lucky," she said wryly. Here she was, using all sorts of products and curling irons and blow-dryers every day to make sure she looked presentable in public, while *his* beauty routine involved walking out of the shower and that was it. Why was it that God had graced men with the beautiful eyelashes and the perfect hair? Was it some sort of divine joke?

"How's the shop?" he asked.

"Not much has changed since you were in yesterday," she teased.

He rubbed the back of his head and laughed. "I suppose I do come in a lot."

"You're my number one customer," she said with a grin. "I'm thinking of having a badge made up for you."

Now he reddened slightly.

"Out of curiosity," she asked, "can I ask what you're doing with the stuff? I mean, a bottle of olive oil should last more than two days."

More laughter. He opened his mouth to say something, but only a sigh blew forth. "To be honest, it's got its own cupboard now," he said.

"Oh, Sam," she said, not thinking. Like the rest of the town's residents, she'd always called him Dr. Morrison.

"Well, the truth is . . ." he started.

She bit her lip and held her breath.

"Dr. Morrison! Yoo-hoo, Dr. Morrison!" called someone.

Della's shoulders sagged. Sam sighed again at the interruption.

"Excuse me for one moment, Della," he said.

"Sure." She didn't know why, but she felt deflated. Needing a distraction, she walked away, intent on finishing the cleanup as most of the townspeople filed out of the hall. As she pushed through the doors of the kitchen in search of a broom, she spied Sam knee-deep in conversation with Edna Knickerbocker, who had driven over from her home in Lavender Bay and who was a known hypochondriac on this side of the state. Currently, she was rattling off a list of her most recent symptoms to the doctor, convinced she was dying.

When Della finally located a broom and dustpan—whoever had used them last had not returned them to their designated spot—Sam was gone.

Probably just as well, she thought with a sigh. *I'm sure he's too young for me.*

Chapter Four

Days later, Della's DNA test arrived at the shop.

"Is that what I think it is?" Sue Ann asked with a nod toward the package. "Mine arrived yesterday, and I already mailed my sample off this morning." She paused and added, "But it takes eight weeks to get the results."

"Eight weeks?" Della asked, surprised. Though she supposed testing people's DNA for their ancestry wasn't at the top of the priority list. She didn't mention to Sue Ann that she'd paid extra to get the whole thing expedited. She really wanted to see what region of Italy her ancestors came from.

"Go on in the back and do it, Della. There's no time to waste," Sue Ann said with a laugh.

"I suppose not." Della looked around her small shop. There was only one customer there.

Again, Sue Ann said, "Go on, I'll hold down the fort."

"Thanks, Sue Ann," Della said. Not for the first time, she thought hiring Sue Ann had been one of her smarter decisions.

She hurried back to her office, closed the door, and ripped open the parcel. She laid out the instructions over the blotter of her desk and opened up the kit. Within minutes, she'd read the pamphlet twice and assembled the test, ready to collect her saliva sample. You wouldn't think a quarter teaspoon of saliva would be difficult to gather, but apparently, if needed on demand, it took a while. Once she had her sample, she sealed it up in the biohazard envelope and tucked it neatly into the small box provided, taping all sides.

As she made her way through the store, she held up the small box and said to Sue Ann, "I'll run this over to the post office."

Sue Ann nodded. "No problem."

On her way back twenty minutes later, Della spotted Alice Monroe coming along the sidewalk toward her just outside the shop. Alice appeared deep in thought and did not seem to register that she was walking directly into Della's path.

Della put her arms out to prevent Alice from crashing right into her.

Alice blinked and looked up, momentarily startled. "Oh, Della, I'm sorry, I didn't see you there."

Della chuckled. "I know. You seem lost in thought."

Alice looked over her shoulder and with a frown said, "I'm on another planet today. I've passed the drugstore, and that was my destination."

Della studied her for a moment and lowered her voice. "Hey, is everything all right?"

"I have a lot on my mind," Alice said a little too quickly.

Della sighed in sympathy. "There's a lot to planning a wedding. All the details." Not that she knew from first-hand experience, but she'd known a ton of brides personally and had stood up in enough weddings to get the general idea that any kind of affair required a lot of planning, reserving venues, and then it was hurry up and wait until the final week, when it was an insane flurry of last-minute activity.

"Yes, here's hoping I remember everything," Alice said, looking less than convinced.

"I'm sure you will," Della reassured her. It was amazing how different the Monroe girls were from each other. "And I'm sure Isabelle and Lily are a great help."

Alice's expression lifted and brightened at the mention of her sisters. "They've been wonderfully supportive. Seriously, I couldn't have done it without them."

"It's as I expected."

"Right now, Lily and Simon are in Italy," Alice said enthusiastically. This was more like the Alice Della knew.

"I'd heard that through the grapevine." Della was envious of Lily and Simon. She'd get there too, someday. But she could hardly take off two weeks from the shop and go gallivanting around Europe. Not right now. When you were in business for yourself, it all fell on you, every single bit of it. You answered to no one, but you were accountable for everything. Still, she wouldn't trade it for the world. A smile tugged at the corners of her mouth. Some dreams were worth having.

Alice appeared thoughtful. "You know, Della, I don't think I've ever seen you in a bad mood."

She shrugged, not knowing what to say. It was true, it took a lot to upset her, but generally she considered herself lucky: she was happy.

"I'm sure I've been in a bad mood from time to time but . . ." Her voice trailed off, unable to finish as she couldn't remember the last time she'd been angry or irritable.

"You're a regular Pollyanna!"

Della winced at this description. "Ugh, not that."

Alice leaned forward slightly. "It was meant as a compliment."

"I know." Remembering the advice her father had given her years ago, she added, "Thank you."

"I really need to get to the drugstore now. Great talking to you, Della! You're like a tonic," Alice said, and she pivoted on her heel and headed back in the direction of the drugstore.

Della watched the young woman bounce off, glad she was able to help. Pushing through the front door of her shop, she thought how much she loved this town and her life.

Chapter Five

Alice

Alice had paperwork strewn across the dining room table, the beginnings of her search for the previous owners of the house on Star Shine Drive. Buoyed by everyone's enthusiasm at the genealogy meeting, she'd approached the genealogist with her questions, thinking the woman might have some ideas for her. Alice hadn't known where to start.

"It must be a very special house," Dina Carruthers said when Alice explained her project.

"It certainly is," Alice said. She relayed the tale of how it had been her grandparents' house, a house full of happy memories, and how she and her sisters had inherited it.

"Some families really do make a house a home," the genealogist had said.

That sentiment had played all week in Alice's mind. If her grandparents had lived in a tent, she would have loved that, too, as they had created a home full of love and laughter, affection and kindness for all of them.

But Dina had been a treasure trove of information for Alice. She'd suggested searching for the deed with the tax assessor's office and the town's archives, if they had such a system. And the library. Find out the previous owners and then search the old newspapers that the library would have on file to get a better sense of them in the context of the times in which they'd lived. And finally, Dina had suggested asking any neighbors who might remember. Alice thought she might try Martha Cotter as her family had always lived in the house on the corner, and Martha's mother or grandmother might have passed some information about the previous owners along to the current Martha. As ever, she was hopeful.

Over the period of a week, Alice spent her lunch either at the County Assessor's office or the town hall, looking into the previous deed holders. From there she went to the library and looked through old newspapers with the help of the librarian. Surprisingly, she had been sucked into the vortex while she wasn't looking. It was all fascinating information, knowing the names of the people who had lived within the walls of the house on Star Shine Drive.

She looked up from all the paperwork spread out before her to check the time on her phone.

Lily and Simon were due in at some point that day, returning from their two-week trip to Italy. They hadn't been in contact once, not even to check on Charlie. But Lily knew her dog was in good hands with Isabelle and Alice. Alice looked over at the dog, who was fast asleep in the corner of the dining room, his loud snores filling the space. She returned her attention to the list of names before her.

If someone had told her two years ago that she would be living with her sisters—and happily at that!—she would have scoffed. Even now she couldn't quite believe it. Maybe their age and maturity had something to do with them getting on so well. Maybe it had to do with the fact that each one of them had landed back in Hideaway Bay and had ended up satisfied with their return. And then maybe it was because of the family that had loved and raised them: their mom and their grandparents. They were all gone now, leaving just the three of them. She wished it could always be like this.

From the front of the house, she heard the door open, and Isabelle appeared in the dining room a moment later. Charlie woke, lifted his head, and thumped his tail a couple of times against the floor but did not get up.

Isabelle smiled at him and then swept her gaze around the room, landing on the paperwork littered across the table. Alice rested her elbows on the table, pen in hand.

"You've been busy."

"Searching the previous owners of the house has turned out to be far more interesting than I thought it would be," Alice responded.

"Anything juicy?"

"Not yet. All I have is a Cecil and Catherine Bernard having built this house in 1902. He was a businessman from Buffalo, and this was their summer home."

"Interesting."

"But they were only here until 1928."

"What happened to them?"

Alice frowned. "I don't know. I'm hoping to find that out at the library, or I could ask Martha Cotter, she might know."

"Good luck."

"Are you going to Joe's tonight?"

"Yes. Tonight's game night with the kids, wouldn't miss that," Isabelle said.

"There's a chocolate cake in the kitchen to take with you."

"They'll love that."

"Have you heard from Lily?"

Isabelle shook her head. "They're not landing in JFK until this afternoon, and they won't be in Buffalo until this evening. She didn't know if they might get a hotel in the city and drive home tomorrow or tonight. She said it depends on how tired they are."

"I can't wait to hear all about their trip," Alice said. Italy sounded like the trip of a lifetime.

"Aren't you and Jack supposed to meet the florist?"

Alice did not look at her, continuing to pore over deeds and old newspaper clippings. "I rescheduled that," she said.

"What? Why?"

"That time didn't work for me," Alice said.

"Alice! You're researching old records, for crying out loud. What are you doing?"

Alice looked up at her sister. "Nothing!"

Isabelle wouldn't let it drop. "What is going on with you? Your wedding is less than two months away."

"Nothing is going on. I rescheduled it, that's all." She used a tone that indicated she didn't want to talk about it.

But Isabelle wouldn't let it go. She lowered her voice. "Is everything all right between you and Jack?"

"Everything is perfect! Why wouldn't it be?"

Isabelle narrowed her eyes at her sister. "Maybe things are all right between the two of you, but something is going on here."

Alice looked at the paperwork without seeing it and muttered, "Don't quit your day job, Izzy."

The following evening, Alice stood in the kitchen, wrapping up trays of baked goods for Jack's veteran's group, which met weekly at the parish hall. Lily and Simon had decided to stay overnight and were due in Hideaway Bay soon.

Lily and Simon arrived around six, all smiles. Lily looked radiant, making Alice think the trip must have gone well.

The four of them stood in the front room with Charlie whining, his tail a blur as he circled Lily and leaned his weight against her, happy to see her. Lily bent and wrapped her arms around him, cooing at him. Charlie whined and thumped his tail harder.

When the dog finally settled down, Isabelle asked, "How was Italy?"

Lily and Simon exchanged a glance as if they shared a secret joke. Alice's eyes widened slightly. These two were up to something. Isabelle glanced at Alice and raised an eyebrow as if to say *What's going on here?*

They both spoke at once.

"It was amazing."

"Wonderful. Trip of a lifetime."

"That's great," Alice said, tucking their glowing recommendations away for future reference. She and Jack still had to make a decision about where to go for their honeymoon. It wasn't that they didn't want to go away, but Alice couldn't make up her mind. Europe? USA? Tropical? A cruise? All these decisions. Jack kept telling her he'd be happy to go anywhere.

"Let's sit down," Isabelle suggested. "Alice and I are anxious to hear all about it."

"Do you want something to eat?" Alice asked. "I can whip you both up a BLT if you want."

"I don't think I can eat any more. We stuffed our faces in Italy," Lily said, glowing. "The food was amazing!"

Simon wrapped his arm around Lily's waist and smiled at her. "Maybe we should tell them our news."

Lily leaned against his shoulder, smiling, and placed a hand on his chest. "Yes, let's."

They looked at Alice and Isabelle, and Lily announced, "We got married in Italy!"

"What?" Isabelle said, her mouth hanging open.

Alice clapped her hands against her mouth in disbelief.

Lily thrust her hand forward to reveal an emerald-shaped diamond solitaire with a matching diamond wedding band on her ring finger.

"I don't believe it!" Isabelle said excitedly and clapped her hands.

Alice's eyes filled with tears as both she and Isabelle rushed the couple to hug them and congratulate them. Alice was delighted for her sister; she had had some heartache with her first marriage and then widowhood, and no one deserved this happiness more than Lily.

"This calls for a celebration. Let me get the wine," Isabelle said.

"I'll get the snacks." Alice followed Isabelle out of the room. "Get comfortable because we'll want to hear all about it."

A charcuterie board and a dessert tray were quickly assembled. Alice and Isabelle carried them, along with a bottle of wine, out to the front porch, where Lily and Simon sat on the wicker two-seater shoulder to shoulder, thigh to thigh, their hands entwined.

Alice could not remember ever seeing Lily as happy and radiant as she was at that moment. The bottle of wine was opened and poured, and they all lifted their glasses and toasted the happy couple again.

"To Lily and Simon," Isabelle said.

"I'm dying to know," Alice said, "did you go to Italy to get married or was it a spur-of-the-moment kind of thing?" She set her wine glass down and popped an olive and a piece of cheese into her mouth.

"It was spontaneous," Simon replied. Grinning, he leaned over and kissed Lily on the cheek. "I consider myself the luckiest man on the planet."

Alice clapped her hands. "How romantic!"

"We thought so." Lily picked up a small dessert plate and put some crackers, cheese, and olives on it.

"What brought it on?" Isabelle asked.

"By the end of the first day, we knew that this trip was going to be something special," Lily started.

Simon picked up the story. "And we'd been talking about getting married."

"But we didn't want the fanfare," Lily said quietly.

"And we looked into it while we were there, and it worked out," Simon said with his lopsided grin and a shrug. "Like it was meant to be."

"It was absolutely beautiful," Lily said.

As Lily and Simon recounted the details of their elopement, Alice beamed, her cheeks hurting from smiling so much.

"So, I'm afraid I'm moving out," Lily said.

"We wouldn't expect you to keep living here with us," Isabelle said with a laugh.

The thought hadn't yet occurred to Alice. Lily was leaving. Their little group of three was breaking up, and they'd only recently gotten back together. It was too soon. She hadn't planned on the three of them living apart until she got married in September. But now, unexpectedly, they were down to two.

"And soon Alice will be leaving, and I'll be here all on my own," Isabelle said. Alice regarded her. She didn't sound too upset at that thought.

"It sounds like you don't mind that," Lily said.

"Not at all. I'm used to being on my own."

"All these changes," Alice said thoughtfully, trying to tamp down the sadness that was threatening to rise. Even happy events could be stressful, she remembered Gram saying once. How right she was.

As Lily and Simon spoke about their impromptu wedding and then showed them pictures of Rome, Alice was lost in her own thoughts. All this change. Lily and Simon, her and Jack, and Isabelle and Joe. This was the normal passage of life, and yet there was a part of her that wished they could stay there in the house on Star Shine Drive forever. As conversation bubbled around her, she looked off into the distance over the lake, narrowing her eyes, her nose irritating her as if the tears were right there below the surface, trying to break free.

"You'll be next, Sparrow," Isabelle said with a broad smile, calling Alice by her childhood nickname.

"Won't be long now," Lily chimed in.

Lily and Simon did not stay long. They left to go back to Simon's house, but Lily let Charlie stay at the house one more night at Isabelle's request.

"I'll pack up my things over the next few days," Lily said.

"There's no rush," Alice said.

Alice and Isabelle stood on the porch, smiling as the newly married couple walked arm in arm to their car parked out front along the curb.

"Well, that's that then," Isabelle said. They waited until Simon and Lily drove off with a wave to them both. When the car disappeared, Alice and Isabelle picked up the empty wine glasses, the plates, and trays and carried them into the house and back to the kitchen.

"I did not see that coming at all," Alice said as she stood at the garbage bin, foot on the pedal, scraping plates off into it.

"Neither did I, though I can't say I'm shocked," Isabelle admitted. She rinsed the empty wine bottle out at the sink and stepped into the back hall to set it in the plastic recycling bin designated for glass.

"I'm not either, really, I'm only surprised they chose to elope."

Isabelle shrugged. "To each their own, I guess. But having been to Italy several times, it's a great place to get married. I'm happy for her."

"Me too. She deserves this." Alice snapped the lid back on the brownie pan and set it at the edge of the counter. "That leaves you, Isabelle. Any plans on marrying Joe?"

Isabelle's smile was coy. "Who knows?"

"Evasive much?" Alice teased.

Isabelle shrugged. "I love Joe. Joe loves me. I love his kids. His kids love me. It's that simple."

Charlie walked around, bumping into them.

"Oh, poor you," Isabelle said, bending over and lavishing attention on the dog. Charlie's tail wagged happily in response. "Come on, Clumsy, let's go for a walk."

Excited, Charlie bounded from the kitchen to the front door, where he waited, whining.

Isabelle grabbed his lead from the back hall. "I'll take him for a walk on the beach."

"Good idea."

After the kitchen was cleaned up and wiped down, Alice went upstairs and ran a bath, throwing in a bath bomb and inhaling the soft, fragrant lavender scent. She sighed as she slipped into the water and leaned back. The clawfoot tub was ancient and deep. They didn't make them like they used to. She would miss this tub when she left.

She was truly happy for Lily, but with a lingering, weighty sadness, she pondered the idea of her and her sisters going off in their own directions.

The thought caused her to burst into tears.

Chapter Six

Della

Della rummaged among the papers on the counter next to the cash register and then turned her attention to the shelves below.

"Sue Ann, have you seen the invoice from Campanella and Brothers?" Della asked. She'd printed it up earlier and set it beneath the counter, but it was not there.

Sue Ann was looking out the front window of the shop, apparently not registering Della's question.

"Sue Ann?" Della gently prompted.

Her friend spun her head around. "Huh?"

"Have you seen the invoice? From Campanella and Brothers? I left it right here."

Sue Ann frowned and hurried behind the counter. "I did some cleaning up and tried to organize things, I must have misplaced it."

Earlier, in a fury of industriousness, Sue Ann had gone through the shop, rotating stock, lining up each and every product facing forward on its shelf and wiping everything down with a damp cloth. There had been no shortcuts.

"It's all right. I'll print up another one."

Sue Ann bent over, pushing through things on the lower shelf. When she had no luck there, she picked up the wastepaper basket and dug through it. Della grimaced, grateful it was only paper trash.

Finally, Sue Ann pulled out the invoice as if it were a winning lottery ticket. "Here it is!" And with that, she slapped it down on the countertop.

"Sue Ann?" Della regarded her friend with concern.

"Yes?"

"What is wrong?"

"What? Me?"

Worried, Della asked, "You're not yourself today. Are you okay?" Briefly, she wondered if Sue Ann and Dylan had had a disagreement, but she quickly dismissed it; they seemed pretty solid. And Sue Ann's son Noah had visited a couple of weeks ago and she'd been in a great mood after that.

It was as if a cloud had descended and shrouded her golden-haired, blue-eyed friend in a sad fog.

"Is it the boys?" she asked, almost dreading the answer.

"No," Sue Ann said. "No, the boys are fine." The mention of her sons brought a smile to her face.

"Then what is it?"

Sue Ann folded her arms tightly against her chest and looked around the empty shop, her eyes filling with tears. She bit her lip and sighed. Della hoped the store would remain quiet for a bit if only to give her friend some space and time. Sue Ann was clearly upset.

"I had a call from my older brother last night. My father died."

Of all the things she'd expected Sue Ann to say, this wasn't it.

"Wow, how old was he?"

Sue Ann snorted. "One hundred and two."

Della didn't know what to say. She knew Sue Ann's story. Her father had been her mother's third husband, and he'd made it clear he wanted no children. Somewhat older than Sue Ann's mother, Barb, he had children from a previous marriage and wanted no more. But then Sue Ann came along, and the marriage hadn't been able to recover, and Barb moved back to Hideaway Bay with Sue Ann in tow.

"My brother wanted to know if I was coming out to California for the funeral."

Della waited, deciding it was best to let Sue Ann get it out in her own good time. Sometimes, the need to unburden was great and could not be rushed.

Sue Ann shook her head and scoffed. "Do you know when the last time was that I heard from my father?"

"No."

"When my mother died, almost thirty years ago! He sent a huge floral bouquet and then after that, nothing. Never heard from him again." Pain was evident in her voice.

It must have been heart-wrenching to be abandoned by a parent like that. Della had been raised by a father who had adored her. She couldn't imagine that kind of hurt. She was full of empathy for Sue Ann.

"Are you going to go?" she asked gently.

"That's just it, I don't know. I mean, technically, he is—or was—my father, and I suppose I should go even if our link is purely biological. But then I mean, really, do I have to? Where is the rule that says you have to go to the funeral of a parent who never acknowledged your existence?"

Anxious to comfort and support her friend, Della said, "Sue Ann, don't torture yourself. There's no obligation to go."

Sue Ann sighed and bit her lip. "I don't know what to do."

"What about your brothers and sisters?" Della asked. Sue Ann hardly ever mentioned them, but she did keep in touch with at least some of them.

"I think my brother called me because he'd like me to come out. They're not getting any younger either. They're all in their seventies."

"Look, why don't you take the rest of the day off. As you can see, it's quiet here, and I can handle it."

Sue Ann protested. "I can't do that. I won't leave you high and dry."

Della gave her a reassuring smile. "You're not leaving me high and dry."

Sue Ann hesitated, and it was the opening Della needed. "Go home. You've got a lot to think about. It's a beautiful day for a walk. You should go up to the corner and see the sunflower field. It's in full bloom."

Behind the Anderson fruit and vegetable stand was a large field of sunflowers, the legacy of the late librarian, Carol Rimmer. It was lovingly tended every year from seed by Jackie Arnold. Residents loved it so much they brought their own lawn chairs and set them up behind the farm stand to enjoy the flowers.

When Sue Ann appeared to hesitate, Della added, "Summer is winding down, you should get out and enjoy it while you can."

Very slowly, almost reluctantly, Sue Ann tugged off her shop apron.

"All right, but if it gets busy, call me and I'll come back."

Della laughed and held her hand out for the apron. "I'm sure I can handle it." She didn't point out that she'd worked in the shop by herself for a couple of years before she'd hired Sue Ann.

Sue Ann folded the apron up carefully and handed it to Della. "Thank you for being so understanding," she said.

"That's what friends are for. Now go on."

"All right. I'll be back in the morning."

"Okay."

Sue Ann left with the weight of the world on her shoulders, and Della felt sorry for her. It was a tough call, and it was one she was glad she didn't have to make.

A man entered the store and looked around the place. He was tall and appeared to be in his sixties. He was tan and fit with a mop of gray hair. His skin was the color of caramel, like someone who'd spent a lot of his life in the sunshine.

"Hello and welcome," she said, stepping out from behind the counter. He was unfamiliar but that was fine, it wasn't only locals who came into the shop.

"Thank you. Nice place you've got here," he said, looking around.

"Thanks," she said proudly.

"Are you Della Rossi?"

"I am," she said.

"I saw your name on a flyer around town for the social club and thought there could only be one Della Rossi."

She smiled, but she was confused.

"You probably don't remember me. I was fifteen when you were born," he said, thrusting out his hand. "Mark Nugent."

"Oh wow! Yes." His mother, Betty, had been a childhood friend of her mother's. "Are you back for a visit?" She knew some of the Nugents lived out of town, but her mother kept in touch with all of them.

"Actually, I retired from teaching this year," he said. "And I've moved back to Hideaway Bay."

"Good for you."

"Would I be able to visit your mom?"

"Of course, she'd love to see you. I'll let her know you might stop by."

"Please. We need to catch up."

They made small talk for a few minutes, and he bought some olive oil and balsamic vinegar. As he was leaving, Della promised she'd pass on the message to her mother.

After lunch, business picked up, and currently there were several customers browsing through the shelves and the special displays on the endcaps. In the midst of this, there was a ping on Della's phone, notifying her of a recent email. She glanced at it quickly just as a customer approached the counter, and a frisson of excitement pulsed through her when she spotted the familiar Ancestry logo. The DNA results were in. She was so excited her feet barely touched the ground. As she'd sent Sue Ann home, it would have to wait until the end of the day when she locked up the store and retreated to her office at the back of the shop.

Despite being busy, the day dragged. She helped customers, matching up the right vinegars and olive oils to taste and then upselling some sea salt or popcorn toppers at the register.

When closing time rolled around, she flipped the sign on the front window around to read "closed." She bolted the door and turned off the lights in the front of the shop. Across the street, the sun was just disappearing behind the shops as it descended toward the horizon.

Lights had been left on in the back of the shop, and she made her way through the small storeroom to her office. There was one small window in her office, which overlooked the parking lot behind the buildings on this side of Main Street.

Atop her desk were piles of paperwork, all of which needed attending to, but she pushed them aside and cleared the space to make room for her laptop, which she opened and powered up.

Excitedly, she logged into Ancestry.com and clicked on the DNA icon for results. The ethnicity estimate opened up first, and she scanned it quickly. Expecting to find Italy at the top of the list, she laughed when it wasn't. Her gaze ran the length of the list, her lips moving silently as she read the geographic regions mentioned. Germanic Europe was at the top with 40 percent, followed by equal parts England, Ireland, and Scotland, which accounted for her mother's side.

No Italy.

She narrowed her eyes in confusion. Glancing up quickly to the top of the report, she verified it was her name and that there hadn't been a mix-up. But still no Italy. Nothing at all in that region or even the ones surrounding it.

"That can't be right," she muttered to herself. Finally, she shrugged it off and chalked it up to a technical glitch. Yawning, she decided she'd look into it the next day. All she wanted to do was go home and soak in the tub. There were a few things that needed to be done before locking up and going home, and she shut down her laptop and thought no more of it. She went through her evening ritual of locking up the place and turning on the alarm before exiting out the back door. She cut through the parking lot behind the storefronts, came out on Beach Street and headed north, crossing Erie and landing on Starlight Drive, where she and her mother lived.

As she approached their home, she smiled. It was the house she'd grown up in, and it held so many wonderful memories she didn't think she'd ever be able to leave it. It had a deep porch and a low, clean roofline. The landscaping company had been there earlier as evidenced by the freshly edged flower beds and the newly mown lawn. She missed the presence of her father in the garden. It was the one place that reminded her most of him. Someday, she promised herself, she was going to grow tomatoes and eggplant and zucchini just like he had. That brought a smile to her face, and she picked up her pace, eager to get home and relax.

As usual, Della's car was parked in front of the garage—she rarely used it, preferring to walk everywhere—and her mother's behind it. But there were several other cars parked by the curb in front of their house. She'd forgotten tonight was her mother's game night, when she had three of her friends over for Scrabble. It seemed like fun, Della thought, and once in a while when they were short a player, she would sit in. Despite the fact that they were all over eighty, they were an active, feisty group of women.

All were accounted for: Mary, Rose, and Lois. The four women sat around the card table Jeanne had set up in the living room. A Scrabble board was parked in the middle of it. Each woman had her tiles on a wooden rack in front of her and a drinking glass sweating on a coaster next to her. Mary and Lois were lifelong friends of her mother's, and Rose had been around for as long as Della could remember; she and Jeanne had worked at the hospital together. Snacks had been laid out on the sideboard on the far side of the room: there was Rose's pineapple upside-down cake; a tray of subs cut into two-inch pieces, compliments of Lois; and Mary's pinwheels—soft tortillas spread with cream cheese, sprinkled with diced black olives and red and green peppers, rolled up and sliced. Della hoped to get a piece of the cake later.

She said her hellos, and they exchanged small talk for a few minutes.

"You'll never guess who came into the shop today," Della said.

All four women looked at her.

"Mark Nugent."

The expressions of her mother, Mary, and Lois softened, as they'd been good friends since childhood with Mark's mother.

The questions began.

"How is he?"

"Is he still in Chicago?"

"What's he doing in Hideaway Bay?"

"He's retired from teaching," Della replied.

"He's that old?" Mary asked with a shake of her head. "How can that be?"

"The same way that we're in our eighties, that's how that can be," Lois said, amused.

"He's moved back to Hideaway Bay," Della said.

"Good for him," her mother said.

"He said he might pop in and visit."

"Good. I'd like to see him."

"I hope he stops by and sees me too," Mary said.

Message delivered, Della headed upstairs, where she closed her bedroom door and removed her clothes, tossing them on the chair next to the window. In the bathroom, she ran the bath, slipped out of her robe, and stepped into the tub as it was filling. As much as she wanted to soak for a while, she was so tired she was afraid of falling asleep, and she didn't treasure the thought of waking up in a tub full of cold water.

After she dried off, she dressed in shorts and a T-shirt and got herself a glass of lemonade and a plate of cake. She used her elbow to push through the screen door in the front, balancing the plate in one hand and the glass in the other.

"You should put something on your feet," Rose called out after her.

Della smiled; not even her own mother would suggest that. For if there was one thing Della loved, it was being barefoot. If she could, she'd go barefoot at work, but she supposed her customers—not to mention the NYS Department of Health—would frown on that sort of thing. She looked westward, liking the soft violet of the sky. She parked the glass on the table beside her, held the plate of cake in her hand, and forked a piece off, sliding it into her mouth.

Nothing could have surprised her more when she spotted Sam Morrison strolling by, his hands tucked in the pockets of his khaki shorts. It dawned on her that she'd never seen his bare legs before. Immediately, she blushed, thinking she shouldn't be entertaining thoughts of the doctor's bare legs or any other bare parts.

She sat up straighter, unsure as to whether to wave or not. Would he think she was beckoning him? Would he think she was rude if she ignored him?

Sam made the choice for her. He'd spotted her, and threw his hand up in a wave, cut across the grass, and made his way toward the porch steps. Pieces of fresh-mown lawn clung to his shoes.

Happy to see him, she set the plate down next to the glass and checked the front of her shirt for any stray cake crumbs. From inside the house, she could hear the twitters and giggles of her mother and her friends.

"Della."

"Hello, Sam. What brings you around to these parts?" Starlight Drive ran parallel to Star Shine, and most walkers preferred the beach or did the loop from the end of Star Shine Drive to Main Street, circling around the town's gazebo. Only those who were dedicated to getting their steps in would walk the side streets that ran off of Erie Street.

"Actually, I'm here for a reason," he said. He put one foot on the bottom step and leaned forward.

She stood from her chair, aware that her feet were bare, her face devoid of makeup, and her hair clipped back messily from her face. Suddenly, she felt self-conscious. She joined him at the bottom of the steps.

"Come up and sit down," she said. "Would you like something to drink? Some pineapple upside-down cake?"

He shook his head. "I might not be here for that long." He laughed nervously and then coughed into his elbow to cover it up.

She tilted her head and regarded him with a benevolent smile, slightly confused. She folded her arms across her chest and waited, expectant.

"I have two tickets to the concert in the park up in the city on Friday. Would you like to go with me?"

This caught her off guard. Did she want to go with him—yes, of course. But that didn't mean she should. There were so many reasons not to. They were both prominent in the community; did she want to be the object of gossip? What if it became messy? She was a no-fuss, no-drama type of person.

He let out more laughter and rubbed the back of his head. It was a gesture she'd seen him do before in her presence; maybe it was something he did when he was nervous. Which begged the question *Why would he be nervous around her?*

"Your hesitancy does not bode well for me," he said.

"Can I ask you a question?"

"Answering a question with a question. I didn't know there was going to be a quiz."

A bark of laughter escaped Della's lips. His humor alone was very sexy.

"Go ahead." His smile indicated he was humoring her. Boy, she couldn't help but like him. She could get used to seeing that smile every single day.

"How old are you?" she asked. A foolish question perhaps, but important to her nonetheless.

"What?" he asked as if he hadn't heard her correctly.

She lowered her voice, realizing it might sound ridiculous. But she had to know. "How old are you?"

His answer came in the form of a question. "Forty-four?"

Shoot. She was three years older than he was. She winced at the thought of it.

"Too old or too young?" he queried.

"Not you. Me."

"Is this going to turn into one of those 'it's not you, it's me' moments?"

He was funny and he did make her laugh, but there was no way around the age difference.

"It's me. I'm three years older than you."

"So?"

The evening was punctuated by the increasing drone of crickets, the buzz of a lawn mower on the next street over, and the tinkle of the conversation and laughter floating from the house.

"You don't think it's a problem?" she asked.

"It'd be a problem if I was fifteen and you were eighteen, but not now. Unless you think I'm not finished growing and maturing?"

She burst out laughing. This guy was such a joker. "No, of course not."

"That's a relief. But seriously, we have to wrap this up because my mother wants me home before the streetlights go on."

Grinning, she asked, "Are you ever serious?"

"Sure, all day long," he said.

Even though he wasn't her primary care physician, she'd heard from other townspeople that Sam Morrison had a great bedside manner. His patients loved him.

His charm was irresistible, but still she hesitated.

"Can I think about it?" she said.

"Sure," he said easily.

And they left it at that. Della wanted to go out with him, but the age difference bothered her. She'd talk to Sue Ann the next day at work and ask for her feedback.

As she watched Sam walk up the street, away from her, she wondered why she needed to confer with Sue Ann. Wasn't she able to make the decision herself?

Sue Ann had other things on her mind the following morning at the shop, and Della didn't want to bother her with something as trivial as her dating life. Besides, she was a grown woman running a successful business. She should certainly be able to decide for herself whether she wanted to go out with Sam or not.

"Have you decided what you're going to do about your father's funeral?" she asked Sue Ann when there was finally a lull in the brisk trade of the morning.

"I have, and I wanted to talk to you about it. I'm going to go," Sue Ann declared.

"Okay," Della said. She was glad Sue Ann had made a decision. Sometimes once a decision was made, it made you feel better.

"I'm sorry for the short notice, but I'll need some time off."

Della gave her friend a reassuring smile. "Don't worry about a thing. This is more important."

"It's not for my father that I'm going. It's because of my brother. He's kept in touch with me sporadically through the years, which is more than anyone else on the West Coast did."

Della nodded sympathetically.

"Dylan is going to go with me. We're leaving the day after tomorrow. I'll be gone a week."

Della made a mental note to make changes to Sue Ann's schedule. She never understood bosses who gave their employees a hard time for taking off for funerals and such. Family was so important. Probably the most important thing. It was how she'd been raised. Growing up, every Sunday was spent at her grandmother Rossi's house.

As Sue Ann was preoccupied, Della didn't bother her with her question about Sam. The more she thought about it, the more she thought, *Why not?* So what if she was three years older than him. What did that have to mean, if anything? He was kind and she found him very attractive. Her being a bit older didn't have to mean anything unless she wanted it to.

She dashed off a text and told him he could pick her up at seven in the evening. It took him a while to respond, but she knew he was probably busy with patients. He eventually sent a one-word text: *Great!*

After Sue Ann left, Della went to the back room and logged into Ancestry. She'd put it off, dreading the phone call to their customer service. She'd rather pull out her eyelashes than dial a customer service line. Invariably, it was either an automated system that did not offer the options you wanted, or worse, the wait was so long you'd grow old.

She looked at her results again, thinking there was no way they could be right. There had to have been some mistake. Scrolling down the page, she was considering her options when her older brother Terry's name popped up. He'd done a DNA test? She was surprised; he'd never mentioned it. But even more surprising was the phrase *half sibling* beside his profile.

What?

Now she knew there was definitely something wrong. Her two older brothers, Terry and Joey, were most certainly not half siblings. She pulled the handset of her office phone from the cradle and dialed the toll-free number for Ancestry. It was obvious that her results had been mixed up with someone else's. At the back of her mind something nagged at her, but she was unable to define it.

The wait time was ten minutes. As she waited, she stared at the results and in the quiet of the on-hold elevator music, a thought seeded in her mind, took hold, and mushroomed. But the thought was so awful that she laughed out loud and dismissed it, feeling guilty for even entertaining such an outrageous idea.

The woman at the other end of the line was courteous and helpful. No, Della's DNA results hadn't been mixed up. Yes, she could take the test again, but the results would be the same. She was sorry that no Italian heritage showed up in her ethnicities, but those were the results. And, the woman stressed, their DNA tests were fairly accurate.

The whole conversation was an exercise in frustration. Della felt she was no further ahead. So much for genealogy being an enjoyable hobby.

Finally, she said, "But it doesn't make sense. My brother is on Ancestry, and he's showing up as my half sibling. How can that be?"

There was a long, drawn-out silence, and then finally the customer service agent spoke. "If he's your half sibling, then you either have two different mothers or two different fathers."

Della dropped the phone and collapsed in her chair. The receiver dangled from the desk, swinging by the cord. In the background, sounding far away, the customer service agent said, "Hello? Hello?"

But Della didn't hear her.

Chapter Seven

Della arrived home later that evening with no recollection of how she got there. She could not remember cutting through the parking lot, pausing to look both ways as she stepped off the curb onto Erie Street, and couldn't even remember if she had locked up and set the alarm of her shop. For all she knew, the place could be ablaze with lights with the front door wide open.

She bounded up the porch steps and didn't even see her mother sitting there in the rocker, doing a Sudoku puzzle. When her mother spoke, it startled her.

"Are you all right, Della? You look like you've seen a ghost." Concern etched her features. Despite her age, Jeanne had beautiful skin, a feature Della had inherited from her.

Without bothering to answer, Della went into the house and straight up to her room. The upstairs was always warmer than the downstairs, but that night Della didn't care.

She sat on her bed and picked up a framed photo from her nightstand. It was a shot of her and her father at some cousin's wedding more than twenty years ago. They were dancing, their arms extended, and her father wore a suit and was laughing that big open-mouthed grin of his. How she missed him! She studied him closer. His hair, his eyes, his nose, his mouth. She'd always thought she shared the same hair and eye color as her father: a variation of brown. But upon closer inspection, it wasn't exactly the same. Her father's hair was dark, almost to the point of being black, whereas hers had shades of red in it. She didn't have her father's aquiline nose, not like her older brother Joey, but then on contemplation, she didn't have her mother's classic nose either.

All this begged the question *Was her father her biological father?* The idea that he wasn't was so ludicrous she practically scoffed at herself, and was momentarily consumed with the impulse to rush downstairs and seek reassurance from her mother.

Of course her father was her father! Her parents had been married up until her father's death. The DNA results were erroneous, they had to be. But still, a niggle of doubt had crept in and parked there. The urge to vomit was strong.

"Are you coming downstairs?" her mother called up from the bottom of the staircase.

Della swallowed hard but her mouth was dry. "I'll be down in a minute."

She went to the bathroom and splashed some cold water on her face, trying to revive herself.

As she made her way downstairs, a heated flush crept up her cheeks. It dawned on her that she might not be able to face her mother. What would she say? How would she not bring it up? What would her mother say? How would she respond? Della realized her mother's answer might have severe consequences on her life, or at least the life she'd thought she had.

Her mother set aside her small magazine of Sudoku puzzles and, resting her elbows on the arm of her chair, looked up and smiled at her daughter.

"How was your day? Busy at the shop?"

Della could only nod. "The usual."

"It's a great little business, Della." Her mother had always been supportive with her shop. Always encouraging.

"How was your day?" Della's voice was barely a squeak.

"The usual." Jeanne Rossi launched into a litany of her day. Della had difficulty paying attention. Above her lip, a fine sheen of perspiration had broken out.

Her mouth had gone dry, and her stomach rebelled, its constant churning increasing her nausea.

Half paying attention to her mother, Della looked around. Everything from color to sound seemed sharper, and it made her feel sick. As if it was too much stimulation. The air was heavy like a blanket and settled down around her, threatening to suffocate her. The smell of mulch from the recent landscaping—a wet-earth aroma she usually enjoyed—made her want to retch. The sun dipping behind the houses across the street was a bright orange fireball. Next door, their neighbor started up his lawn mower, and the ensuing buzz was obnoxious.

"Della? Della?" Jeanne's voice sounded far away. It was similar to the sensation of being underwater and hearing someone outside of the water speaking.

She turned her head abruptly to her mother. "What?"

"I was asking if you wanted any ice cream."

Della shook her head.

"What's wrong? You're not yourself tonight," her mother commented.

She couldn't not ask. She had to know. "Funny you should ask."

Her mother looked at her and waited.

Della drew in a deep breath and prayed for some fortitude. "You know how we're doing that genealogy project in the social club?"

"Yes?"

"I sent away for my DNA results . . ." She locked eyes with her mother. The older woman gave nothing away, but Della could have sworn there was a flicker of something—maybe fear? Worry?—behind her eyes. But just as quickly, it was gone. It happened so fast that Della thought she might have imagined it. "And strangely enough, mine don't make sense. It says I have no Italian ancestry." Here Della frowned. Even now, to suggest that she wasn't of Italian heritage was incomprehensible. "And it says that Terry is my half sibling."

Della waited for her mother's reply, never removing her gaze from her face. There were a few missed beats of silence and during that silence, the bottom of Della's stomach fell out.

Then her mother announced in an unnaturally loud voice, "I wouldn't put too much stock in those computer-generated results." This coming from a nurse, who was a strong advocate of science.

Jeanne didn't say anything reassuring like "Of course your father is your father, who else would be your father?" No, there was nothing along those lines.

Della went to say something, but her mother stood quickly and said, "Now, I'm going in for some ice cream. Are you sure you don't want some?"

Her mother did not look at her as she passed by, but her gait seemed a bit unsteady. When the screen door closed and her mother was out of sight, Della sank in her chair, realizing the possible truth. And it came like a punch to the gut: the man she thought was her father was quite possibly not. With her head in her hands, she sobbed, her heart broken.

On Friday night, Della was home alone as her mother had gone out with her friends for dinner. There was relief in not having to share the same space with her mother. She sat on the porch, her legs up on the railing, and ran a hand through her hair, thinking she should wash it but not having the energy to do so. It could wait until the morning. She'd closed the shop early; with Sue Ann gone, she didn't want to stay open and since she so rarely closed early, she gave herself permission and then thought no more of it.

There hadn't been much contact between her and her mother since the previous night, her mother having left as soon as Della had gotten home. But it felt as if there was this great big impenetrable wall between them.

Even though her father had been gone a long time, she could still remember the sound and timbre of his voice, especially when he was singing "Volare." Her wonderful father, whose favorite holiday was Christmas, who put on a big party for St. Joseph's Day, and who grew prizewinning tomatoes in their backyard.

What did all this mean for her if her dad wasn't her dad? The idea of it was unfathomable and too painful to consider.

Tears began to spill over onto her cheeks just as a car pulled up to the curb. The next-door neighbors must be having company, she thought as she brushed the tears away. Or maybe the family across the street.

When Sam Morrison stepped out of the car, Della pulled her legs off the railing and whispered, "*Oh no.*"

She'd forgotten about their date. What kind of message would that send to Sam? Why hadn't she written it down in her diary? Because she'd been so excited she didn't think she'd forget about it.

He whistled as he strolled up the driveway, hands in his pockets. He wore a cream linen shirt and a pair of khaki shorts with boat shoes. When he spotted her on the porch, he threw his hand up in a wave and smiled.

"Della."

Embarrassed, she forced herself to her feet.

"Sam, I'm so sorry, I completely forgot about tonight," she said. She felt awful. What was he going to think?

"Oh." He narrowed his eyes at her. "Have you been crying?"

Quickly, she shook her head. "Allergies."

"We have plenty of time if you need a few minutes to get ready. We could still make it."

Oh, Sam.

She really liked him, and she didn't want to hurt his feelings. She decided to go for honest.

"It hasn't been a good couple of days." Her chin quivered as she spoke. She didn't want to say too much because the tears were right there, just below the surface, threatening to return in full force. "I'm so sorry."

"Anything I can do?"

"No, thank you."

"You have my number if you need me."

"Thank you." But she would be mortified to share this bit of news with him, especially since she didn't know the whole story.

He stood there for a moment, hands on his hips, regarding her. He turned his head, seeming to take in the sights of the street, and then looked back at her.

"Okay, Della. I'll see you around," he said.

"Again, I'm very sorry, Sam." She thought for a moment and added, "I was looking forward to it."

"Me too."

"Another time," she said.

"Yeah, sure." And he left.

She watched him get into his car, do a three-point turn in the street, and drive off. A part of her was torn between wanting him to stay and needing to be alone. She hated this feeling of discombobulation, of not feeling herself, as if her peg was off-kilter and not fully inserted into its hole. It was disorienting.

She remained on the porch until it got dark. The crickets had gotten louder, and the mosquitoes had come out. And after getting bit several times despite an apparently useless citronella candle, she gave up and went inside. Was her mother purposely avoiding her? It seemed so. It was no secret that Della went to bed at ten. She was up by six and liked to be at the shop by eight to start the day.

She settled on the couch in the living room, leaving the front door open. She liked to listen to the sounds of summer through the screen door. The sound of kids laughing and shouting as they rode by on their bikes. The screech of tires and the odd firecracker. Although she wasn't much of a television watcher, she turned it on anyway. She half paid attention to some show she was unfamiliar with, pressing the mute button every time a car drove by. But when there'd been no sign of her mother by ten thirty, she flipped off the set and headed up the stairs. As she climbed into bed, she heard her mother's car pulling into the driveway, the beam of headlights sweeping across the front of the house.

Della lay back, her head on the pillow. Yes, her mother was definitely avoiding her. She supposed she could go downstairs and talk to her. But what was the hurry? Did she want her worst fears confirmed? She didn't think so.

A big lump formed in her throat, and tears rolled out of her eyes and down the sides of her face.

Everything was all wrong.

Chapter Eight

The following morning, Della delayed the opening of the shop to call Dina Carruthers, the genealogist who had given the social club a tutorial.

"It's great to hear from you," Dina said at the start of the call.

"How are you?" Della asked politely. She leaned forward and stirred sugar into her coffee before taking a sip.

"I'm fine, thanks for asking. How's everyone doing with their genealogy projects?"

"Well, everybody is excited. Some have met with dead ends, as you can imagine, but they're determined and thinking outside the box as you recommended," Della said.

There had been some interesting finds. Some of the members of the group had reached out to distant cousins to get a more rounded picture of their family history. Jackie Arnold learned that her great-grandfather and his brother fought in World War I and had survived the Battle of the Argonne Forest. After the armistice, the brother was waiting his turn to go home when he contracted the Spanish flu and died in a military hospital in France.

The Andersons, who'd farmed land near Hideaway Bay for generations, could trace their relations back to the arrival of the Mayflower, along with thirty-five million other Americans. And before their arrival in America, the Andersons had been a landed family in England, to which Ben Anderson had quipped, "I guess the land is in our blood."

Baddie Moore found a whole other line in Australia; apparently the brother of an ancestor had gotten on the wrong boat and ended up on a different continent.

The stories abounded, but it seemed to Della none was more heartbreaking than hers. She kept that thought to herself.

She summoned her courage and asked Dina, "Something has come to my attention, and I wanted to run it by you."

"Sure, go ahead."

"One of the residents, who wishes to remain anonymous, has a problem with her DNA results," Della said.

"In what way?"

"Well, it came up that her brother was listed as a half sibling instead of a full sibling." Della thought of something but took a minute phrasing it, careful to conceal her identity. "And the heritage she thought she had through her father did not show up on her ethnicity map."

Dina did not hesitate in her response. "Unfortunately, as exciting as these DNA tests are with linking us to our relatives, for some people it opens a can of worms and can reveal long-kept family secrets."

I'll say, Della thought.

"It's called an NPE, which can stand for *non-paternity event* or *not parent expected*. It's not the first time this has happened."

"So, the father they thought was their biological father really wasn't?" Della could feel her heart sinking further into the depths of despair.

"DNA rarely lies."

When Della didn't respond, Dina said gently, "You might want to suggest that this person bring up the results with their mother. Unless of course the mother in question is deceased."

"I will do that. I mean, suggest they talk to their mother," Della said.

They made small talk for a few more minutes before hanging up.

Della gave some thought to Dina's advice. But what if her mother didn't want to answer her questions?

She opened up at ten, turning on the lights in the interior of the shop and unlocking the front door.

She pulled the sandwich board out from behind the counter, erased the previous day's specials and took a piece of colored chalk from a bin beneath the counter and wrote the current day's specials on it. She held the front door open with her foot as she carried the sign out and set it up in front of the shop near the curb. Mr. Lime was outside the five-and-dime, hunched over a broom, sweeping the pavement like he did every morning. They exchanged hellos and pleasantries about the weather before Mr. Lime returned inside. She looked up and down Main Street. It was just coming to life. Cars went by slowly, and pedestrians began to fill the sidewalks.

In the distance, she spotted Sam walking from his home and heading toward his office at the other end of Main Street. She went inside and found herself waiting for him. She made herself busy behind the counter, not wanting to appear overly eager. When she spotted him through the front window, nearing the shop, her heart skipped a beat and a smile emerged across her face. She felt awful about how she'd forgotten their date but had decided she would try and make it up to him.

But he didn't open the door and stroll in as he did almost every day. Without so much as a glance toward her shop, he kept on walking right by the front door, heading to his practice.

Disappointment could now be added to her feelings of despair. Still feeling a bit raw, she blinked several times, fearing that tears might be imminent. She had no one to blame but herself.

"Mom, I think it's time we talked. Seriously," Della said.

Over the last few days her mother had been scarce, and that had hardly buoyed Della's confidence that it somehow had all been a mistake. That the man she'd loved and adored had been her biological father. Her mother was not up before she left for work in the morning and when she arrived home at night, she was gone, out with friends for various social activities. Della had tried to hang on at night until her mother got home but as soon as her eyelids started drooping, she headed off to bed, figuring if she couldn't keep her eyes open, she was in no shape to be having a serious conversation with anyone, especially about a topic as important as this.

The ironing board was set up in the kitchen, and her mother had their clothes in the basket on a chair, ready to be pressed, all the wrinkles erased.

"There's nothing to say, Della," her mother said shortly. It was a tone Della had rarely heard from her mother. Short, abrupt, and no give.

"Mom, please."

"I don't want to talk about it." Her mother turned away and shifted her attention back to the ironing. She shook the can of spray starch vigorously and sprayed it onto a blouse, the air around her becoming a mist of starch.

"Mom, please look at me. Forget the ironing for a second. I need some questions answered."

"I'm sorry, Della, but this is none of your business," her mother said without turning around.

"If it's about me, then it is my business!" She couldn't understand why her mother was being so obstinate.

"Let it go," her mother said quietly. She draped the blouse over the board, spreading out the front of it, the remainder hanging over the edge.

"Then I'll call Terry and ask him."

Her mother's shoulders stiffened. Slowly, she turned and glared at her. "Do not contact Terry or Joey. It's none of their business either."

She'd never seen her mother like this. Never. Normally, she was so even-keeled. Della was almost afraid of her. But not quite.

"Is Dad my father?" she asked.

"Of course he is."

Tears stung Della's eyes. Her mother could be so frustrating.

"Is Dad my biological father?"

"No," her mother said sharply, and she turned and picked up the iron and continued pressing the blouse.

It felt as if Della's life had leeched out of her with that one-word reply. She expected to look down and find her entire being in a big puddle on the floor. Her life as she knew it, as she understood it, ebbed away from her.

"What happened? Were you a victim? Were you—"

Her mother turned and leveled her gaze at Della. "I was not the victim of a sexual assault."

Although relieved to hear that, all Della could think about was her father. "How could you do that to Dad? To *Dad*? Of all people," she cried.

But her mother kept right on ironing.

Chapter Nine

When Sue Ann returned from California, she wasn't herself. She was quiet and distant. The Sue Ann that Della knew—the kind, bubbly one—was nowhere to be found. Della had picked up on that right away. It was hard not to be in tune with someone else's thoughts and emotions when you spent so much time with them in a small space. Originally when Sue Ann had started working at the shop, it was a part-time job, no more than twenty hours a week. But as the shop became busier, Sue Ann sometimes put in forty-hour weeks.

Della was concerned about her friend. Sue Ann was almost always in a good mood; she hadn't even let a bitter divorce drag her down, deciding instead she was going to rebuild her life in Hideaway Bay.

Taking advantage of a lull, when the store was empty, Della inquired about the funeral.

"It was the usual," Sue Ann said. "Lots of flowers and a nice eulogy from his best friend, but the whole time, I was thinking how strange it was to be sitting in the front row at the funeral of a man who was your father and who you hadn't seen since you were a child. And that had been his choice."

"It must have been difficult."

"It was and it wasn't. I mean, that decision to be a crappy father is on him. I spoke to my older brother and sister, and his relationship was minimal with them as well. They lived in the same state and they rarely, if ever, saw him."

"It's kind of sad, isn't it?" Della asked.

"Yes, it is," Sue Ann said. "The will was read after the funeral, and a lot of his estate went to charity, which is a nice thought, and he left all of his children a sizeable legacy. To be honest, I'm surprised he even remembered my existence."

"How does that make you feel?"

"I don't even know. I mean, is the money supposed to make me feel better about him falling down on his job as a father? The one thing I think any child wants is the parent's time and attention, but he was incapable of that." She shook her head, her lips pressed together in a thin line.

Della's own father came to mind. He'd been a great parent. But now all that was up in the air.

"Anyway," Sue Ann continued, "it wasn't all sad and bitter. Dylan and I went to Monterey one day and Sausalito the next. And we went to Sonoma. Beautiful. If I wasn't so in love with Hideaway Bay, I'd seriously consider moving out there. I can see why my mother loved California so much."

"It sounds lovely."

"It must be in my blood," Sue Ann said with a laugh.

And what was in her own blood, Della wondered, coming down her paternal line? It was heart-wrenching that she didn't know.

"Anyway, enough about me. What's new around here? Is the doctor still coming in every day?" Sue Ann asked.

"No, I haven't seen him in a while." Della did not want to get into how she'd forgotten her date with Sam, because then she'd have to explain why she forgot about it, and she wasn't ready yet to share that with anyone. Not even Sue Ann.

At home, the tables were turned. It was she who was going out of her way to avoid her mother, leaving the house early in the morning and either staying late at the shop or going home and going right up to her room. When she was forced to share space with her mother, the communication was minimal and the air tense around them. Jeanne had attempted to make small talk several times, but Della gave her one-word replies, and finally her mother gave up.

But Della was dying to ask her questions like *why*, *how*, and not least, *who*? Who *was* her father?

Who am I? It was a brand-new question that plagued her day and night. A question she'd never had to ask herself before, because she'd been so confident in her past and who she was. But now everything was upside down and nothing made sense. The Italian American heritage she'd worn like a badge of honor felt tarnished. She prided herself on her sauce and her Italian-inspired dishes that had been passed down for generations. She even made her own pasta from scratch using flour and eggs, having been taught by her father when she was just a child. She could still remember the day she'd mastered rolling the dough with her grandmother's long, skinny rolling pin with a slap and a flourish, and how he'd clapped and declared her a master. Had it all been for nothing? Had she and her father been unwitting victims of her mother's deceit?

She couldn't even think of her father without getting upset. She'd been spoiled and doted on by him up until his death. Did he know? He must not have, and every time she came to this conclusion, a painful lump would appear in her throat and she'd have difficulty swallowing. It was one question she was terrified to ask her mother. If her father hadn't known, then their father-daughter relationship had been based on a lie. She shuddered at the thought that things might have changed between them if he'd found out.

Days later, Sue Ann said, "Don't you find it odd that Sam Morrison hasn't been in the shop? I mean, we couldn't get rid of him." She laughed at this.

The truth was, Della missed him. She liked their flirty banter. And she realized she'd looked forward to him coming into the shop. Sometimes, it had been the highlight of her day. But it couldn't be helped that he never came back.

"He must be really busy," Della said. What else could she say? That she'd forgotten about their date, sending him a clear message—albeit an erroneous one—that she wasn't into him as much as he was into her?

"Nobody's *that* busy," Sue Ann countered.

Della shrugged, and when a customer pushed through the door of the shop, she felt nothing but relief that that particular topic of conversation would end. It was painful to talk about. She liked Sam like she hadn't liked anyone else in a long time, and she'd blown her chance.

The following week when Sue Ann came to work, she bounced in full of energy. It was good to see the old Sue Ann back.

"Guess who I ran into last night?" Sue Ann said as she went around the shop with a damp cloth, wiping everything down.

Della looked up from a brochure she was reading. She was thinking of going on a cruise by herself to get out of town for a week and to think about things. To be alone and away from everyone and everything.

Sue Ann's eyes were bright. Della hadn't any intention of guessing and waited patiently for Sue Ann to land the plane and get to the point.

"Sam Morrison!"

"Oh."

"Oh?" Sue Ann repeated, her disappointment in Della's reaction written all over her face. "That's all you've got? *Oh*? I said Sam Morrison."

"I know," Della said.

Sue Ann pursed her lips in disapproval at Della's reaction, or lack thereof. But she soldiered on. "He asked about you, asked how you were doing."

Della was aware that Sue Ann's gaze was pinned on her.

"Oh, did he?"

She narrowed her eyes and studied Della for a moment before slapping her hands on her hips. "Why don't you tell me what happened between you and Sam while I was out in California?"

Tears sprang to Della's eyes.

At the sight of Della's tears, Sue Ann's brightness partially dimmed. "What's wrong? What *did* happen?"

Her horror unabated, Della's tears fell.

"Come on." Sue Ann took her gently by the arm and led her from the shop to her office in the back room and commanded her to sit at the desk. "Hold on." She disappeared to the outer area of Della's office, and the sounds of the Keurig machine filled the silence. Within minutes, she returned with a cup of coffee and set it in front of her friend.

"Take some time for yourself. I'll take care of the store."

Della pulled a tissue from the box and wiped her eyes and blew her nose. Concern distorted Sue Ann's features.

"I appreciate it," Della said quietly.

"Don't worry about it. Maybe later, if you're up to it, you could tell me what's happened to put you in such a state." Sue Ann appeared to think for a moment and then narrowed her eyes. "Did he insult you or hurt you in some way?"

Della waved her arms in front of her lest Sue Ann get the wrong idea about Sam. "No, definitely not. He's not at fault here."

Before Sue Ann could reply, someone called out from the front of the shop.

"Della? Sue Ann? Is anyone here?" Della recognized the voice of Thelma Schumacher.

"I'll take care of things. Don't worry," Sue Ann said, and she disappeared from the office.

Della was lucky to have a friend like Sue Ann, and that made her cry harder.

In dire need of a distraction, she looked at the clock, allowing herself five more minutes to sit and stew in her funk, but then she had to get back to work. Because this—this wallowing—was not her. It served no purpose and did no one any good.

When the allotted minutes were up, she pulled herself out of the chair and stood at her desk, gulping down the rest of the coffee for a much-needed jolt, not caring that it had gone cold. In the tiny bathroom outside her office, she splashed cold water on her face and returned to the front of the shop with a big smile pasted on her face to greet her customers. They deserved the best from her, and she'd have to put her personal problems aside and give it her all. Everything she had accomplished and everything she had was because of the patrons of her little olive oil shop. And that thought alone was enough to lift her spirits and help her make it through the rest of the day.

When the day was done and the shop was closed up, Della breathed a sigh of relief. She'd gotten through the day. Now she could go home. As she stood behind the counter, pulling out the day's earnings for the bank deposit, she spotted Sam walking by the shop. Her heart lurched at the sight of him: the beautiful wavy brown hair, the strong profile, the straight posture. But he sailed past as if in a hurry and did not look into the shop window.

She supposed she could text him, but would that make her appear desperate? Maybe he'd moved on. And her heart was tender and couldn't possibly handle any more rejection.

Sue Ann stood next to her, emptying leftover pieces of French bread they'd had out for samples with the various dipping oils, into the trash. Her gaze followed Della's, and when Sam disappeared from view, she asked, "Do you want to tell me what happened while I was gone?"

Della bit her lip. Did she want to tell her? It wasn't that she didn't trust Sue Ann, because she did. Sue Ann was the very model of discretion. Since she'd started working there, the two of them had had many heart-to-heart talks, often over a bottle of wine and some crusty French bread and dipping oil.

"He asked me out on a date," Della said.

Sue Ann's expression bloomed, full of joy. "That's wonderful!"

"It was until it wasn't."

Sue Ann's happy expression caved in on itself. "You've lost me."

"We made plans and I totally forgot about them," Della said, wincing as she said it.

Sue Ann looked at her in disbelief. "You forgot about a date with Sam Morrison? Did you lose consciousness or something? Slip into a coma? Bang your head?"

Despite her sadness, Della smiled. It was all she could manage. She sighed, looking around. "Do you have time to hear this?"

"Sure."

"Let's finish up here, and we'll go to the back and I'll tell you what's happened."

"Okay."

Once the lights were turned off in the front of the shop, they retreated to the back room. As Sue Ann followed her, she asked, "Do we need a bottle of wine?"

"It probably wouldn't be a bad idea."

"I'll grab one."

They were now stocking Tom Anderson's label, Hideaway Bay Winery, and the wine was very good. It was proudly displayed on its own table with the banner identifying it as the product of a local vineyard.

As Sue Ann grabbed the wine, Della took two clean coffee mugs down from the cupboard of the mini kitchenette in the back. Sue Ann uncorked the bottle and set it on the table to rest.

"Now, how did you forget that you had a date with the dishy doctor?" Sue Ann's expression was one of disbelief and confusion. Actually, Della couldn't believe it either. She'd been crushing on him for a long time and perhaps if she hadn't forgotten, there might have been a second date.

"I found out something awful."

Sue Ann's eyes widened. "What?"

Della took in a deep breath even though it hurt her chest, where it felt like a lump of lead had taken up residence. "I found out that my dad isn't my biological father."

Sue Ann's mouth fell open, and the shock that registered on her face mirrored Della's. "What?"

Della went to speak, but her friend put up her hand. "Wait a minute. We need wine." Sue Ann poured a liberal amount into their mugs and handed one to Della. Cradling the mug in her hands, Della took a sip.

"Now, what happened?" Sue Ann asked. "And how did you find out your dad isn't your real father?"

Della looked away, suddenly feeling embarrassed. Sue Ann reached out and laid her hand over Della's, giving it a gentle squeeze. "It's all right."

"Is it?" Della launched into her story. Telling it out loud did not make the pain go away.

Verbalizing the whole awful affair had brought all those raw emotions to the surface. She'd thought if she shared her story with someone, she might feel better. But she felt worse. Somehow, sharing the story had made it seem more real. Truer. And there was a whole ton of heartache in that.

Sue Ann asked lots of questions.

"Do you know who your real father is?"

"No, my mother has clammed up."

"Do you think your father knew?"

Della lowered her head. How could he have known? He'd raised her as his own. He'd cherished her. "I don't think so."

"Did you ask your mother?"

Della's laugh was brittle. "She doesn't want to talk about it. Any of it. Flat out refuses."

Sue Ann made sympathetic noises. "How awful. Do you want to find your real father?"

"I don't know," Della said, shaking her head, her hands in her lap. "I don't even know who I am anymore. My life was built on a lie."

Sue Ann sighed. "I'm sure it must feel like that. But your dad loved you. And no matter who your biological father is, nothing changes that."

"But the question is, would he have loved me if he knew I wasn't his own flesh and blood."

Sue Ann poured more wine into their mugs. "You can't do that to yourself, Della. That's pure speculation. You had a great relationship with your father. End of."

Della wasn't entirely convinced. "I suppose."

"It makes sense now why you forgot about your date with Sam. You've been handed a lot to deal with, and deal with it you must. It doesn't necessarily change your past, who you were, but it does affect your future."

Della blinked. "I don't even know who I am anymore."

"Who you are right now at this point in your life shouldn't be altered by this new information. You are the sum of all your experiences and all your relationships, good or bad."

A rare smile broke out on Della's face. "You're full of wisdom, Sue Ann."

"Aren't I just?" she grinned. She leaned over and patted Della's hand. "I can imagine how it feels, as if the bottom of your world has fallen out, and I suppose in some ways it has. But remember, nothing lasts forever. This too shall pass and all that."

"Hopefully," Della said, inhaling a large breath.

Picking up the bottle and emptying it of its contents into their mugs, Sue Ann said, "Come on, let's finish this wine, which is pretty good, and go home."

"It's a good thing we walk to work."

Sue Ann chuckled. "Getting back to Sam. I think you should text him. Ask him out."

"What?"

"Hear me out. Everyone fears rejection, even successful, confident men like Dr. Morrison. It's understandable you forgot about your date, but he doesn't have the benefit of the context behind it."

Della thought there was some truth to what her friend said.

"It's unfortunate," Sue Ann said, "but someday, when you're feeling a little stronger and a little better, you might want to explain things to him. He's a nice man. He'd understand."

Della nodded. "I'll think about it."

Chapter Ten

Alice

Alice had become immersed in her new hobby. Spread out before her on her desk at the law office of Enright and Monroe were photocopies of the now-defunct *Hideaway Bay Gazette* from more than one hundred years ago. Unwittingly but pleasantly, she'd been sucked into the vortex of the past, curious to see former residents and the ancestors of current ones. She found delight in looking at the shops of Main Street and the homes that had been newly built at the time. One of the constants was Lime's Five-and-Dime. She'd stumbled across an old newspaper article with an accompanying photograph featuring the store's founder standing outside his establishment, hands on his hips, bearing an eerie resemblance to his grandson, the current Mr. Lime.

There were even a few old photos of the lake that looked as if they could have been taken yesterday. It was comforting to see those connections between the past and the present.

One newspaper clipping in particular grabbed her. It showed three young women in 1912, dressed from head to toe in Edwardian-style lace and silk and sporting complicated hairdos. She loved looking at all the old fashions of the era—the opulent gowns with all the fabric and trimmings, and the impossibly wide-brimmed hats. They were gorgeous. The women in the picture stood at the shore, barefoot, arms linked, all three of them lifting the hems of their dresses above their ankles as they took a tentative dip. One of the women had her head thrown back, laughing. Alice could feel the happiness from the photo taken over a century ago, and goosebumps broke out on her arms. It reminded her of herself and Lily and Isabelle.

She'd discovered in her search through the deeds that the first family to occupy the house on Star Shine Drive was the Bernards, who featured prominently in Buffalo's society pages of the day. Mr. Bernard, an industry scion in Buffalo, was short, rotund, and looked gruff in most photos. His wife, Catherine, despite her middle-aged years, appeared delicate and fair. Alice couldn't tell if her hair was blond or light brown. She couldn't imagine anyone as stern-looking as that occupying her home. There was an article about their eldest daughter's debut at the age of eighteen up in Buffalo. The young girl, named Cecelia, was sheathed in a lacy white gown with her voluminous hair in a low but expansive pompadour with a diamond diadem appearing to hold it all together. Cecelia Bernard had been photographed with the other debutantes at the time—ten in all—decked out in white and no one smiling. All appeared delicate and waifish. The previous night, Alice had read through more clippings about the Bernards, mostly about the father and his business ventures. But she had stumbled across a rare family photo of them taken on the front porch at Hideaway Bay.

Flabbergasted to see the house as it was over one hundred years ago, Alice sank back into her chair, her mouth slightly open. Then she leaned forward to study it further, trying to glean anything from it.

An impromptu snap had been taken of the family in the summer of 1916. Mr. and Mrs. Bernard were there, seated in white wooden rockers, surrounded by their five daughters of various ages. The youngest daughter appeared to be about twelve. The oldest, the former debutante, had to be in her thirties. But gone was the father's dour and serious expression, to be replaced by twinkling eyes and a mouth wide open with laughter. His wife, now white-haired, looked at him, laughing too. In fact, all the girls were laughing, some with their eyes closed.

Without realizing it, Alice was smiling too. Content that this was a happy family, she studied the details of the house. The porch was the same, but the screen door was different—she'd been sure the current creaky screen door must have been there since day one. But apparently it was a replacement. Because the photo was black and white, it was hard to tell the color of the house. Had it always been white with green shutters? But no, in the picture there were no shutters!

Her overall impression was that the house looked nice and sturdy. And the obviously spontaneous picture of the Bernards reassured her that it had been filled with love and laughter right from the beginning.

"Hello? Alice?"

It was Jack. Immediately, she smiled, the past forgotten.

"Where is everyone?" he asked as he made his way toward her, leaning on his cane. He carried a white paper bag that smelled fantastic, and Alice's stomach growled in response.

Leaning over, he kissed her on the lips. Tenderly, she reached up and placed her hand along the side of his face, loving the feel of the stubble against her skin.

"Everyone is out for lunch, and I'm holding down the fort," she told him.

He lifted an eyebrow. "Have you had lunch?"

"No, I forgot," she said, her brow furrowing. That was always a problem for Alice when she became engrossed in something.

He held out the bag. "I took a chance and picked up a couple of samosas for you."

She broke into a smile at his thoughtfulness. "I knew you were a keeper!"

Jack set the bag down in front of her, and Alice ripped it open and used it as a placemat, the spicy aroma filling the air as she took out the paper-wrapped samosas.

He sank down into the chair across from her desk. Alice looked up from her lunch as she shoved half a samosa into her mouth, and caught him staring at her. When their eyes met, he grinned.

"What's so funny?" she asked, wiping the corners of her mouth with a napkin.

"I've never seen anyone look so beautiful as they're shoveling food into their mouth," he said with a laugh.

A blush crept up her neck at the compliment. She was going to like being married to Jack Stirling. She took another bite of the delicious samosa, chewed thoughtfully, and swallowed before asking, "Can I make you some tea or coffee?"

"No, sweetheart, I'm good. Eat your lunch."

"I'm doing just that," she said, taking another bite. She took a swig from her water bottle.

"How's your day going?" he asked.

She nodded, wiping her hands on the napkin, swallowing the bite in her mouth. "Great." All the days at the office were good. She was so much happier working at a small-town law firm than she had been working for a big-city firm in Chicago. Sometimes she had to pinch herself at how lucky she'd gotten with this job. She'd fallen into it. With her tongue, she felt around her teeth for any stray food. If Jack thought she was beautiful, there was no sense in disabusing him of that notion with food stuck in her teeth. Satisfied, she said, "Don't forget, we have an appointment with the caterer."

He tilted his head to one side. "You haven't rescheduled this one again?"

"No, smarty," she said with a laugh. "We need to go over the menu."

"Good," he said. "I was beginning to get worried that we'd be making boloney sandwiches for our big day."

"Ha-ha."

"I found out some more info about the first owners of the house," Alice said, crumpling up the empty wrappers, folding the torn bag around them, and tossing them into the trash bin next to her desk.

"Really?"

She nodded and relayed the tale of the lovely Bernard family, and showed him the photo of the house taken more than a hundred years ago.

He smiled. "It hasn't changed that much."

She agreed. She bent closer and looked at it. "I'm looking at those pots of flowers at the base of the porch steps. You know, I think they're the ones that have been sitting in the back of the shed for years and years."

"Didn't Lily throw them out when she remodeled the shed?"

Alice shook her head. "No, I asked her to hang on to the really old stuff. I'm going to have to investigate that further."

Jack laughed.

"The Bernards were only there until the late twenties. Then another family moved in. I wonder what happened to them."

"That's life for you. We live. We die. We move on."

"Well put!" she teased. "Concise and succinct. I like it."

He shrugged and held out his hands, palms up, with a devilish smile. "It's all I got."

She laughed and looked at him from beneath her eyelashes. "Will you have more later?"

He burst out laughing again. "You know it. Now I better get going. I don't want you to get in trouble with your boss."

"She's tough to work for," Alice joked.

"I can imagine." He struggled briefly to stand. His leg had been injured in the war. But Alice knew he wanted no sympathy. He'd gotten on with his life and accommodated his injury.

"Do you think I'm high maintenance?" she asked as he got up to leave, wondering if by marrying her, he had taken on a full-time project. He made his way around to her side of the desk and placed a hand on the back of her chair. His smile was full of mirth.

"You?" He bent down and placed a long, lingering kiss on her lips. "I wouldn't have you any other way."

She watched him as he left, thinking how she loved him a little bit more now than she did only a few minutes ago.

She straightened up her desk, humming to herself, gathering her research into a pile and pushing it aside. It was time to get back to work.

At the end of the week, Alice carried a loaf pan of fresh-baked blueberry lemon drizzle cake down to Martha Cotter's house. It was still warm, and the aromas of sugar, lemon, and blueberries with a hint of vanilla made Alice's mouth water. Now she was glad she'd made two; its twin waited on the countertop at home. She knew this cake to be a favorite of Martha's. Her granddaughter, Mimi, had told Alice as much.

Martha Cotter sat on the porch outside her house at the corner of Star Shine Drive and Erie Street, sporting a pair of oversized sunglasses. Hers was the grandest home on the block. She threw up a thin arm in a wave when she spotted Alice approaching.

Years ago, neither Alice nor her sisters would ever have considered visiting their elderly neighbor. Known for being spiky and short-tempered, she caused residents of the beachside town to cross the street when they saw her coming. But the arrival in town of her granddaughter, Mimi Duchene, had changed all of that. The effect of the teenaged girl living with Martha had been transformative for both, by all reports, and the newer, improved version of Martha Cotter was nothing short of amazing.

It was with these thoughts in her head that Alice stepped up onto the porch.

Martha was dressed comfortably in linen trousers and a lace blouse with a cardigan. The weather was warm, but Alice suspected elderly people got colder easier.

"Hello, Alice," Martha said. When she spied the loaf pan, she leaned forward and said impishly, "That smells wonderful. I hope it's for me."

Alice laughed. "It is. Blueberry lemon drizzle cake."

Martha broke into a generous smile. "My favorite. How did you know?"

"A little bird told me," Alice said.

Martha smiled, leaning back into her chair. "Would that little bird be named Mimi?"

"It would be."

"Would you mind putting it into the kitchen for me? Mimi isn't here and—well, my legs don't move as fast as I'd like them to." A walker stood next to her chair.

"Not at all," Alice said, making for the front door.

"Why don't you pour us each a glass of lemonade? You'll find the glasses in the upper cabinet next to the sink."

"Okay."

Alice made her way through the house, catching glimpses of the cavernous rooms with high ceilings and crown molding. She set the loaf pan down on the kitchen table and went about pouring two glasses of lemonade. Not wanting Mrs. Cotter to think she was dawdling and gawping at her things, Alice hurried, practically dashing back through the front of the house, glasses three-quarters full, careful not to slosh the lemonade over the sides.

"You're almost out of breath. What did you do, sprint?" Martha asked with a laugh as she accepted the lemonade from Alice. She took a dainty sip before she set it down. "Mimi makes wonderful lemonade. I didn't think it was possible, but it's even better than my grandmother's."

Alice smiled, taking the seat next to Mrs. Cotter. "I heard she's going off to college in Buffalo soon."

"Yes. UB. Both her and her friend Kyle Koch are going."

"You'll miss her."

Martha's gaze clouded over. "I will, but this will be good for her. She can't hang around an old woman forever. She needs to live her own life."

"It's hard to let go, isn't it?" Alice asked, thinking of her own situation with her sisters.

Martha sighed, her elbows on the arms of the chair and her hands clasped over her crossed legs. She stared straight ahead at the lake. "It is. But we must. It's not healthy to cling to the past."

"No, I suppose it isn't," Alice agreed.

"Mimi says she'll be home every weekend. And that might be true in the beginning, but I bet once she gets a taste of college life, she might not come home as much." Her voice sounded wistful, not sad.

Alice sipped her lemonade.

"But I'll have her here at Christmas, and Martine and Edgar and Micah will be coming here for the holidays as well, so I have something to look forward to."

"That's wonderful."

"How are your wedding plans coming along? Mimi said she'd definitely be home for your wedding."

"I'm glad to hear that." Mimi and Kyle were good kids. Alice had met them several times up at Anderson's fruit and veg stand up on the highway, where they both worked through the summer. They were polite and friendly and helpful.

Alice launched into a brief account of her plans, and Martha asked questions. When a natural pause occurred, Alice said, "I stopped by because I'm looking into the past owners of Gram's house."

"Whatever for?" Martha asked.

Alice shrugged. "I'm curious to find out about the people who lived there before my grandparents. I know Valerie Fisher's grandparents lived there in the 1950s but other than that, there are a lot of gaps. I'm looking for any information on the owners before the Brandts. I was hoping that your mother or grandmother might have passed some knowledge on to you."

Martha looked away, choosing to look out at the lake. The water was dotted with sailboats and their crisp white sails, and kayaks and surfboards closer to the shore.

"I've discovered that Cecil and Catherine Bernard were the first owners," Alice prompted.

Martha picked up the thread. "My grandmother spoke about them often. Catherine Bernard was a bit older than my grandmother. And grandmother said she was a bit in awe of her. She said that Catherine was one of the blue bloods of Buffalo, social register, that kind of thing. But Cecil Bernard came from nothing and worked his way up in the business world, all the while climbing the social ladder. Grandmother said that all the Bernard daughters were quite beautiful. Fair and delicate like their mother." Martha paused, seeming lost in her thoughts.

Then she laughed. "Mr. Bernard was said to be a practical joker of sorts. I don't know how he found the time with running a business, but I suppose even magnates need to let off steam. He'd do foolish things like replace the sugar with salt." She shook her head, smiling, as if it was a memory she'd forgotten.

She continued, "Mr. Bernard used to do this thing where he'd have one of his daughters toss one of the grandchildren out of an upper window, and he'd catch the child below. I'm sure at the time it was great fun, and thankfully no one was ever hurt. But you couldn't pull a stunt like that these days. Child Protective Services would be all over that in a heartbeat, as they should be.

"When I was growing up, mother and grandmother used to tell me all these stories about the Bernards. But I don't remember most of them anymore." She folded her arms and looked out at the lake. "I wish I had paid more attention."

"Don't we all," Alice said. Even her own memories of her mother and grandparents were blurring at the edges. "I hope you don't mind me asking you all these questions."

Martha shook her head. Her voice was wistful when she spoke. "It's how we keep the dead alive and with us, by speaking of them." She nodded in the direction of town. "Some of the Bernards are buried in the Hideaway Bay cemetery."

"Do you know who moved in after them?"

"Yes, of course. The Bernards passed away, and there had been no son. The house was left equally to all the girls. They sold it to a widow from Buffalo who'd had no children. Mother said the house remained empty while she owned it—she never stepped foot in Hideaway Bay. Whatever her reasons were for that, they remain unknown."

Alice was glad she'd sought out Mrs. Cotter; she was a wealth of information.

Martha continued her story. "But that was only for a year or two. When this woman died, she left it to a niece. This would be a Laura Bartlett from Cleveland. She was supposedly a poor relation, but she'd married into money. Not the kind of money the Bernards had, but *some*," she said with a sniff.

Alice had to suppress a smile.

"They rarely came out to Hideaway Bay. Mr. Bartlett didn't like sand." The expression on Martha's face suggested that she thought this attitude reprehensible. "The husband passed away, and Laura moved permanently to Hideaway Bay with her young son. And even though it was just the two of them, it was a happy home. She doted on the boy. But the second war came and Johnny Bartlett went off and was killed soon after. Laura, now elderly, followed him into the grave. My mother used to say there was comfort in knowing they were together. The house was left to some shirttail relative, a shifty sort." Martha made a little moue of distaste with her mouth.

Alice let her tell the tale at her own pace.

"He didn't own it long. Wasn't here long enough to know him when he lost the house to Wayne Brandt in a card game. Scandalous. Disgraceful." She shook her head.

Alice sat back, staring straight ahead at the rippling gray hues of the lake, letting all this history sink in. It was a fascinating, colorful history. The house had seen good times and bad, but that was life. Its happiest moments seemed to have been when it was filled with families, especially children. Granted, there were the occasional blips of downtimes, but that was life. Overall, it had a lovely history. It was a house that was meant to be filled with people, especially children.

"Now, I don't know about you, but I think it's time for a slice of that blueberry lemon drizzle cake," Martha said.

Alice laughed and had to agree with Mrs. Cotter.

Part Two

Jeanne

Chapter Eleven

1949

Nine-year-old Jeanne Becker chased her three older brothers down Erie Street. The sun shone bright in the mid-morning sky behind them.

One of her brothers, Doug, looked over his shoulder and yelled, "Go home, Jeanne!"

Jeanne stopped abruptly, breathless. She leaned forward with her hands on her hips and her feet wide apart. Her chin jutted forward, defiant. "I wanna play too."

"Aw come on, Jeanne. Go home already." This exasperated plea came from her oldest brother, Roy.

She continued to follow her brothers and their gang of friends, which included Cal Cotter and the Nowak boy, whose family had recently moved into the house on the corner of the street.

Her three brothers, Roy, Doug, and the youngest, Ernie, ran toward the beach, their friends trailing behind them. Jeanne brought up the rear but kept some distance between them until she knew what they were up to. It seemed they were always doing fun things, going on adventures, and she was interested in joining in the fun. She hated being excluded simply because she was a girl.

As the boys reached the boardwalk, Ernie turned around, waved his hand at her, and scowled. "No girls allowed!"

"Shut up, you little pipsqueak," she yelled.

Jeanne continued to chase them onto the beach, the heavy sand slowing her down. The boys ran along the shoreline, where the surf-flattened sand was easier to navigate, but Jeanne knew if she got her brand-new shoes wet her mother would have a fit.

As the boys got farther and farther away, looking over their shoulders and pointing and laughing at her, she threw up her hands in frustration. "Arrgh!" she wailed. The injustice of it all, of being left out. Excluded.

"What's the matter?" asked a voice behind her.

Jeanne spun on her heel and came face to face with two girls. She knew them to see, they were in the other third-grade class at George Washington Elementary School in Hideaway Bay. Lois Thomson and Betty Enfield. Immediately, she forgot about her ire with her brothers and their friends.

"They're in a gang and won't let me join," Jeanne explained.

Lois, the taller girl with the blond hair, shrugged. "So what?"

"I want to have fun! I want to be in a gang," Jeanne wailed.

"We all do. Come on, there's three of us, we'll make our own gang and have more fun than those stupid boys," said the blonde, puffing out her chest. "I'm Lois and this is my sidekick, Betty."

The dark-haired girl with the small blue bow in her hair let out a giggle. It was the first time she'd made any sound.

"I'm Jeanne. Jeanne Becker."

Lois stuck out her hand and shook Jeanne's hand vigorously. "How do you do, Jeanne Becker!"

More giggles from Betty and this time, she covered her mouth with her hand.

With a nod toward Betty, Jeanne said, "Does your sidekick talk, or does she only laugh?"

"Sure, she talks, but only when she has something important to say."

Betty stopped laughing and spoke up. "I've got to go; mother will redden my bottom if I don't get this milk home." And she held up the glass jug of milk she'd been holding at her side.

"See what I mean?" Lois said. "We'll meet up in the morning."

"Can I bring Natalie and Marjorie?" Betty asked, eyes bright. Jeanne thought there were going to be a lot of girls in this gang. She didn't know these other girls and wondered if they went to the same school as the rest of them.

"Sure, they're always welcome," Lois said.

With a promise to see them tomorrow, Betty skipped off, the sweaty jug of milk dangling at her side.

As soon as Betty disappeared, Jeanne asked, "Who's Natalie and Marjorie?"

Lois laughed. "Those are her dolls. She likes to bring them everywhere she can. She wants to have lots of babies someday."

Oh. Jeanne never thought about having kids. But thinking about it now, she decided she'd only want girls. After dealing with her fair share of her brothers' smelly socks, it was a no-go for boys.

Jeanne stood there for a moment, pivoting to see that her brothers were no longer in view. Forlorn, she looked longingly into the distance, at the space previously occupied by her brothers and their friends.

"Come on, forget about them," Lois advised. She began to walk toward the shore and despite the new shoes, Jeanne followed her. She said nothing, preferring to let Lois do the talking.

"There's another girl, too, that can join our gang. Mary."

Jeanne nodded.

Lois looked over at her. A slight breeze lifted her blond hair from her shoulders. "I've seen you at school."

Jeanne nodded again, surprised the other girl had noticed her at all. She wasn't impressive like Lois, who stood out for being tall and blond.

"Let's meet with Betty and Mary and we can decide what to call our gang," Lois said. As she rambled on about her ideas for the gang, Jeanne nodded and agreed with what the other girl said. It all sounded swell to her. She'd show her brothers.

A question popped into Jeanne's head, and she asked, "Will it only be us or will we let other people join?"

Lois appeared contemplative for a moment. "We can let others join, but they must pass a test to get into the gang."

Jeanne had a moment of panic. "Do I have to take a test?"

Lois rolled her eyes. "Of course not, silly! You're one of the founding members!"

Relief flooded Jeanne. Test-taking wasn't her strong suit.

"Come on, let's go find your brothers."

"They'll be mad," Jeanne mumbled.

"We're going to spy on them, not let them see us!" Lois said.

Jeanne was beginning to think that this girl with hair the color of sunshine had a lot of good ideas. The day had started out sour, but things were looking up.

"And you know what the best part of our gang is going to be? We won't allow boys!" Lois threw her head back and laughed, revealing white teeth no bigger than corn niblets, and Jeanne joined in. "Let's go find those rascals. And remember, they're boys so they're stupid, and we'll find them with no problem."

Lois had been right. The boys were easily found on the other side of the town green, past the gazebo in a wooded area.

"How did you know they'd be here?" Jeanne whispered.

"Because this is where everyone goes."

They did? Jeanne hadn't known this.

"Come on, but keep down so they don't see us," Lois said.

Jeanne mimicked Lois's crouched posture, walking along but keeping low, her back horizontal with the ground, like a crab. They cut down a driveway to a house and slipped through the gate of the white wooden fence.

Lois carefully opened the latch and beckoned Jeanne in with a wave. Just as quietly, she closed the gate, wincing at the squeak of the latch. She put her finger up to her mouth to tell Jeanne to be quiet, and glanced up at a window on the second floor.

Whispering to Jeanne, she said, "No talking."

They ran to the back of the fence line, where Lois parked Jeanne in front of a small opening where the wood had rotted away. Closing one eye, she squinted through the hole in the fence and easily spotted her brothers and their friends in the thin and reedy trees of the wooded copse. Her eyes widened when she saw Doug pull out a cigarette from his back pocket, looking around as he did so. The Nowak kid pulled out a Zippo lighter and lit it.

"They're in so much trouble!" Jeanne hissed.

"Let me see," Lois said, nudging Jeanne gently out of the way.

Lois watched them and said, "Where did they get the cigarette?"

"Probably from the pack on my father's dresser," Jeanne said. On one hand, she was miffed that they were smoking without her and on the other hand, she was practically gleeful that she was in possession of this information.

Lois pulled back from the fence. "Now you have leverage."

Jeanne frowned. Leverage? Where had a nine-year-old girl learned a word like that? And what did it mean? Dumbfounded, she repeated, "Leverage?"

Lois nodded, her eyes bright. "You can blackmail them. What would your father do if he found out they were smoking in the woods?"

They'd get the belt, that's what would happen, Jeanne thought. She shivered at the thought of it, but then thought it served them right for excluding her. Maybe Lois was right; she might be able to use this to her advantage.

"Quick, look!"

Jeanne put her eye up to the opening in the fence and watched as Doug took a long drag, trying to look cool, and ended up bent over at the waist, coughing his brains out. Jeanne clapped her hand over her mouth to stifle her giggles. Even her oldest brother, Roy, looked green around the gills as her mother was apt to say.

"Lois Thomson! Is that you in my backyard spying through my fence?" yelled a shrill voice from the upstairs window.

Lois's cornflower-blue eyes grew big and round. "Run!"

They ran all the way up Main Street, stopping only when they reached Erie. Both were sweaty and out of breath.

"I've got to go home," Lois said, twisting her mouth in an expression of displeasure. "If I don't get my chores done, Mama will tan my hide."

"Oh." Jeanne tried to hide the disappointment in her voice. She wanted to suggest to Lois that she do her chores before she left the house, as that's what the rule was in the Becker house, but she didn't think they were at that stage of their friendship yet.

"Meet me here tomorrow morning at nine," Lois said.

"Make it ten, I have to do chores first."

Lois regarded her with an odd expression and then said, "Okay then. I'll bring Betty and Mary with me."

Jeanne nodded, smiling. They waved to each other as they parted.

It was going to be a great summer.

Chapter Twelve

1957

Jeanne stood back and looked in the mirror, touching the side of her hair absentmindedly. Bobby preferred her hair like this. For the last six months, they'd been going steady, and she really liked him. She could see a future together with him. Placing her hands on the front of the short dresser, she leaned forward and inspected her lipstick, making sure there was no smear on the front of her teeth. The mirror was old, as was the dresser. When she and Bobby got married, she'd get all new furniture, something sleek and modern, nothing like this, all mismatched and old and handed down. They hadn't talked about marriage yet, but it felt like a conversation that was on the horizon. In the fall, he was going away to college on a full scholarship, but Jeanne had already decided she'd wait for him. She'd bought some nice stationery to write to him when he did go away. And she had that brand-new perfume that she could spritz onto her letters.

The phone rang downstairs. She took one last look in the mirror and then glanced at her wristwatch. Bobby was picking her up in fifteen minutes. She flipped off the lights on her way out of her bedroom and made her way down the staircase.

"There you are," her mother said when she appeared. "Bobby's on the phone."

Jeanne trotted to the kitchen and picked up the handset from the phone on the kitchen counter. Handset to her ear, she leaned against the Formica countertop, twirling the cord between her fingers.

"Hello?"

"Hey, Jeanne, how are you?"

"Good. But what are you doing calling me? Aren't you supposed to be picking me up in fifteen minutes? We don't want to be late." They were going to see *Jailhouse Rock* at the cinema. It wouldn't have been Jeanne's first choice; she'd wanted to see *Peyton Place*, but Bobby had scrunched up his nose and said no way. He wanted to see Elvis.

"That's what I'm calling about," Bobby said. "I can't make it tonight. My aunt and uncle are here in town and, well, you know, I have to spend time with them."

"I don't mind meeting your aunt and uncle," she said. She'd have preferred to go to the movies but as long as she was with Bobby, she didn't care what they did.

"That's all right, Jeanne. You don't want to spend your Saturday night with a bunch of old fogeys," he said.

"I don't mind," she said truthfully. She got on so well with his mother and father, and she didn't want to spend a Saturday night at home alone. That much she was sure of.

"That's okay, sweetheart. We'll go to the movies tomorrow night," he said. Before she could protest any further, he added, "I'll call you tomorrow." And he hung up, leaving her to stare at the phone, the dial tone faint. She placed the handset back in its cradle and sighed.

"Did Bobby cancel?" her mother asked. Mrs. Becker was no fan of Bobby Hendricks and had once commented that she thought he was "slippery." Whatever that meant.

"Family is in town. He has to spend some time with them." She tried to sound as nonchalant as possible because she didn't want her mother to know she was upset.

Her mother didn't look up from her sewing, only nodding and making no comment, which relieved Jeanne to no end.

Jeanne figured that while she had her mother alone, she'd broach a topic she'd been wanting to discuss but had been a little nervous to bring up. She pulled out a chair from the kitchen table and sat, crossing her legs. Her mother looked up briefly from her sewing and smiled.

"Mother, I wanted to ask you something," she started.

"If it's money for a new dress, the answer is no," her mother said without looking up from her task.

"No, of course not." Jeanne frowned. "It's something else."

"Yes?"

"I was thinking of my plans after graduation."

A perplexed expression clouded her mother's face. "Plans after graduation. What do you mean? You'll get a full-time job."

Jeanne sighed. "I was hoping to take a two-year secretarial course at the business college."

"A secretary?" her mother repeated, her hands still, the sewing forgotten in her lap. Now Jeanne had her undivided attention.

Jeanne was the image of her mother: brown hair the color of a glossy chestnut, a high forehead, big brown eyes, and the same beauty mark at her temple next to her left eyebrow.

"Yes, it's something I've been thinking of doing," Jeanne said. She liked the idea of having a proper job.

The thought of going into an office to work, wearing stylish clothes and working with nice people, kind of excited her.

"But you'll be able to get a job with no problem. All the shops in town are always looking for help. I know that Roy's Drugstore is always hiring. And Elvira is looking for a clerk at the grocery store."

Jeanne shuddered. There was a permanent "help wanted" sign in the front window of the drugstore because there were rumors that old Mr. Roy was handsy with the young female staff. And Milchmann's grocery store? The turnover there among staff was high because Mrs. Milchmann was so difficult to work for.

"I'd like to be a secretary," Jeanne repeated, this time with conviction.

Her mother chuckled, not unkindly. "And I'd like to be the queen of England and yet here I am." She returned her attention to her sewing, picking it up and pulling the threaded needle through the material.

Jeanne uncrossed her legs and leaned forward to shorten the distance between her mother and herself. "Mother, it's only two years and when I finish, I'll get a proper job and be able to support myself."

Her own mother had never worked outside of the home, and all through her childhood Jeanne had watched her father paying the bills and giving her mother money for groceries and any other household items.

But if her mother wanted a new dress, she had to ask for money, and that had always bothered Jeanne. Why couldn't women make their own money and then they wouldn't need to ask their husbands?

Her mother smiled benevolently at her. "But Jeanne, honey, you won't need a proper job! You're a pretty girl who's kind and intelligent, and you'll find a husband with no problem. Your husband will support you."

The conversation was exasperating. "But I don't want to depend on my husband. I want my *own* money."

Her mother pursed her lips as if the topic had become unpleasant, and lowered her voice. "Jeanne, we didn't raise you to be greedy."

Jeanne leaned back and looked up at the ceiling. "Ugh!" she cried in frustration. "Mother, it has nothing to do with greed. It's about being self-sufficient."

"But you will become self-sufficient when you get married and have a home of your own," her mother pointed out. "You'll be running a household and taking care of a family, like all wives do."

Was she really not getting it? Sure, there was a generation gap, but was her mother really that obtuse?

Jeanne tried one more time. "I'm talking about a different kind of self-sufficiency. The kind where you're not dependent on a man for your money."

Her mother stiffened. "When you're married, everyone contributes in their own way to the running of the household. No one is less important just because they don't earn the money."

Jeanne sagged in her chair. "Mother, I didn't mean to offend you. Of course what you do is important! You're the glue that holds us all together." Being the only daughter, Jeanne had spent her whole life helping her mother with the cooking and cleaning and anything else that was deemed an "inside chore." Meanwhile, shoveling snow, painting, and cutting grass were done by her father and three brothers. From an early age, Jeanne had seen the imbalance.

Before she could continue, the phone rang, its heavy trill startling them both. Jeanne jumped up to get it.

"Hello."

"Jeanne?"

Jeanne recognized her friend Mary's voice. "Hi, Mary. What's up?"

"Where are you?"

Jeanne rolled her eyes at the ludicrous question and quipped, "Take a guess."

But Mary ignored her and lowered her voice. "I thought you were going to the movies with Bobby."

"No, he had to cancel. His aunt and uncle are in town."

"Well, that's funny, because Sid and I were just driving down Main Street and I saw him walking arm in arm with Sheila Kelp into the Pink Parlor."

"What?" Jeanne whispered. Her knees buckled, and she pulled the nearest chair from the kitchen table toward her and fell onto it. She was aware of her mother's gaze pinned to her, but she ignored her. "You must be mistaken."

"I know what I saw, Jeanne. I'm sorry to be the bearer of bad news but if Sid was stepping out on me, I hope one of my friends would have the decency to tell me."

Jeanne said nothing as she was trying to process the information Mary had thrown into her lap. Bobby wasn't with his out-of-town relatives? He'd lied to her to take another girl out? And Sheila Kelp, of all people?

"Look, I gotta go," Mary said. "Sid's waiting. I'm at a payphone."

Jeanne still didn't say anything. She blinked rapidly, trying to fit this information into her world.

"I'll call you tomorrow, Jeanne." And the line went dead.

Even though Mary had disconnected, Jeanne remained seated with the earpiece pressed against her ear. When she jumped up, her mother started.

"Is everything all right? You look peaked," her mother said.

"Everything is fine," Jeanne said, her voice low. She hung up the phone and headed out of the kitchen.

"Where are you going?" her mother called out after her, but Jeanne was already sailing through the front door.

She walked with purposeful expedience in the direction of Main Street. The air was muggy and thick. Pedestrians strolled along the streets through the dusk, and people wandered back from the beach.

Mary *had* to be wrong. There was no way Bobby was out with that tramp Sheila Kelp. Impossible. Rumors swirled around Sheila like bees around honey. Older by one year than Jeanne, Sheila had a reputation for being fast and loose. She went through a lot of boyfriends. And although Bobby had broached the subject of "going all the way," and with more frequency as of late, Jeanne had held firm. She was saving herself for marriage. Her mother had had a long talk with her the previous year when Jeanne had first started dating. She'd made it very clear that her virginity was a gift that was reserved for her husband. And Jeanne, being the dutiful daughter, would do what her mother had advised. She looked forward to being with Bobby that way, but *after* they marched down the aisle.

The night air was still; she couldn't even hear the water hitting the shore. There were the muted sounds of traffic, and she could hear laughter and shouts from children and the loud chirping of the crickets, but all that became white noise as she focused on her destination:

the Pink Parlor. A mosquito buzzed near her, but she swatted it away angrily. More than anything, she wanted to prove Mary wrong.

Bobby wouldn't cheat on her, would he?

He was popular. He'd been voted most likely to succeed, but that didn't mean he was without integrity, did it?

Illumination from the interior of the ice cream shop spilled out onto the sidewalk, casting a pale rectangular swathe of light onto the pavement. She could hear loud voices from inside as she approached. The place was packed. It was the end of June and school was out and the weather was hot. The town had its summer vibe in full swing. Hadn't she and Bobby made all sorts of plans for the summer? Starting with the Fourth of July festival the following week.

As she neared the front window, her step faltered. Did she really want to find her boyfriend with someone else? If it was true, it would be the end of them. Could she really break up with him? If she turned around right now, then he was still her Bobby.

She paused for a moment and then decided she had to know one way or the other. To suspect or doubt would be ten times worse. Better to find out either way and let the chips fall where they may.

She braced herself: lifted her shoulders and squared her chin. With a sudden determination, she marched into the Pink Parlor and stood there for a moment just inside the door, her gaze bouncing around the place. Booths and tables and the swivel chairs that lined the counter were all occupied. It was as if everyone who lived in town had made a beeline for the ice cream parlor. There were families, elderly couples, and young couples sharing ice cream floats with two straws.

Relief slowly filled her. Mary had obviously gotten things wrong. She was about to turn and leave when she spied Bobby in the back booth.

And he wasn't alone.

A group of guys rushed through the door, jostling her and knocking her off balance. Quickly one of them righted her and mumbled, "Sorry."

She couldn't stand there all day. Shaking, she marched toward the booth where Bobby and Sheila sat side by side on the pink vinyl seat, his arm around her shoulder, just like he did with Jeanne. Jeanne scowled at the sight of them. In front of them on the table sat a large banana split. Bobby dangled the cherry in front of Sheila. Jeanne recalled that he'd done that with her a few times. Fury replaced her shakiness.

When she arrived at their booth, Bobby looked up, smiling, looked back to Sheila, did a double take, and returned his glance to Jeanne, the smile gone.

"Jeanne!" Quickly, he dropped the cherry and pulled his arm away from Sheila's shoulder, putting some distance between him and the other girl. Sheila reacted with a pout and crossed her arms.

Aware that the volume had decreased inside the ice cream parlor as all eyes were on them, Jeanne said nothing, choosing instead to turn on her heel and exit the shop. It was satisfying when she realized Bobby had chased after her.

"Jeanne! Wait up!" he called.

But Jeanne lifted her head and kept walking.

Bobby laid a hand on her arm to slow her down. Jeanne stared down at it as if it was something distasteful, like a bug or an insect.

He removed his hand. "It's not what you think."

He must think I'm stupid, she thought. "Really? What is it then?"

"I'm only helping her out."

Jeanne snorted. "I thought you were spending the evening with your aunt and uncle."

He rubbed his hand through his hair and said nothing.

To Jeanne, there was nothing more to say. As much as it saddened her to break up with Bobby, he'd lied and obviously cheated, and there was no coming back from that.

With a nod in the direction of the ice cream parlor, she said, "You better get back to Sheila. I'll be going now."

"Come on, Jeanne, she doesn't mean anything to me."

"Does Sheila know this? Because the two of you looked pretty cozy about five minutes ago," she said, her voice rising.

"It's nothing, really," he insisted.

"Is that what you told Sheila about me? That it's really nothing?" Jeanne was beginning to get tired of this circular conversation. She wanted to go home and be alone. "Goodbye, Bobby." With pronounced effort, she pulled his high school ring off of her finger and threw it at him. The ring flew wide to the right and hit the sidewalk with a *ping*. He reached down and picked it up, slipping it into his pocket.

"If you want your jacket back, you'll have to stop by the house and pick it up," she said. He'd lettered in football and basketball, and she'd been so proud when he'd given it to her. Now she wanted to burn it. She left him standing there, never looking over her shoulder, not wanting to give him the satisfaction.

Going straight home was not an option, because she had started crying and wanted to stay out of sight. As she walked up and down the side streets of Hideaway Bay, she wiped her eyes, wishing she'd brought a handkerchief with her. She couldn't believe he'd do such a thing! How had she gotten him all wrong?

It was dark and by now, she had circled back to Main Street, choosing to remain hidden in the shadows. As she passed the barbershop, a voice caused her to jump.

"You're going to wear out the pavement, miss."

Jeanne stopped, sniffled, and peered into the shadowy darkness of the doorway. She hadn't seen the man sitting on the stoop. It was the son of the barber. Sal, was it? Her father and her brothers came here for their haircuts. She didn't really know him that well. He was at least four years older than she, and if she remembered correctly, he'd gone to St. Thomas, the Catholic high school.

The man stood, not that much taller than Jeanne. He smelled nice, some aftershave she didn't recognize. In the glow of the streetlamps, she could see that he had dark hair, and his dark eyes glittered in the evening light.

"I was going for a walk," she said feebly.

The man pulled a folded handkerchief from his back pocket and handed it to her. "It's clean."

"Thank you," she said, her eyes filling at this unexpected kindness. She turned her back slightly to him so she could blow her nose, which made her sound embarrassingly like a honking goose. She was mortified. She wiped her eyes and crumpled up the handkerchief in her hand.

She held up her balled fist. "I'll wash and press it and return it to you."

He held up his hand, and there was kindness in his smile. "Not necessary. I've got plenty where those came from."

She laughed a bit, finding it ironic that she could laugh. Two minutes ago, she felt as if it was the end of the world.

He held his hand out. "Salvatore Rossi, but my friends call me Sal."

She transferred the hankie from her right hand to her left and shook his hand. "Jeanne Becker."

"Ah, the Beckers. Your father and brothers come into the barbershop."

Jeanne smiled and nodded. "That's right. Sometimes, Father treats himself to a hot shave."

Sal laughed. "Everyone should treat themselves to a hot shave." He cleared his throat, looked down at the pavement and kicked at something that wasn't there. "Men, that is."

For a moment, neither said anything, and finally it was Sal who spoke first. "What's a nice girl like you doing walking around by herself in the dark?"

She shrugged. She didn't want to reveal that she'd just broken up with her boyfriend. For some strange reason, she didn't want this Sal Rossi to know that she had a boyfriend, even if he was a former one. "I needed to clear my head."

He nodded, accepting her answer. "A good walk and some fresh air will do that."

There seemed to be nothing more to say, and standing there, idling, seemed foolish to Jeanne, though she'd be the first to admit she didn't want to leave him. There was something about him that was magnetic, this son of a barber. And his voice was lyrical. She liked the way it sounded in the semi-darkness.

Finally, she said, "I better get going." But she dragged her feet.

"I can walk you home," he offered.

"No need. I don't live far from here," she said. She didn't want to inconvenience him any further; she'd already destroyed his handkerchief. His short conversation had been a good distraction.

"Well, good night, Sal, and thanks for the handkerchief," she said, walking slowly backward, mindful of the pavement behind her.

"Any time," he said, lifting his hand in a goodbye wave.

In the darkness, she smiled at him and slowly turned around, not really wanting to put her back to him but not wanting to fall flat on her behind either.

As upset as she was about Bobby, she already felt slightly better.

Behind her, Sal whistled a familiar tune. She recognized the song immediately.

"Only You."

Chapter Thirteen

Two days later, Jeanne made her way to the barbershop to return Sal's handkerchief. She'd washed it and ironed it herself as she had promised she would.

The sky was overcast, and fast-moving clouds threatened rain, but she carried her umbrella with her as a precaution. She'd ironed his handkerchief into a neatly folded square and carried it wrapped in tissue paper inside her pocketbook as if it were the most precious thing. He'd told her it wasn't necessary to return it, but she wanted to see him again. She was curious to see if she was as drawn to him in broad daylight.

Bobby had called the house several times, but she refused to take his calls. The speed with which she had moved on from him had amazed even her. All she could think about was the barber's son, Sal Rossi.

The barbershop on Main Street had a large plate glass window with "Salvatore Rossi and Son, Barbers" in black and gold etching. A barber pole with its trademark red, white, and blue stripes was mounted next to the front door.

She caught sight of him through the plate glass window. A man lay horizontal in one of the barber chairs, and Sal was giving him a hot shave. Sal spoke animatedly the entire time, and this made Jeanne smile. When he raised the chair and the man was sitting in an upright position, Sal removed the barber's cape with a flourish. A laugh escaped her. He caught sight of her through the window and his smile deepened. Jeanne pulled out the handkerchief from the tissue paper in her pocketbook and held it up. He nodded in response and held up his finger to indicate he'd be with her in one minute. She didn't mind waiting.

The wait wasn't long. The door to the barbershop opened and Sal stepped outside.

In the daylight, she was able to see his features better. Although he wasn't much taller than she, he was solid. He was tanned, and his eyes were the color of espresso. His hair was thick and dark, almost black, and as was the rage at the time, he wore it in a pompadour style with a curl landing right in the center of his forehead. She'd seen similar styles on Elvis Presley and Tony Curtis. She wondered if he spent a lot of time on it. It looked just as good on Sal Rossi as it did on the celebrities.

"I wanted to return this to you," she said, looking up at him. She handed the handkerchief to him, and he tucked it into the pocket of his shirt without taking his eyes off of her.

"Thank you," he said. Although his nose was a little crooked and some of his features seemed too large for his short stature, she liked the overall look of him: strong. Dependable.

Two men side-stepped him to enter the barbershop.

"Are you all right?" he asked Jeanne.

She looked at him quizzically.

"The other night, you seemed upset," he elaborated. He stood there with his hands on his hips, regarding her.

There was something about him that was serene. She gave him a small smile. "I'm fine, thank you." That was a truthful statement.

He went to say something, but they were interrupted by a succession of raps on the window from inside the shop.

They both looked up. It had to be Sal's father, Jeanne concluded, because he looked like an older, more mature version of Sal. The older man wore a white apron over a white short-sleeved shirt, just like Sal. He mimicked cutting with scissors and waved Sal in. Through the glass, the older Mr. Rossi spoke quickly in Italian. Before he turned away, he looked at Jeanne and smiled and winked.

"I've got to get back to work," Sal said. He rubbed the back of his neck.

Jeanne nodded, sad that their interaction was coming to an end. Now she had no excuse to come back.

"Would you like to go dancing on Saturday night?" he asked.

She didn't have to think about it. "Yes, I'd like that."

His father wrapped on the window again.

"Give me your address and I'll pick you up at seven," he said.

Quickly, Jeanne rattled off her address, and Sal repeated it.

"See you Saturday at seven," he said with a wave and a smile, and he disappeared back into the barbershop.

Jeanne walked home with a smile on her face, counting the days until Saturday.

After a night out dancing with Sal, Jeanne began to see him in earnest, regularly. He was a gentleman and although her parents preferred him over Bobby, agreeing with her assessment that he was an upstanding person, they had two concerns: he was Catholic, and he was the son of immigrants. Immigrants from a country the United States had fought against in the recent past. But Jeanne was quick to point out that Sal was born here in the United States and that his parents had come to America long before the start of World War II. She got around the religion argument by noting that Catholics practiced Christianity, as they did in their own Lutheran church. On the former matter, her parents begrudgingly agreed that they couldn't hold it against the Rossis that their home country had picked the wrong side, but they were more reticent about the latter, worrying that if the relationship proceeded, any children that were born would be raised in the Catholic faith.

But to Jeanne none of these things mattered. In fact, they made her feel protective of him. In a way, she supposed these things about Sal, his steadfastness, his "outsiderness," made her love him even more. And if he asked her to marry him and stated his intention to raise any children Catholic, it wasn't going to be a dealbreaker.

By the time she graduated from high school the following year, secretarial school was forgotten, as Sal had indeed asked her to marry him. And although her parents had reservations, they couldn't say no. Her mother said, "He's such a good and kind man, it's hard to be against it." Even her father admitted that she was not likely to find a better man than Sal Rossi. Wedding plans went ahead for the fall.

What did come as a shock was that Sal's mother was not keen on Sal marrying Jeanne. She'd been holding out hope for a nice Italian girl. It wasn't that anything was said directly to Jeanne, and Sal insisted that his mother was quite fond of her. But Jeanne pointed out that his mother spoke only Italian when she was present, and never appeared to smile. Sal reassured her that his mother was a wonderful, kind individual, but Jeanne had yet to witness any of those attributes.

February 1960

Jeanne walked along Main Street carrying a brown paper bag full of groceries. Tonight was going to be a special night. After work, she'd got off at the bus stop on the highway, walked down Erie Street, and made a left onto Main, heading over to Milchmann's grocery store to splurge a little on a better cut of meat. It would be nice to give ground beef and chicken a break for a change. And although she'd spent a little extra on a strip steak—only one, as two would have broken their budget—she and Sal could share it.

It was getting dark, it was chilly, and the air was brisk, but Jeanne didn't mind. She was in too good of a mood. She pulled her wool coat closer to herself.

Jeanne had concluded that she liked being married. Well, she liked being married to Sal. Seven months into their marriage, they were having a great time. They'd rented an upstairs apartment on a side street off of Erie that was within walking distance of the barbershop. It made her feel all grown up to have a place of their own. And her wedding shower had yielded a lot of brand-new kitchen appliances. It had felt like Christmas morning for a long time. Her favorite gift had been the

Corningware set in the Cornflower Blue pattern. There were a few casserole dishes and a tall coffeepot, and she took great care with them, treasuring them. She'd never owned anything as nice.

Once home, she set the bag on the chair in the kitchen, unloaded everything onto the table, and put the items away. There was something to celebrate, and she'd planned a meal of baked potatoes, the strip steak, green beans, and a small salad.

An early morning visit to the doctor before work had confirmed her suspicions: she was finally pregnant. She couldn't wait to tell Sal. He'd be over the moon. He wanted a large family. As they'd been married for so long, she was beginning to worry when nothing was happening. But by the fall, they'd have their own baby.

At six thirty sharp, Sal came sailing through the door, whistling, like he did every evening. Jeanne paused from turning the steak on the broiler, trying to identify the tune. After a moment, she gave up and returned her attention to the steak, flipping it and sliding the broiler back into the oven and closing the door.

"Something smells wonderful," Sal said as he waltzed into the kitchen. Jeanne tilted her face up to him, and he laid a kiss on her lips.

"How was your day?" she asked.

"Great. I can't complain," he said. Sal was one of the few people she knew who actually loved his job. He liked people, was a natural with them, and liked what he did. She supposed they couldn't ask more than that. He never complained or grumbled like Mary's husband, Sid. Sid told anyone who would listen all the things he hated about his job. The list seemed never-ending. She didn't know how Mary stood it. Jeanne was grateful that Sal wasn't like that.

As for herself, Jeanne worked at the grape jelly factory, Gibson's Grapes, down in Lavender Bay. In a short time, she'd moved from the factory floor to the upstairs office, answering the phones. It was rare to get off the floor. She knew men and women who'd been working down on the floor since the '30s and '40s. But one day, as the elderly owner of the company, Mr. Gibson, was doing a walkabout on the factory floor, he chatted with Jeanne for a few minutes and said he liked the sound of her voice, thought it would be perfect for answering phones, and would she be interested in moving upstairs?

It was a big factory as the region was one of the largest grape-growing areas in the country. During her engagement, she purposely left her engagement ring at home—this had been on Lois's advice—and told no one she was getting married. After the wedding, her boss had reminded her of the company policy forbidding pregnant women from working there.

With a smile, Sal asked, "What's for dinner?"

"Baked potatoes, green beans, and I thought we could split a strip steak."

He raised an eyebrow. "What's the special occasion?"

Jeanne blushed and felt the heat creep up her neck. She was at a loss for words, and suddenly felt shy about telling her husband her news.

But she needn't have worried about that, because his smile morphed into a grin, his gaze traveled to her belly, and he raised his eyebrows in question. Relieved, Jeanne nodded and leaned against him so he wouldn't see the scarlet of her cheeks. Sal immediately wrapped his arms around her and held her in a tight but comfortable embrace.

He leaned his cheek against hers and whispered, "That's wonderful news. You should have bought two steaks—this is cause for celebration!"

Jeanne laughed. Sal always said the right thing. Always made her feel good.

Chapter Fourteen

As it was her first pregnancy, Jeanne didn't start showing until her fifth month. She said nothing about it to anyone at work, not even the girls she was friendly with. She wanted to keep her job as long as possible. The truth was, she enjoyed working. She liked earning her own money, even if it was only a little bit. It gave her a sense of independence.

For the most part, she'd been feeling pretty good during her pregnancy. She'd had no morning sickness, not like her friend Mary, who always seemed to have her head in a toilet bowl during the first months of her pregnancy. Because she wasn't sick, Jeanne's mother-in-law, Mrs. Rossi, feared the worst. But not Jeanne. It reassured her that she'd be able to keep her condition a secret at work. Nothing would tip them off faster than her running to the bathroom to throw up.

But the very same morning she first had trouble zipping up her skirt, she was called to the office of her boss, Mr. Cline, the factory manager.

There were three desks in the reception area outside Mr. Cline's office, each occupied by a woman responsible for her own set of administrative tasks contributing to the smooth running of the company. The room was filled with the sound of clacking typewriter keys and the constant ding of the carriage returns. There wasn't much chat, only the odd whisper or giggle, as Mr. Cline frowned on that sort of thing. As Jeanne walked past the three women, she was aware of their eyes on her, and in response, she lifted her head a little higher.

She knocked on the door of his office and waited for the invitation to enter. When summoned, she drew in a deep breath and turned the door handle and stepped in.

The rumor throughout the office was that Mr. Cline was only fifty, but he looked seventy. He'd been married a long time, served in the war, and had four daughters. The other rumor was that his daughters ran roughshod over him. Jeanne had trouble believing either. He was so severe-looking, and wasn't known for his humor. It was difficult to picture anyone taking advantage of him. She had a hard time imagining a bunch of young girls ordering him around.

"Sit down, Jeanne," he instructed from behind his desk. His hair was salt-and-pepper gray and cropped short. Wire-rimmed glasses were perched on his large nose. His suit was gray, his shirt white, and he wore a thin black tie. It was his uniform; he never deviated.

Jeanne sat up straight in the chair directly across from his desk, keeping her hands folded in her lap, her right hand over her left to cover her wedding band. As he did the only other time she'd been summoned to his office—when she got married—he appeared engrossed in a ledger in front of him. It was his way to keep her waiting. Finally, he closed the ledger, squared it up with the edge of his desk, and folded his hands on top of it, lifting his gaze to make eye contact with her.

"Jeanne, I had an interesting telephone conversation that I wanted to discuss with you."

Jeanne tilted her head slightly to one side, taken aback by his opening line and unsure of where this conversation was going. She hoped one of the customers hadn't complained about her. Still, she felt totally in the dark.

"Your mother-in-law"—here he glanced down at a small spiral notebook to his right—"a Mrs. Salvatore Rossi, has informed me that you're in the family way and demanded to know how I could allow a woman in that condition to work in a factory."

His clasped hands revealed white knuckles. Under his intense scrutiny, Jeanne sank in her chair. Her mother-in-law had been harping on her to quit her job since the day she learned Jeanne was expecting. Had said that a job was unseemly for a pregnant woman, or something along those lines. The word she'd used was an Italian one, but Jeanne had gotten the gist. Now she was sorry she'd told her. She should have waited until the child arrived.

"To be quite frank, Mrs. Rossi," Mr. Cline continued, "I was at a loss. I felt as if I was caught on the back foot. I made it clear to the other Mrs. Rossi that I had no idea."

Sal's mother most likely had delighted in that fact. Jeanne sighed and sank further into her seat, her posture crumpling. There was no way she was walking out of that office with her job intact. And forget about her pride.

"Now I am put into the unenviable position," Mr. Cline said, "of having to ask a delicate question of a young woman. Are you in the family way?"

She didn't hesitate. She couldn't hide the truth any longer. "I am."

"You know company policy forbids pregnant women from working here."

"I'm aware of that, but I'm pregnant, not ill." This notion that pregnant women couldn't continue to work was ridiculous. She was tired of being treated like she was spun glass. Human civilization had lasted this long and women in the past had performed harder tasks then Jeanne's job entailed. Answering phones wasn't that difficult.

But Mr. Cline ignored her. "Twenty years ago, married women weren't allowed to work here." His ensuing sigh was one of displeasure. "Why Mr. Gibson got rid of that rule is beyond me."

Jeanne waited for the boom to drop. Because it was coming.

"Unfortunately, Mrs. Rossi, I'm going to have to let you go," he said. His face was a mask of gravity, but Jeanne suspected he derived a perverse pleasure in firing people, especially pregnant women.

She didn't wait for the rest of it, choosing to stand up. "I'll clear out my desk." As she stepped away, he called after her, "We'll mail out your final check."

She was glad she had her back to him, as the heat in her cheeks was intense and she was sure there was an accompanying scarlet blush. She didn't look back.

She cleared her desk of her few meager belongings, piling them in a small cardboard box the company readily supplied, and exited the building for what she supposed was the last time. She made her way home and dumped the box onto the kitchen table, abandoning it to be sorted out later.

Her ritual of a cup of tea after work was skipped and she sat there on the sofa, fuming, with her arms folded tightly across her chest and her legs crossed, one leg swinging. It was late morning, and Sal wouldn't be home for hours. What was she supposed to do? Their apartment wasn't that big, so there was no cleaning to be done. The little laundry they had, she'd caught up on over the weekend, and she'd done all the ironing the previous night.

She didn't know if she was more furious about being fired or about her mother-in-law meddling in her affairs. It seemed about equal. There was nothing she could do about her lost job; it was just the way things were. Married and pregnant women weren't expected to work. But she could do something about her mother-in-law. Jeanne felt compelled to nip that right in the bud, or the older Mrs. Rossi would be running interference for the rest of her life. As it was, Sal's mother had hijacked Sundays, and they were expected to spend every Sunday with them as his mother made sauce and pasta. Jeanne had grown up in a meat-and-potatoes house. When she met Sal, she was introduced to all kinds of Italian dishes and customs. Some she loved: sauce, meatballs, lasagna, stuffed shells and manicotti were at the top of her list. She did not care for tripe, squid, artichokes, or dandelion wine. She pushed herself up off the sofa, deciding she had time before Sal arrived home from work to pay a short visit to her mother-in-law.

May had been a wet and rainy month. A slight breeze ruffled Jeanne's hair as she walked over to her in-laws' house. They occupied a redbrick house over on Luna Drive, a side street between Seashell Lane and Moonbeam Drive. They'd had the house built years ago, when the barbershop had turned successful. It was one of only a handful of brick houses in Hideaway Bay. Sal's uncle had been a bricklayer, and he'd insisted that Sal's father build his house of brick.

It was a small, neat, two-story home with an archway on the right-hand side of the porch, over the front door. It dawned on Jeanne that she had never been here uninvited or without Sal. But then, she'd never been fired from a job before either.

The concrete driveway was clean and free from debris. Her father-in-law swept it every evening and hosed it down on the weekends. There were a few red clay pots lining the side of the house, full of potting soil and waiting for the annual flowers, and a green garden hose was coiled on a metal reel against the side of the house.

Jeanne went around to the back and let herself in through the gate. Immediately, she spotted her father-in-law, home for lunch, stretched out in a metal lawn chair, holding a straw hat against his chest, his head hanging back with his mouth open as he had a short nap. No matter the weather, the older Mr. Rossi liked to be outside as much as possible. On more than one occasion, Jeanne wondered if it had anything to do with the fact that his wife was inside.

As quietly as possible, she opened the back door, trying not to wake him.

The house always smelled of garlic and onions and although it usually made Jeanne's stomach growl and her mouth water, today it had the opposite effect: her mouth went dry, and a slight wave of nausea rolled over her.

When she stepped into the kitchen with its bright cream tiles, light wallpaper, and maple cabinets, Mrs. Rossi stood at the stove, stirring a large pot. When she turned to see who had entered her kitchen, the smile disappeared from her face.

"Mrs. Rossi," Jeanne said by way of a greeting.

"Jeanne, what are you doing here?" The elder Mrs. Rossi removed the wooden spoon from the sauce and set it down on a small plate on the counter next to the stove. She made a production of wiping her hands on her apron, then waved Jeanne toward the kitchen table. "Sit down. I make you something to eat."

Jeanne shook her head. "I'm not hungry."

Mrs. Rossi scowled. "You need to eat. You're too thin!" This was a constant refrain from her mother-in-law, even though the older woman could be described as scrawny herself despite her hearty appetite and all the cooking and baking she did.

Mrs. Rossi stood with her hands on her hips and stared at Jeanne.

Jeanne narrowed her eyes at her. "I lost my job today."

The older woman looked away, choosing that moment to wipe down a counter that did not need it. "That's not so bad. You shouldn't be working in your condition. You should be home taking care of your husband and getting ready for the baby." These sentiments were a common theme with Jeanne's mother-in-law.

The insinuation that she didn't take care of Sal properly prickled Jeanne, but she bit her tongue. For the moment. She shook her head. "There'll be plenty of time for that."

It was time to address the reason she'd been fired in the first place. "My boss told me you called him and told him I was pregnant."

"In the family way," her mother-in-law corrected.

Jeanne rolled her eyes, and she didn't care if the other woman saw it or not. "You had no right to do that."

Mrs. Rossi lifted her chin, planted her feet slightly apart, and placed her hands firmly on her hips. "I did what I thought was right."

Were the two of them always going to butt heads? Jeanne already found it exhausting, and she and Sal hadn't been married that long. And this woman was the picture of health, which indicated a long life of annoyance for Jeanne.

"It wasn't your business to interfere in mine," she said firmly.

"If it concerns Sal, it concerns me," said the other woman. Her dark eyes glittered. "You belong at home. You're going to have a baby. You need to look after yourself."

"I had a nice job," Jeanne cried, but she suspected her attempts to make the other woman see reason were futile.

Mrs. Rossi waved her hands in front of her in a short gesture. "No!"

Who did this woman think she was to interfere in her life? Jeanne's own mother didn't tell her what to do. A small yelp of frustration escaped Jeanne's lips.

She took a few steps closer to her mother-in-law and pointed a finger at her, her eyes full of tears. The other woman's eyes widened. Jeanne raised her voice to make sure she'd be heard. "If you ever interfere in my life again, I promise you, you will never see this grandchild." She lowered her finger and her voice. "I mean it."

Mrs. Rossi looked at her and shrugged.

Jeanne hissed, "I know you understand me, so don't play dumb."

The other woman went off on a rant in Italian, but Jeanne refused to be cowed.

The back door opened, and Mr. Rossi stepped in. Both women immediately went quiet. Jeanne was fond of her father-in-law and hoped he'd heard none of the exchange between her and his wife.

"Hello, Mr. Rossi."

"What are you doing here?" He looked over to his wife and said, "Anna, give Jeanne something to eat. She has a bambino to feed."

Mrs. Rossi sniffed, and Jeanne looked over her shoulder at her and narrowed her eyes. "That's all right, Mrs. Rossi already offered me something to eat, but I can't stay."

"Does Sal know you're home?" he asked, obviously delighted. What was with their attitude against her working?

Jeanne shook her head and put her finger to her lips. "No, I want to surprise him." And with a small smile at her father-in-law, she gave a wave goodbye and sailed out the back door.

Later that evening, Sal couldn't understand why she was so upset about being let go from her job. She couldn't bring herself to use the word "fired," especially since she'd done nothing wrong to incur termination. Being pregnant, to her, was not a fireable offense. It annoyed her to no end.

"But you would have had to quit anyway. Once the baby got here." Sal tried to reason with her, but Jeanne wouldn't budge. It was as if she was being dinged because she was a woman and she was pregnant. It wasn't fair.

"I have some news," Sal said.

She looked up from the edge of the bed where she sat. He was smiling, and her reflex was to smile back. Unlike her announcement, it looked like he had good news. She did not want to drag him down into the morass of her own self-pity.

She forced a brightness to her expression that she did not feel. "Tell me."

Sal sat down next to her on the edge of the bed and took her hands in his. It was late in the day, and his five-o'clock shadow was coming on strong. She liked it; it gave him a swarthy countenance. There was a hint of his aftershave circling him, which she also liked.

"I've bought us a house!"

Jeanne's mouth fell open, and she blinked. "What?"

Sal grinned. "I found us a house, and I've signed all the paperwork. We move in in four weeks. I stopped by to see the landlord to give him our notice that we'd be moving out in a month."

Jeanne looked down at their clasped hands, her lips parted, and she shook her head slowly. "Say that again. You bought a house? For us to live in?"

Sal laughed. She usually loved his laugh as it came from deep within him, but at that moment, it annoyed her. Did pregnancy make you mean and miserable?

"Of course!" he said. "Who did you think was going to live in it?"

"And you've purchased it already?" Disbelief laced her voice. What a day she was having.

"With a mortgage, yes."

"But I haven't seen it," she pointed out. Her voice sounded shrill, but she didn't care.

An expression of confusion clouded his face. "I thought you'd be happy."

"I would have been if I'd been involved in the decision-making." She pulled her hands out of his and folded them in a huff across her chest.

He looked at her, dumbfounded. "But we're starting a family, we're going to need a bigger place."

"I know that. But you went and made a major purchase without my input." Sheer frustration set in. Tears stung the back of her eyes. She knew she should be grateful, but she had a hard time summoning anything akin to that feeling. In this world, she had no say in anything. Her husband, her boss, even her mother-in-law had more control over her life than she had.

Sal was speechless and appeared wounded. She hated herself for being such a shrew about this but if she didn't stand her ground now, he'd be making all the major decisions for the rest of her marriage, and she'd only be going along for the ride.

"What if I don't like it?" she asked. "Not to mention we'll be making less now that I've been let go from my job."

"I make enough to cover our bills," he said. "I thought you'd be happy to have your own home."

His repetition of "I thought you'd be happy" began to erode her anger. Sal was an honest man; he had genuinely been trying to please her. His last statement made her feel like she was being unappreciative, which she wasn't. Still. She would have liked to contribute, to be a partner instead of a beneficiary. "I am, but I would have liked to go with you to look at houses."

"I only looked at one," he admitted.

That was worse, but she didn't say anything. She sighed. She felt so powerless.

"You don't want to see it?" he asked.

"Of course I want to see it if it's going to be our new home," she said begrudgingly.

"Maybe you'll feel better after you see it," he said.

She shrugged. "Who knows."

"What's for dinner?" he asked.

The last thing she felt like doing was cooking. "I've got cube steaks for tonight."

"How long before it's ready?"

"Half hour." She forced herself off the bed and made her way to the kitchen to get the dinner ready. At the doorway, she paused and walked back to him. There was a slight droop to his shoulders now. Why did she have to go and ruin his good mood? What was wrong with her?

As she slipped her arms around his waist, he wrapped his around her, and she began to feel better.

"I'm sure it's a perfect house, and I can't wait to see it." There was some truth in the last part of what she'd said. Even if she hadn't been consulted, they had a home to call their own and she was curious about it. Their current apartment was tiny and although she thought it was romantic at present, she was practical enough to realize that it wouldn't be so romantic after the baby arrived.

Coyly, she looked up at him. "Can I choose the color for the carpet and the paint? Wallpaper maybe? Can I have a say?"

Sal grinned. "You can decorate the whole house in polka dots for all I care."

She pressed her face against his chest and held him tighter.

Over the weekend, Sal managed to get the keys from the realtor and drove Jeanne over to see the house.

From the outside, it looked big. Two stories, and she noticed with some satisfaction that it was slightly bigger than the houses either of them had grown up in. It did need some work. There was a shutter missing on the front window, and the siding was in desperate need of a paint job.

As she followed Sal through the house, she remained silent, deciding to reserve her judgement until she'd seen the whole place. It was spacious, with a large kitchen in the back, a dining room and large front parlor downstairs, and three bedrooms upstairs. There was an additional room at the end of the upstairs hall, and although Sal enthused about how it could be used for a fourth bedroom, Jeanne was doubtful. The bathroom had been recently redone with dark pink ceramic tiles with black trim. The toilet, tub, and sink were also pink. She could have sworn she'd seen Sal wince when looking in through the door. Smiling to herself, she thought it served him right for buying the house without her.

They ended up back at the front door. She really liked the house, and that disappointed her. She wanted to hate it if only to teach Sal a lesson.

"Well, what do you think?" he asked, watching her expression.

She nodded, looking around. "I like it."

Sal breathed an audible sigh of relief and came at her, wrapping his arms around her and lifting her off the floor. He was hard to resist. She couldn't help but smile.

When he set her back down, he said, "I know we have a lot of work to do here, but at least it's ours."

She was only half listening. "Sal, I have one thing to say. Don't ever again make such a big decision as this one without including me." Before he could answer, she turned and marched out the front door. She had things to do. Everything in their apartment needed to be packed up, and she was already envisioning where she was going to put all their furniture and what color she would paint the walls.

Chapter Fifteen

1964

Jeanne pulled up a chair to the kitchen table in Lois's apartment. The two of them, plus Mary and Betty, met up once a month at Lois's for cards. Initially, they'd tried for once a week but with the demands of motherhood on Jeanne, Mary, and Betty, that soon became impossible, and they settled for monthly get-togethers. This one night was a night Jeanne looked forward to with relish. There were no dishes to wash or diapers to change or anyone crying. It was a little bit of heaven for a couple of hours. She loved being a wife and mother, but sometimes she liked a break and a chance to be herself.

All were married with children except for Lois. She worked as a secretary in the county clerk's office. Jeanne envied her life: the other woman was free to come and go as she pleased, with no one making any demands on her.

Lois carried over a tray of cheese and crackers and a bowl of cheese puffs, which were a personal favorite of Betty's, even if they did leave orange dust all over her fingers and then the cards.

"Highballs all around?" Jeanne asked, giving Lois a hand.

"None for me," Betty said demurely. She didn't look at her friends, her eyes busy on the cards she was shuffling.

But all three looked at Betty. There was only one reason Betty would turn down a drink.

Lois, bold and forthright, asked simply, "Are you pregnant again?"

"Yes," Betty said, not looking at them. She had four children already, all under the age of five.

Jeanne said nothing, only raised her eyebrows slightly. Betty was chronically tired. Her husband was a great provider, but he worked a lot of doubles at the factory, and Jeanne was surprised he had the time or energy to procreate. But she supposed where there was a will there was a way.

"I thought you were going on the pill," Mary said.

Betty reddened. "Chuck didn't like the idea."

Lois frowned. "But it's your decision too."

Betty's husband was very conservative, and roles were clearly defined in their marriage.

"Do you want another baby?" Lois asked, highballs forgotten.

"Of course. I love babies," Betty said. But her gauntness and the ever-present purple circles beneath her eyes told a different story.

Mary shook her head. "No more kids for me. Three is enough. I went on the pill right after Denise was born." Mary's youngest was the same age as Jeanne's son Joey: one. She appeared thoughtful as she picked up the cards Betty dealt. "It's so nice not to have to worry about getting pregnant."

Jeanne couldn't agree more. Joey, her second child, hadn't been an easy baby. Lots of colic and too many sleepless nights. And Terry had been so easy. If they were all like Terry, she'd have ten of them. But the more she talked to other mothers, the more it seemed the second child was the handful. The first one was easy, to lull you into having more, but the second child tested you. When Joey was six months old and her period had been late, she'd had a scare and realized she didn't want another baby. Immediately, she made an appointment with her doctor, who did not hide his displeasure when she requested contraception. But she would not back down. Unlike Mary, who hadn't told her husband she'd gone on birth control, Jeanne had been honest with Sal. He'd been against it: he was Catholic after all, and it went against the Church's teaching. But as Jeanne had pointed out, she *wasn't* Catholic. "Only for a little while so I can catch my breath," she'd assured Sal. Her friends were aghast when she told them she'd discussed the issue with her husband. But it wouldn't be right, she concluded. If she demanded to be included on decisions regarding big issues, then she had to afford him the same courtesy.

As far as she was concerned, this was between Betty and Chuck. And Betty had always wanted to have lots of kids; she shouldn't be made to feel bad about it. It was none of their business.

In the small apartment kitchen, she mixed three highballs in tall glasses, putting a colorful stir stick in each one. She uncapped a bottle of Pepsi and poured it into a glass for Betty.

She looked around the kitchen, and not for the first time, thought how she'd love to have her own apartment, wondering what her life would be like if she hadn't gotten married so soon out of high school. She liked the idea of making her own money and spending it on herself and an apartment. But that was not her life. There was no sense in dwelling on what might have been.

As Lois and Mary chided Betty on her pregnancy, Jeanne felt her own feathers being ruffled. She carried the Pepsi and one highball over to the table. After setting the Pepsi down in front of Betty and the highball down in front of Mary, she pivoted and grabbed the other two highballs. When she returned the second time, she noticed Betty had her head bent, and Jeanne scowled at Lois and Mary. Mary shrugged as if to say, *What?*

What her friends failed to remember was that Betty was the sensitive sort and took things to heart.

"Are we ready to play?" Jeanne asked, trying to inject a light-hearted tone into the conversation. This was her only night out in the month; she didn't want drama.

Lois and Mary studied their cards.

Betty's bottom lip quivered. Jeanne sighed. They'd gone and done it now. She reached over and patted her friend's hand.

"It's all right, Betty. Don't be upset. You have to do what's best for you. And really, honey, it's between you and Chuck."

Unable to speak, Betty nodded.

There was a grim set to Lois's mouth. "Cheer up. It's not the end of the world. Mary and I are sorry if we came on a bit strong. Jeanne is right. You have to do what's best for you and Chuck." She gave Betty a reassuring smile.

Jeanne took a big gulp of her highball and helped herself to a Ritz cracker and a piece of cheese. "Okay, who's going first?"

Betty raised her hand, and the pads of her fingertips were covered in orange dust. The three of them burst out laughing.

The following morning, Betty called Jeanne after breakfast. She'd been expecting her call and had hurried to give the boys their breakfast and wash the dishes in a pan of sudsy water.

Betty started the conversation with "I don't think I'm going to Lois's to play cards anymore."

Jeanne sat down on the kitchen chair that had a straight-shot view into the front parlor, where she'd temporarily parked Terry and Joey in the wooden playpen. She took a sip of her now half-gone, half-cold tea.

"Why not?" But Jeanne could guess the reason. Sometimes Lois and Mary together could overwhelm Betty. "Look, Betty, ignore those two. They tend to come on strong, and they think everyone should be in line with their way of thinking."

Betty faltered. In the background was the noise of Betty's kids. Some crying, some shouting, some laughing. She seemed to take it in stride. That sort of thing didn't bother Betty at all. Maybe she was better cut out than the rest of them for motherhood.

"I don't know. Are you mad at me, Jeanne? Do you think I'm stupid for having another baby?"

Jeanne could hear the upset in her friend's voice, and she immediately sought to reassure her. "Not on your life. For as long as I've known you, you've always wanted babies."

"Ever since I was a little girl."

Jeanne had known that since they were young. Betty had dragged those dolls around with her everywhere until she was thirteen. "Betty, if it's what you and Chuck want, then it's the right thing to do. To hell with everyone else."

1966

Jeanne and Sal drove home from their usual Saturday night out. They spent their Saturday nights at a cocktail lounge, drinking and dancing. She always looked forward to it. And one Friday a month, they went to the movies. She liked being married to Sal; he was so easygoing and such great company. Her friends complained of their husbands but truthfully, she couldn't say anything bad about him.

From his side of the car, he winked at her and reached for her hand. "Let's get home and get to work on baby number three."

Jeanne laughed. She'd gone off the pill the previous year, as they'd decided they'd like another child or two. But every month when her period arrived, she had to admit to a small sense of relief, a feeling she did not share with her husband.

"Sal, do we have to go to your mother's house for dinner tomorrow?"

He looked over at her with an expression that suggested she'd uttered something blasphemous.

"But we always go to Mama's on Sunday for dinner."

Jeanne refrained from rolling her eyes. "I know, but I was thinking this Sunday, I'd like to stay at home. I could cook us a roast."

He frowned. "But we can't cancel now. She'll be up early to make the sauce and the gnocchi."

Jeanne sighed. "How about next weekend?"

"But you know how much Mamma looks forward to our visits," he said.

It was true that the elder Mrs. Rossi enjoyed seeing Sal and the boys. She lavished a lot of attention on the boys, and yet Jeanne always felt as if the other woman barely tolerated her.

When Jeanne didn't respond, Sal added, "Especially since Papa died."

That had been awful. Mr. Rossi had ended up with some kind of rare cancer and was dead within a month of his diagnosis. Jeanne had been mortified at her own uncharitable thoughts in wishing it had been Mrs. Rossi instead.

"I don't want to spend *every* Sunday at your mother's house. I wouldn't mind going to see my parents for a change," she said, trying to keep the hostility out of her voice.

"We could see your parents on Saturday."

Jeanne rested her elbow on the car door, tapping her knuckles against her bottom lip. She closed her eyes, feeling a headache coming on. Where was it written in stone that they had to eat sauce and pasta on Sundays with Sal's mother? Maybe she wanted pork chops or a roast chicken instead. But she decided it wasn't worth the fight. She was tired, and she didn't want the night to end with them sleeping with their backs to each other, tense. Best to bring it up another time. Maybe some night during the week.

As Sal swung the car into the driveway, the headlights swept broadly across their home, illuminating the two-story house. In the years since they'd moved in, she grown to both love it and hate it. She loved it because it was theirs, but she hated it because sometimes it felt like her prison.

Chapter Sixteen

April 1975

After seventeen years of marriage, Jeanne Rossi was ready to cry over the sheer boredom of her routine. If she had to spend one more night in the house, she was going to scream. The desire to get out after being cooped up all winter was strong. She was always antsy come spring. You could smell the better weather that was coming in the air. The new earth. The fresh breeze. She was anxious for the warmer weather that would mean she could at least sit outside.

Sal had suggested she join the PTA if she wanted to get out of the house. But she wasn't looking to fill the time with more tasks. She wanted to do something fun, something new.

She was in a rut.

Sal was a homebody; he liked staying at home in the evenings. He said he did enough socializing at his barber shop during the day that he looked forward to the quiet of the evening at home with his family. But Jeanne was stuck inside all day and chomped at the bit to get out. When she suggested they go out during the week, he'd looked at her like she'd grown a second head. He suggested she try a new craft, knitting or sewing. At that suggestion, all she could think of was jabbing him with a knitting needle. The years were going by, but she was still young and wanted to have some fun before she got too old to care or remember what having fun meant.

Jeanne was a dutiful wife: she kept the house clean, the beds made, and the toys picked up and put away. Every evening, she had a hot meal ready for Sal when he returned from work. She'd even learned how to make sauce like his mother. She helped the boys with their homework and volunteered at school functions. The previous year, she'd broached the subject again of maybe getting a part-time job now that the boys were older, but Sal had firmly said no. Said she didn't need to work, and his own mother had never worked outside of the home. The very idea of it had been distasteful to him.

Across the room, he sat in his easy chair reading the newspaper. He lowered the paper and looked at her. But there was nothing to say. A glance passed between them and within moments, Sal picked up the paper again. Once she sat down on the sofa, that would be it. And she couldn't. She wouldn't. With a sigh of displeasure, she turned and headed back to the kitchen, picking up the handset from the rotary phone on the wall.

She dialed Betty's number first. Her friend might like a night out for a change too. Get a break from her six kids. Maybe they could go out to the Old Red Top and have a cup of coffee and a slice of pie. The line was busy. Jeanne tried three times and then gave up. Betty had a lot of sisters and even though they lived within walking distance of each other, they spent most of their time on their phones, sitting at their kitchen tables, smoking cigarettes and talking to each other. Next, she tried Mary's number. But her husband, Sid, answered the phone and said she was putting the baby to bed. Mary's oldest kids were the same ages as Jeanne's boys, but she'd had a baby the previous year, an unexpected surprise. She hadn't been happy about it as she'd thought she was done having babies, but when the little boy had arrived, she and her husband were over the moon. Desperate, Jeanne dialed Lottie Moloney's phone number. They had never hung around together but their kids were the same age, and they'd had some nice chats when they saw each other at school functions.

"Hi Lottie, it's Jeanne," she said when the other woman answered.

There was a pause on the other end of the line. Admittedly, she hadn't had Lottie's number and had to flip through the pages of the phone book for it.

She cleared her throat. "Jeanne Rossi. Our kids go to school together."

"Oh yes! I'm sorry, Jeanne, my mind went blank. How are you?"

"I'm good, Lottie, thanks, and you?"

"Up to my neck in it, but other than that I'm fine," Lottie said.

There was a momentary lull as neither said anything. Jeanne soldiered on. "I was wondering if you'd be interested in going to the movies tonight." She groaned inwardly. It sounded like she was asking her out on a date. "*Three Days of the Condor* is up at the show." She loved any movie with Robert Redford.

"Oh, I can't. I have ceramics tonight," Lottie said.

"I understand," Jeanne said, her shoulders sagging.

Lottie lowered her voice and whispered. "I've seen it three times already at the show. Dennis would kill me if he knew." She laughed, and Jeanne laughed along with her.

"Another time," Jeanne said.

"Sure. Give me a call sometime."

Finally, Jeanne dialed Lois's phone number. It rang and Jeanne leaned against the wall, fingering the corkscrew telephone cord that hung from the base. She wasn't hopeful.

Lois had never married, and continued to work full time as a clerk in the Hideaway Bay municipal offices.

And because of that, she had drifted away from Jeanne, Betty, and Mary, though they still ran into her from time to time. It wasn't that there'd been a falling out, but their lives were drastically different. Lois was still dating and living the single life while the other three were raising kids, and growing apart, although sad, seemed inevitable. They no longer had anything in common.

It went both ways, Jeanne reminded herself. Lois was hardly ringing her phone off the hook either.

When Lois picked up on the fifth ring, Jeanne was surprised.

"Hi Lois, it's Jeanne. Jeanne Rossi."

"You didn't have to add your last name, silly. I know who you are." She paused. "It's been a long time."

Jeanne had to agree with her. "It has."

"To what do I owe the pleasure of this phone call?"

Jeanne decided she detected no hostility in Lois's voice.

"I was hoping to pop over. Thought we could catch up." Maybe they could play cards or have a few drinks or something, like they used to do.

"Actually, I'm getting ready to go out," Lois replied.

Jeanne couldn't hide her disappointment and sighed loudly. She didn't have to be in the living room to know that her husband was comfortable in his chair, his head still buried in the paper. On the shag carpet, the boys would be stretched out on their bellies, their hands propping up their faces as they watched *Happy Days*. It was the same thing every night; the only thing that changed was the television show.

"Why don't you come with me?" Lois said.

"Where are you going?"

"Out to a dance club. Come on, it'll be fun."

Jeanne didn't need much convincing; she jumped at the chance.

"What should I wear?"

"No mom clothes, that's for sure. Do your hair and your makeup,"

"Okay," Jeanne said.

"I'll pick you up in fifteen minutes," Lois said.

A moment of panic set in. That wouldn't give her enough time to plug in her rollers. "Can you make it thirty? I mean, I have to get ready."

"Okay, sure. I've got to stop and get cigarettes. See you in thirty," Lois said, and she hung up.

Jeanne jumped up. She said to Sal, "I'm going out for a little while with Lois."

The boys didn't look up, and Sal lowered his paper halfway so that his eyes met hers. "Lois? You haven't seen her in a long time."

"I know. Too long."

"Sure, get out for a little bit. It'll do you good."

Jeanne headed up the stairs, pondering what she would wear. She looked down at her jeans and her

T-shirt, thinking they were a little too casual for a nightclub. The first thing she did was plug in her Remington hot rollers, then headed for her bedroom closet to pick out an outfit.

In the end, she opted for a beige dress she'd worn to a wedding months ago. She left it on the bed and returned to the bathroom, where she expertly took sections of hair one at a time, combed them out, and rolled rollers around them, securing them with hair clips until rollers covered her entire scalp. She stood in front of the bathroom mirror, leaning over the sink with the vanity drawer open, applying green eyeshadow, mascara, a little dab of rouge, and clear lip gloss. When she finished applying her makeup, she put all her cosmetics away in the drawer, wiped off the counter, and removed the hot rollers from her hair, brushing it out before she applied a liberal dose of hairspray.

She slipped on a pair of pantyhose, and it got caught on her fingernail, starting the beginning of a run. "Shoot." She grabbed a bottle of nail polish off the top of her dresser and dabbed the run before it could go any further. She rummaged through her drawer, found her slip at the back of it, and slipped it over her head, followed by a brown turtleneck. Finally, she pulled the dress over it, a light material with a V-neck and a pointy collar.

On her way out of the bathroom, she peeked into her bedroom and glanced at the clock on Sal's dresser. She'd gotten ready with five minutes to spare. She slipped on a pair of wedge shoes, which were high enough that she had to hold on to the banister on her way down the staircase.

Sal looked up from his newspaper and raised his eyebrows, shock registering on his face.

"You're all dressed up to go to Lois's house?"

"I'm not going to Lois's house. We're going out dancing!" She smiled, then self-consciously ran her lip against her front teeth, looking for evidence of any errant lip gloss.

"Oh." Sal's tone was underwhelming. But then he was caught in the cocktail era of the 60's and still listened to Frank Sinatra and Dean Martin. Although he was only four years older, sometimes it felt like he was fifty. The gulf of differences and preferences had grown wider between them over the years, as if they were heading in opposite directions.

Before she could respond or explain, there was the honk of a car horn outside.

"I'll be home later." She looked over to the boys, who were engrossed in *Laverne and Shirley*. "Good night, boys."

Not turning their heads, they both called over their shoulders, "'Night, Mom."

As an aside, she said to Sal, "Remember, no *Three's Company*." That show was a little too racy for her tastes.

Sal nodded and lifted his chin and puckered his lips.

She almost sighed but didn't, leaning down to kiss him. "Good night, Sal."

"Not too late, Jeanne."

Okay, Dad.

Lois's orange 1970 Plymouth Barracuda idled at the curb. For the life of her, Jeanne couldn't understand why Lois had bought a muscle car. She'd seen her tooling around town in it but had presumed it must belong to her boyfriend, if she even had a steady boyfriend. But then Mary had told her that the car belonged to Lois. Jeanne supposed since Lois was single and answered to no one, she could do whatever she wanted. It irritated Sal, and he attributed her choice of a car to attention-seeking behavior. He had never been a big fan of Lois's. They were at opposite ends of just about everything. During the Vietnam War, Sal had tied a yellow ribbon around his barber pole at the shop, while Lois was marching in protests, demanding that the soldiers be brought home. When she burned her bra during another protest, Sal had been horrified and asked Jeanne, "You're not going to stop wearing a bra, are you? That would be indecent."

At the time, Jeanne had rolled her eyes and said, "Of course not." But she'd be the first to admit that removing her bra at night was sometimes the highlight of her day.

When she opened the car door, she was confronted with the smell of cigarette smoke and perfume. Immediately, she recognized the scent—Charlie—because Sal had given her a bottle for Christmas. She slid into the passenger seat and Lois peeled away from the curb. Jeanne wondered why she did that; it was such a masculine gesture. Was it because she was trying to make a point, draw attention to herself as Sal said, or was it simply because she could?

"Let's go," Lois said, looking over at her.

"Where are we going?"

"To the Paradise," Lois replied.

Located right on Main Street on the beach side, Jeanne had passed it a million times but had never been inside. The name, she'd concluded, sounded corny.

Lois pushed in the knob for the cigarette lighter on the dashboard and nodded toward the carton of Virginia Slims on the seat between them. "Help a girl out and tap me out a cigarette."

Jeanne opened the carton, pulled out a pack, removed a cigarette, and handed it to her friend. Sal would have a fit if she ever took up smoking, but she found herself drawn to those ads for Virginia Slims. They seemed so sophisticated. If she ever started smoking, she'd smoke the same brand as Lois.

The Paradise nightclub shared a common parking lot with the Old Red Top. And despite it being April, the lot was packed with cars. Jeanne was filled with a combination of anxiety and excitement. Nerves because she wasn't a very good dancer and had never been out to a nightclub by herself. And excitement because she was out of the house on a Tuesday night and doing something fun. Adult. For a change.

Without further ado, Lois pulled into the fire lane in front of the building, put the car in park, and pulled the key out of the ignition, cigarette hanging from her mouth, the ash lengthening.

"You can't park here, it's a fire lane," Jeanne pointed out.

"I park here all the time," Lois said with a confidence Jeanne envied. "The bouncer, Jed, is a good friend of mine," she added with a wink.

Tension coiled and unwound in Jeanne's stomach as she followed Lois toward the entrance of the nightclub. The door opened and music with a fast beat spilled out. She bit her lip.

"Hold on a minute," Lois said, turning around in front of her. She reached out and removed Jeanne's glasses. "Put those in your purse. They make you look like a schoolmarm or something."

"Oh, okay," Jeanne said, slipping her spectacles quickly into her purse. She squinted to see better.

"And don't squint like that! You look like you need glasses."

"But I do need glasses," Jeanne countered.

At the entrance stood a man wearing a brown leisure suit with a matching brown patterned shirt. The front of his shirt was open, revealing a gold medallion around his neck, nestled against a hairy chest. He had a thick brown mustache and a headful of dark hair.

"Hey, Jed." Lois grinned as she approached him.

He nodded, crossing his arms over his chest. With a glance toward her car, he said, "I see you've parked in the fire lane again, Lois."

Lois responded by tossing him her car keys, which he caught midair with one hand. "If the fire department should need the space," she said, "would you be a love and move it?"

Jeanne raised her eyebrows and stared at her friend. She'd practically cooed at the man.

Inside, the noise increased exponentially, but Jeanne smiled as she recognized the song playing: "I Love Music" by the O'Jays. Without even realizing it, she began to tap her feet along to the beat of the music.

Lois indicated she should follow her to the coat check, and Jeanne felt a surge of excitement. Underneath Lois's short rabbit fur coat was a stunning aqua-colored dress that complimented her blond hair. On her feet were a pair of strappy silver sandals that made her slim legs appear even longer. Next to her friend, Jeanne felt old and frumpy. They checked their coats and made their way to the bar. Lois leaned over to get the bartender's attention.

"The usual, Lois?"

Lois glanced at Jeanne beside her and held up her fingers in a "v" sign. "Make it two, please."

The bartender went to work and while they waited for their drinks, Jeanne took the opportunity to look around the place. It was a long rectangular room. They were at the back of the building where the bar was located. Between the bar and the dance floor were booths and high tables. She couldn't believe how many people were out on a Tuesday night. Although some of these faces looked familiar, she didn't really know anyone other than Lois. She could feel the vibration of the music beneath her feet. A big silver strobe light hung over the center of the dance floor, its pulsating light flashing around the room.

The bartender set their drinks down in front of them. Lois pulled money out of her purse and slapped it down on the bar.

As the bartender picked it up, Lois said with a wink, "Keep the change, Chad."

He held up the bills toward her and said, "Thanks, Lois."

"Let me give you money for my drink," Jeanne said.

"Don't worry about it. You can get the next round."

"What is this?" Jeanne asked, taking hold of the stem of the margarita glass. The beverage was a slushy blue concoction. Hanging off the rim of the glass was a chunk of pineapple and a maraschino cherry that had been speared with a pink plastic sword. She sipped it, immediately thinking, *tropical.*

"It's a Blue Hawaiian. It's my absolute favorite drink, and no one makes them like Chad," Lois said. She held the straw between her lips, smiling at the bartender.

Jeanne readily agreed that it was the best drink she'd ever had. Her drink of choice was normally a highball, but she'd been drinking them all her adult life and was ready for something different. Something new. And in more areas of her life than alcoholic beverages.

"Come on, let's find a table closer to the dance floor."

Jeanne carried her drink in one hand and slung her purse over her shoulder. She tried to see in the dim, smoky light, wishing she could put her glasses on for a second to get a better look at the place and the people. The music throbbed and the lights flashed constantly. The noise was so loud she couldn't hear herself think.

And she absolutely loved it.

There was one high table at the far corner against the railing that divided the seating area from the dance floor. Her gaze focused on the dancers. The floor itself was a checkerboard of different-colored illuminated lights.

There was no waltzing around like the dancing she and Sal did at family weddings or the odd Saturday night at the cocktail lounge. This was the disco dancing she'd seen on television. She stared, mesmerized, as couples did intricate footwork in tandem. It was so beautiful. Still watching the dancing, she pulled her purse off her shoulder and set it on the table next to her drink.

The music ended and the DJ announced, "Time for your Tuesday night dance lesson. Are you ready to learn the Hustle?"

"Yeah!" Lois shouted along with the crowd, holding her drink above her head.

"Then let's boogie on the dance floor!"

Lois put her drink down and summoned Jeanne with a wave. "Come on, let's go dance."

Jeanne took a gulp of her drink and shook her head. "No. I can't dance like that!"

"Don't be silly! There's an instructor, he'll show you. He gives lessons on all the new disco crazes every week. It's how I learned."

As Jeanne racked her brain for an excuse, Lois glared at her, hand on hip. "What are you going to do? Stand there all night and watch everyone else dancing?"

Jeanne didn't think that was a bad plan; she would have been satisfied with that.

Lois took the drink out of Jeanne's hand and set it on the table. Taking her by the arm, she pulled her onto the dance floor, laughing.

"What about our purses and our drinks?" Jeanne asked, keeping her eye on the table. She could feel the frown between her eyebrows. That's just what she needed: to get her purse stolen or her drink spiked. She'd read all the horror stories of drinks getting spiked and girls being assaulted while they were out of it.

"Watch and learn from the master," Lois teased. She walked around to the dance floor and found a spot by the railing right in front of their table. "See, everything is right there. And if we get thirsty from too much dancing, all we have to do is reach over the railing and grab our drink. Like this." She demonstrated by doing just that and lifting her Blue Hawaiian from the table, taking a long sip, her feet moving to the beat, and setting her drink back down.

Immediately, Lois got caught up in the music and moved her feet and arms in rhythm to the song, the beat, the music. Unsure of what to do and feeling rather foolish, Jeanne stood there for a moment.

"Come on, Jeanne! Don't be a stick-in-the-mud."

Studying Lois, Jeanne tried copying her moves but felt clumsy and uncoordinated.

The DJ made another announcement that everyone who wanted to learn how to do the Hustle needed to meet in the center of the dance floor.

"Come on, you can learn this. This is a great dance," Lois said, pulling Jeanne by the hand and leading her to the center of the dance floor, where a small group of people had gathered.

"I'll keep an eye on our drinks," Lois said as she departed and went back to their previous spot. Or at least that's what Jeanne thought she said. It was hard to hear over the loud music.

Jeanne felt self-conscious and for a brief moment thought it might be time to go home, even though she hadn't finished her drink.

Suddenly a man took her by the arm, and the look on her face must have betrayed her because he laughed and said, "Sorry, honey, I'm putting you all in a line. It's easier to learn that way."

"Oh, okay."

"I'm Randy, by the way."

"Jeanne."

"Hello, Jeanne." He smiled. He was blond and blue-eyed with straight white teeth.

The DJ cut the music while Randy gave step-by-step instruction on the Hustle. There were two lines of roughly five to six people. Jeanne was glad she was in the front line so she could see better. Randy stood in front of them and slowly demonstrated the footwork for the dance. Her eyes remained glued to his feet, and she kept doing the steps and following his lead so often, she didn't realize right away that the DJ was playing the actual song that had inspired the dance.

Randy turned around and said, "That's it, keep it going. You're all looking great. Remember this is the East Coast Hustle, not the West Coast. If you want to learn the West Coast, then I suggest you go out to the West Coast."

That struck her as funny, and she laughed. Randy looked at her and said, "You're a quick learner, Jeanne. Nice footwork."

Heat crept up to her cheeks at being singled out, but she kept moving her feet, following Randy, ignoring the fact that her turtleneck was too heavy and she was beginning to perspire. She didn't care; she'd know for next time not to wear such heavy clothing. She kept moving. And she kept dancing.

As she practiced, she kept her eye on Lois, who was right where Jeanne had left her: in the corner of the dance floor in front of their table. Feeling a little more confident in her footwork, she made her way over to Lois and joined her.

The crushed ice in her drink had melted and it was a diluted, warm glass of blue sweetness. She didn't care. Her mouth was parched, and she gulped it down.

"I'll get us another," she said, grabbing her purse off the table and heading to the bar, not giving Lois a chance to voice her opinion or even raise an eyebrow.

She carried the drinks back to the table, one in each hand, singing along to the song being played by the DJ. She wanted to get back out on the dance floor soon, but she needed a break as her feet ached.

Jeanne handed Lois a drink. Her elbow rested on the edge of the table, and she took a drag off her cigarette. Jeanne studied her face, particularly her makeup: her eyebrows were plucked thin, her eyeshadow was bright blue, and she wore rouge and lip gloss. It was a look Jeanne thought she might try.

"I think someone likes disco!" Lois said.

"I sure do! The dancing and music are incredible," Jeanne enthused, taking a big gulp of her drink.

"Hey, slow down, lady, you're not used to drinking," Lois advised.

"May I?" Jeanne asked, indicating Lois's pack of cigarettes.

Lois scowled. "Since when do you smoke?"

Jeanne shrugged. "I don't. But I feel like having one."

Lois pushed the pack toward her. Jeanne tapped one out and used Lois's lighter to light it. She drew in a deep lungful, feeling the smoke burn her throat and her lungs. As awful as it felt, it also felt good. It made her feel alive.

When she didn't think she could drink another drink or dance another step, she asked Lois what the time was.

Lois glanced at her wristwatch and announced, "It's a little after one."

"One in the morning?" Jeanne asked, aghast.

Lois giggled. "Well, it's not one in the afternoon."

"I've got to go home."

"I suppose I should too, I have to work in the morning."

Jeanne winced. "What are you going to do about work?"

Lois looked at her uncomprehending. "What do you mean? I'll go in like I always do."

"But won't you be tired and . . . hungover?" Jeanne asked. She did not look forward to the headache she was certain was in her future, but it was a small price to pay for the good time she'd had.

"Yeah, so what? I'll go to work. I'll be dragging, of course, but I'll think of all the fun I had tonight, and I'll think of all the fun I'll have again next time."

Jeanne couldn't wait to go out again.

"Come on, grab your purse and let's go."

If Jeanne had known it would take Lois so long to say goodbye to everyone, she would have insisted they leave earlier. First, Lois said goodbye to Randy, who told her that her friend was a great dancer. Then it was on to the bar, where she said goodbye to the two bartenders and was, by Jeanne's estimation, a little flirty. She spoke briefly to some other patrons, wishing them well and telling them she'd see them next time, which made Jeanne wonder how many nights a week Lois went out dancing. On the way out, Lois's longest goodbye was reserved for Jed, the bouncer. Their flirting made Jeanne slightly uncomfortable; it was like she was invisible.

Jed handed over the keys and walked them to the car, which Jeanne thought was ridiculous as it was still parked in the fire lane and only steps from the front door.

But when Lois got in, she rolled down the window and Jed leaned in, resting his elbows on the door.

"Listen, Lois, why don't you come back after you take your friend home."

Jeanne's eyes widened but she kept her gaze directed straight ahead, feeling like an intruder on a private conversation.

Lois giggled at the invitation. "Jed, now don't be naughty, you know I'm not that type of girl."

"Naughty is nice," he whispered.

"Say good night now." Lois was laughing.

"All right, Lois, another time. Good night, girls." And he rapped on the top of the car with his knuckles and stepped back so Lois could pull the car out.

When they pulled out onto the street, Jeanne asked, "Why did he want you to come back? Won't the place be closed?"

Lois leveled her gaze at her. "Really, Jeanne? Are you that naïve? He wants me to come back for a little hanky-panky."

"Oh," Jeanne said. In hindsight, the invitation seemed kind of brazen.

"You have got to get out of the house more," Lois said.

Jeanne couldn't agree more with this off-the-cuff assessment.

When they pulled onto Jeanne's street, she noted how quiet and dark it was, and it dawned on her that she rarely saw it at this time of night. It was rather peaceful.

"Don't bother pulling into the driveway, Lois. I'll get out at the curb." She didn't want to wake Sal with headlights, an engine running, or the sound of a car door slamming.

"Will Sal give you a hard time?"

Jeanne shook her head. Sal had never given her a hard time about anything.

The house was dark, but Sal had left the porch light on for her. It was weird to be out without him or the boys. She was so used to it being the two of them or the four of them that being out by herself was something altogether different. She definitely liked it.

Standing at the front door, she turned and waved Lois off. She dug through her purse until she found her house key. Teetering on her feet, she felt her vision was a little off, and she opened her eyes wider and tried blinking. Slowly, she took the key and inserted it into the lock. Thankfully, she got it on the first try, listening for that satisfying click that told her the lock had been undone.

As quietly as possible, she removed her coat and hung it up in the hall closet. She would have preferred to go straight upstairs, but she had a throbbing headache and made a beeline for the kitchen, where she downed two aspirin and a glass of water. It wasn't that she'd had that much to drink, it was that she wasn't a drinker, and three Blue Hawaiians had the room tilting slightly to one side.

At the staircase, she removed her shoes, carrying them upstairs so as not to wake anyone. She stopped in the bathroom and brushed her teeth and used the toilet. She didn't bother washing her face, she was too tired. She took off all her clothes, letting them fall in a pile on the floor. She sat on the closed lid of the toilet seat, peeled off her pantyhose, and threw them in the hamper. She pulled her nightgown off the hook on the back of the bathroom door and slipped it over her head. Hurriedly, she hung her clothes on the hook. She'd put everything away properly in the morning. All she wanted was to climb into bed.

On the way to her room, she peeked in each of the boys' rooms, satisfied that they were covered before heading to bed. The streetlight shining in their bedroom window illuminated the path to her side of the bed. Tonight, she would not complain about it. Her eyes were closing as she slid beneath the blankets, and a sigh escaped her lips.

"What time is it?" Sal asked in a voice that did not sound groggy. In fact, he sounded wide awake.

"A little after one," she lied. It was almost two.

"Have you been smoking and drinking, Jeanne?" Sal asked.

"We went dancing and the place was smoky," she said. Besides, she only smoked one cigarette; it was hardly a federal offense. "And I did have a couple of drinks."

"Did you have fun?"

"I did."

Her feet hurt and her legs ached, but she couldn't remember the last time she'd smiled so much. Or had such a great time. She was already counting the days until next Tuesday night.

Chapter Seventeen

Jeanne sat at her kitchen table tapping her foot relentlessly, every so often glancing up at the clock, but the minute hand moved agonizingly slow that morning. It had been a week since she'd gone out with Lois. Since then, the memories of dancing and drinking Blue Hawaiians had been the sole occupants of her mind. And as she waited for Tuesday night to roll around again, the week had dragged.

Long forgotten was the pounding headache she'd woken up with on Wednesday morning. Over the weekend, she bought a new dress, something both clingy and swirly, and even the salesgirl had said it was made for dancing. That comment had sealed the deal for her. The whole week while the boys were at school and Sal was at the barber shop, she blared the radio in the house. Every time a disco song came on, she'd stop what she was doing and practice her steps. When the boys arrived home in the afternoon from school, she turned the volume down so it could only be heard in the kitchen. And when she heard the sound of Sal's car pulling into the driveway, she turned it off altogether.

Earlier, she'd been up before the alarm went off, and it still wasn't even ten in the morning. The boys had gone off to school, their brown paper lunch bags and books in their hands. Sal always left at seven thirty for his barbershop, kissing her on the cheek before he walked out the door.

Impatient, she stood from the table, pushed her chair in, and emptied her coffee mug in the sink before giving it a quick washout and setting it on the drainboard to dry. The antidote to the interminable wait was to keep busy. She scoured the kitchen sink, the bathroom sink and tub. Looking at the tile, she frowned at the grout, deciding it was time to tackle that. By early afternoon, she'd cleaned and scrubbed the main rooms of the house. When she was finished, she peeled potatoes, carrots, and onions and set about making a pot roast for dinner. An hour before the boys were due home, she took a bath, soaking in the tub and lathering herself up with a bar of Camay. It would do no good to go out dancing smelling like Ajax, Spic and Span, and Endust. She dried off and slipped on her housecoat. She stood at the sink, leaning forward to see better in the mirror, plucking her eyebrows, showing no mercy, until each one was a thin, arched line.

The only thing she didn't do was think about Sal. She hadn't told him she was going out dancing again. Hadn't told him she'd spent a little more money than necessary on a brand-new dress. She'd used the grocery money, and she'd have to be clever the next few weeks to cover the difference.

The boys came in right after school, throwing their books on the bottom steps of the staircase, to be taken up later after they'd had something to eat. Both breezed into the kitchen, looking for food. Terry, fifteen and now taller than both Sal and Jeanne, made a beeline for the refrigerator, opened the door, and leaned in, surveying the contents.

He tilted his head to one side and then looked at the radio sitting on the counter. Scowling, he asked, "What is that noise?"

"That is dance music. Disco," Jeanne answered. He shook his head in disgust. A glance at her youngest son, Joey, indicated he wasn't paying any attention to their conversation. He was too busy choosing an apple from the fruit bowl on the kitchen table.

"Do you guys want sandwiches?" she asked.

"Boloney," replied Terry.

"Salami," said Joey between bites of apple.

She fixed their sandwiches the way they liked them: butter on one slice of bread, lunch meat, and some Weber's mustard. She cut them on the diagonal and handed a plate to each of them. Joey sat down at the table, finished his apple, and picked up the sandwich. Terry leaned against the sink and wolfed down his food.

One song on the radio ended and another began: "Shining Star" by Earth, Wind and Fire.

"I love this song!" She reached over and turned up the volume. In the limited floor space by the refrigerator, she practiced the steps she'd learned the previous week, just as she'd done every day since.

Joey laughed.

Terry scoffed. "Mom, what are you, a freak? Disco is for freaks!"

Jeanne shrugged, not caring. "Then I guess I'm a freak."

Once the boys finished their sandwiches and headed upstairs, she turned the volume up slightly as she got dinner ready.

She could always tell when Terry was done with his homework, because that's when he would blare his stereo. The previous weekend, Sal had bought him Bruce Springsteen's *Born to Run* album, and he'd been playing it nonstop.

Jeanne stood at the end of the staircase and yelled up, "Terry, turn it down. It's too loud!"

This was met with an "Aw, Mom!" She thought he turned it down, but it was hard to tell. It was still pretty loud.

Sal walked through the front door.

"Something smells good! I'm starving."

"Good," she said, leaning into him as he kissed her cheek. "Pot roast tonight."

"What happened to your eyebrows?" he asked. "You didn't shave them, did you? My cousin Rosalie shaved hers off and they never grew back. She always had to draw them in."

"Oh, Sal," she said, trying to shrug off his criticism. "This is the fashion nowadays. Look at any model on the cover of any magazine and you'll see they're all wearing them thin."

"Just because it's fashionable . . ." His voice trailed off. The music from upstairs picked up in volume.

"Can you do something about that?" she asked. "I've already asked him to turn it down once."

He nodded, heading upstairs. "I'll take care of it."

By the time she reached the kitchen, the music had been turned off.

She pulled the black enamel roasting pan from the oven and set it on the stove. The smell was heavenly. She removed the lid and inhaled. Maybe her sauce wasn't as good as Sal's mother's, but Jeanne made a mean pot roast. The secret was a tablespoon or two of vinegar to keep the meat tender.

Wiping her hands on her apron, she walked briskly from the kitchen to the staircase and called upstairs to the boys that it was time for dinner.

Sal seated himself at the table, and Jeanne served up the plates.

"Looks good!" Sal asked the boys how their day was. Then he turned his attention to Jeanne. "What's new here?"

She shrugged and finished chewing a piece of roasted potato. "Not much. The usual. I'm going to go dancing with Lois later, if that's okay." Having to ask his permission grated on her, but she slipped it in there because that was simply how marriage worked.

Sal's fork paused on his plate, and from across the table she could see the lines and furrows deepening along his forehead.

"Again?"

She braced herself, sitting up a bit straighter and looking at him, ignoring the heat of the flush creeping up from her neck to her face. She smiled brightly. "I love dancing, Sal, you know that. And you yourself said I needed to get a hobby."

His expression relaxed slightly, and he attempted a smile, but it didn't reach his eyes. "I did say that. But I meant something you could do at home."

Jeanne sagged in her seat. "Sal, darling, I need to get out of this house once in a while. That's all I'm asking.

You and the boys are gone all day. But I'm here all day and all night. I just need a change of scenery."

"I can take you dancing Saturday night," Sal said.

Her reactive sigh was one of exasperation. Going out with Sal on a Saturday night would involve a cocktail lounge and Rat Pack music. "I'd like that someday, but right now I really like disco."

"Oh," he said. "Well, if you insist." He went quiet, which was his way of indicating disapproval, but Jeanne decided she'd take it for consent. She was not going to get into a fight. Would not point out that if he'd let her get a part-time job, she'd be getting out of the house and would see their home as a refuge. Instead, it felt more like a prison.

They finished their dinner in relative silence, the boys doing most of the talking amongst themselves. Afterward, Sal retreated to the living room with the newspaper. The boys took off: Joey to a friend's house and Terry back up to his room to listen to his stereo, but at a much lower volume now that his father was home. Jeanne hummed a tune as she washed the dishes and set them in the rack to dry. After tackling the black enamel pan with a scouring pad, she wiped down the counters and table. When everything was in its place, she turned off the kitchen light and went upstairs to get ready.

She loved the way her new dress felt. It made her feel young, feminine, and pretty again, something that had faded after many years of marriage and teenaged children. Leaning over the bathroom sink, she applied makeup and did her hair. For a minute, she studied her newer, thinner eyebrows and concluded that they looked great. Finally, she put on lip gloss, smacking her lips together and making sure she had none on her teeth.

As she made her way downstairs, she glanced at her wristwatch. Lois was due to pick her up in five minutes.

Sal lowered the paper and looked at her. "Is that a new dress?"

"It is."

"How much did that cost?"

"The receipt is upstairs in the bag in the closet," she said. She was in a great mood, anticipating the hours of dancing ahead of her. She wasn't going to ruin that mood with a discussion about how much money she'd spent on her dress. The sound of a car horn honking outside rescued her from any further discussion. Hurriedly, she grabbed her coat from the closet, pulled it on, and kissed the boys good night. She reminded herself not to stay out as late as she had the previous week.

"You look pretty," Sal said.

"Thanks." Why did a compliment from her husband make her feel awkward?

"Don't you need your glasses?"

"I don't need glasses to dance," Jeanne replied. The car horn beeped again. "I better go."

"Okay, have fun. Not too late, Jeanne," he called out after her, but she had already closed the door behind her.

Jeanne's level of excitement rose considerably as soon as she pushed through the doors of the Paradise and felt the pulsating bass of the Jackson 5's "ABC" beneath her feet. Immediately, she lifted up her arms and started snapping her fingers and swaying her hips. As they waited for their coats to be checked, she tapped her foot to the beat, mouthing the words.

Lois smiled indulgently at her. "Someone's in a good mood."

"Happy to be out of the house and can't wait to start dancing."

"First things first, though. Let's get our drinks." Lois put the coat-check ticket into her purse and led the way to the bar. Jeanne followed her happily, swaying to the beat of the next song.

Minutes later, the two of them stood with their backs to the bar, Blue Hawaiians in hand, surveying the scene. It amazed Jeanne how many people came out on a Tuesday night. She'd assumed everyone in town was home like her and Sal. But apparently not. On closer inspection, she noted some of these people were younger than she and Lois and most likely didn't have a spouse or children at home. Images of Sal and the boys came to mind, and a little stab of guilt speared her, as if she had no business being out and enjoying herself. *It's only dancing*, she told herself. It didn't make her a bad mother or a bad wife. She didn't want to be burdened with nagging guilt all night. She took a gulp of her drink, resulting in immediate brain freeze from the icy concoction. She touched the pads of her fingers to the area above her left eye, waiting for it to pass.

"Come on, there's a table over there," Lois said.

Just as they landed at the table, a couple of guys commandeered it.

But Lois was not to be denied. "Sorry, fellas, we were here first," she said sweetly.

The two guys looked at each other and smiled. They were both dressed in leisure suits. One was brown with a green shirt and the other was beige with a brown shirt. Leisure suits were all the rage and Jeanne had tried to convince Sal to get one, but he'd pronounced, "No, they look ridiculous."

The taller one, the blond in the beige suit, smiled. "No reason we can't share the table." With a wide sweep of his hand, he said, "There's more than plenty of room for all of us."

Jeanne sipped her drink, her eyes darting back and forth between the guys and Lois. She didn't want trouble, but she was surprised they hadn't relinquished the table. Was chivalry on its way out the door?

Lois acquiesced. "All right."

"I'm Keith," said the blond. He reached across the table and offered his hand. "This is my friend Steve." Steve was the shorter of the two but the better-looking, in Jeanne's opinion. He had thick dark-brown hair, a full mustache, and dark eyes. He kind of reminded her of Burt Reynolds.

"I'm Lois, and this is my friend Jeanne." Lois offered her hand, with its finely painted red nails, and Jeanne reluctantly offered her own, embarrassed at her short, unvarnished nails, thinking of all the scrubbing she'd done that day and wishing she'd spent some of that time on a manicure. She'd know for next week.

"Nice to meet you, Jeanne," Steve said, holding on to her hand a little longer than was necessary. Jeanne averted her eyes and pulled her hand away. She clasped her hands on the table, left hand over right, so her wedding ring was prominently displayed.

The sound of "Lady Marmalade" by Patti LaBelle flooded the room, and Lois's eyes went wide. She tugged at the sleeve of Jeanne's dress. "Come on, let's dance."

Jeanne carried her purse with her even though Lois left hers parked on the table. When they reached the dance floor, she wrapped the strap around it and set it on the floor near the perimeter so she could keep an eye on it and so no one would trip over it.

"Why didn't you leave it on the table?" Lois shouted over the music.

"I don't know them at all," Jeanne said. Unsure of the dance, she saw that everyone was more or less doing their own thing.

"I got a good vibe off of them," Lois said with an air of authority.

Jeanne hadn't gotten any vibe off of them, good or bad. And honestly, she was there to dance, not make friends.

After a couple of songs, they returned to the table to see that a second round of drinks waited for them, courtesy of Keith and Steve. Lois lifted an eyebrow. Jeanne wasn't totally ungrateful and lifted her Blue Hawaiian with a nod toward the men. "Thank you."

Lois made small talk with Keith. Steve kept his eyes on the dance floor and didn't appear interested in conversing with Jeanne, which was perfectly all right with her. She was dying to ask him what type of cologne he wore; it smelled wonderful. She'd like to get it for Sal for Christmas, instead of the same old bottle of Old Spice.

When "The Hustle" came on over the loudspeakers, Jeanne headed for the dance floor. Lois followed her, laughing. Within seconds, they were joined by Keith and Steve.

"Do you mind if we join you?" Keith asked.

"Not at all," Lois said, smiling at Keith.

Steve parked himself next to Jeanne.

Left, right, left, right, clap. Just like she'd practiced at home. *Turn.* She continued her steps and claps, counting in her head, but out of the corner of her eye, she watched Steve, who seemed a natural. His movements were fluid, and she doubted he was counting his steps. She became so fascinated with his footwork that she didn't immediately notice him staring at her, and when she caught his eye, he winked. Having been caught, she turned beet red and looked away, determined not to stare at him or his feet anymore. She didn't want to give anyone the wrong idea. When they returned to the table after a few sets, overheated and breathless, they took large sips of their drinks, the ice now melted.

As the night wore on, she forgot about the promise she'd made to herself to go home early. Once she'd stepped out on the dance floor and the Blue Hawaiians had loosened her up a bit, the night went by in a blur, and when Lois let out a yawn at the table and announced that it was two, Jeanne stared at her and sobered up quickly.

"I've got to get home," she muttered to herself.

"Aw girls, don't go," Keith pleaded.

Lois finished the rest of her drink in one gulp and picked up her purse off the table, sliding the strap over her shoulder. "No, we have to go. We have to get our beauty sleep. I've got to go to work in the morning and Jeanne has kids at home."

Jeanne slid a side eye to Lois, wishing she hadn't told them that. It wasn't that she was embarrassed about her kids—quite the contrary—but somehow, she didn't want these strangers, these people she'd never met before, to think of her as only a housewife, home minding kids and cleaning and cooking. Without looking at them to gauge their reactions, she headed in the direction of the coat check, anxious now to get home.

The house was dark, and thankfully, Sal was snoring when she slipped quietly into bed.

The following morning, she was up before everyone else, making a breakfast of eggs and bacon in her cast iron skillet. Her head pounded and her feet ached. She kept an eye on the clock, thinking as soon as Sal left for work and the boys headed off to school, she'd crawl back into bed for a few hours.

The boys were slow to come to the table. Sal sat down without a word and tucked into his breakfast. His mother had sent over a loaf of homemade Italian bread, and Jeanne had toasted it and slathered it with butter, the way he liked it.

He did not speak while he ate but when the boys appeared at the table, a smile broke out on his face and he became more animated, even if they were not. Their faces were still full of sleep.

Jeanne ignored him. If he was going to give her the silent treatment, so be it. She kept busy while they ate their breakfast. She made their lunches and lined the brown paper bags up on the counter, and they grabbed them on their way out the door. Sal took his lunch and got his coat from the front hall closet. He did not say goodbye or kiss her on the cheek like he did every other morning.

As soon as she heard the front door close, she finished cleaning up the kitchen and went back upstairs to bed.

In the evening, as she stood at the ironing board, ironing shirts and pants with the smell of spray starch in the air, Sal entered the kitchen, holding the newspaper at his side. Jeanne did not lift her head. He'd given her the silent treatment all through dinner, and that was one thing she couldn't stand.

"I don't want you going out anymore on Tuesday nights," he said firmly.

She looked up from the pair of pants she was pressing and scowled. "Why not?"

"Because it isn't right," he said.

"What isn't right about it?" she demanded.

"You're a married woman."

"And?" she cried. *What did that have to do with anything?*

"It's not right for a married woman to be out until all hours of the morning doing God knows what."

Jeanne blinked as if she'd been slapped. Color and heat rose to her cheeks. "Don't you trust me, Sal?"

"I trust you, but I don't trust other people."

"I'm going out dancing, that's all. Why can't you understand that I enjoy it?" she said.

"I'll take you out dancing Saturday night," he said with finality.

"I want to disco dance," she said, realizing it sounded ridiculous.

"What's the difference?"

Frustrated, she mumbled, "Forget it."

Chapter Eighteen

When Saturday night rolled around, Jeanne pulled on a skirt and blouse and put on minimal makeup. When they were leaving, Sal asked, "Why aren't you wearing that dress you wore the other night?"

"Because I don't feel like it," she said.

They drove in silence to Sal's favorite lounge. The place had a singer, a client of Sal's at the barbershop, who covered Frank Sinatra, Dean Martin, Robert Goulet, and Jerry Vale. They'd been there a couple of months ago and Jeanne had felt no desire to return. But here they were.

The place had low lighting, and small candles flickered inside textured-glass globe centerpieces at each of the tables, which were draped in white linen. She and Sal took a table at the back.

"What will you have to drink?" Sal asked. "The usual? A highball?"

She shook her head. "A Blue Hawaiian."

"What's that?"

She was unsure. Had no idea what the ingredients were. She shrugged. "It's some kind of tropical drink."

He laughed and patted her hand. "One Blue Hawaiian coming up."

Jeanne smiled at him in return. She knew she should be more excited about being out with her husband on a Saturday night, but they'd been married a long time. The bloom was well off the rose, and there were no surprises at this stage of the game. The reward, of course, was that they knew each other inside and out, but lately, she'd been thinking a lot about Lois's lifestyle, and how lucky she was to have no one to clean up after but a cat and a bunch of houseplants in macramé hangers. It almost seemed idyllic. No hampers full of men's and boys' clothes needing to be washed and ironed. No hot dinners to cook every night. She sighed as she waited for Sal to return with her drink. This was unfamiliar territory, and these unknown feelings were strange.

Sal landed in her vision, carrying two highballs back to their table. For his sake, she pasted a smile on her face.

He set a drink down in front of her. "Jimmy never heard of a Blue Hawaiian, so I got you a highball instead. Or do you want me to get you something else?"

"No, honey, it's fine."

He sat next to her, pulling his chair closer to hers. He'd always done this, and she'd always found it romantic, but now it felt claustrophobic. She smiled when he looked at her, trying to feel it.

"It's great to get out for a change, isn't it?" he asked.

Jeanne nodded. "It is." That was true enough. The never-ending evening routine of settling down in front of the television or reading the paper or a ladies' magazine was beginning to wear her down. The best part of her life—her twenties—had been locked into this routine and was now behind her. And pretty soon, she'd be able to say the same thing about her thirties. If she dwelled on it too much, it would depress her.

The cover singer stepped onstage and took the mic. Behind him, his wife sat at the piano and began playing. He started with his cover of Frank Sinatra's "Strangers in the Night." Oddly, Jeanne thought it appropriate.

"Let's dance," Sal said, standing and pushing his chair back.

Jeanne was slow to stand up as Sal waited, hand out for hers. Finally, she placed her hand in his and let him lead her out to the dance floor. She realized this summed up her life: she could simply close her eyes and continue to be led around by her husband.

When he took her in his arms, held her close, and led her expertly round the dance floor, it was familiar. They were so in tune with each other that she could close her eyes and not step on his feet at all. And while, at one time in her life, that had been comforting, it no longer felt that way. What was the phrase about familiarity and contempt?

By midnight they were home and in bed, and it wasn't long before Sal, on his back beside her, was snoring.

Jeanne nudged him and whispered, "You're snoring, Sal." He automatically rolled over onto his side, his back to her, and the snoring stopped briefly, only to start up again a few moments later. But that wasn't what kept her awake for hours.

"But we went out dancing on Saturday," Sal protested, his voice tinged with annoyance, when Jeanne came downstairs all dressed and ready to go the following Tuesday evening.

"What does that have to do with anything?" she said. Although he had mentioned that he didn't want her going out anymore, the truth was, she was sick of him telling her what she could and could not do. Looking forward to going out tonight was the only thing that had gotten her through the week.

Joey looked up from where he was laid out on the floor. "Aw come on, Mom, stay home. You've missed a lot of *Happy Days*."

Sal's gaze swung to Joey and then back to Jeanne. "Come on, Jeanne, give it a rest."

Thankfully, Lois's car horn sounded outside. "Another time. I can't let Lois down." She gave them a quick wave and a good-night, and sailed out the front door, closing it tightly behind her before guilt could make her change her mind.

The following Tuesday, as Jeanne scooped mashed potatoes and sliced chicken onto their plates along with green beans and carrots, Sal said, "I had a customer in today and he said he's seen you at the Paradise."

For a moment, Jeanne froze, unable to shake the feeling that she was being spied on. "Really?"

"Yes, he said you're a terrific dancer." Sal leaned against the counter, arms folded.

Jeanne set all the plates on the table and watched Sal's face, but his expression betrayed nothing.

"That was a nice thing to say." She did one last-minute check to make sure they had everything. The gravy boat, that's what she'd forgotten. She pivoted and grabbed it off the counter.

"I thought so too. He said you never leave the dance floor."

"That should come as no surprise, Sal. You know how much I love dancing," Jeanne said with a smile that felt artificial.

"Yes, but he also said you always dance with the same man."

"What is he, a nosy Nellie?" she huffed. "Yes, I dance with someone named Steve and sometimes his friend, Keith. But it's not what you think."

"Isn't it?" Sal asked quietly.

"Call the boys in. Dinner's on the table," she said.

Sal stepped out of the kitchen, stood at the foot of the staircase, and yelled up, "Dinner!"

When he returned, Jeanne was pouring milk into the boys' glasses.

"Why don't you come with me tonight and see for yourself?" she challenged.

Sal looked at her thoughtfully. "You know, I think I will."

Terry was first at the table and slid into his chair.

Sal asked him, "You don't mind watching your younger brother while your mother and I go out and trip the light fantastic, do you?"

Terry shrugged. "I guess not."

Jeanne sank back in her chair, no longer interested in her dinner. Sal had called her bluff. She hadn't expected that. Had misread him. Now he was going with her to the Paradise, like a millstone around her neck.

After she washed the dishes, she called Lois and told her Sal was going.

"Oh boy," Lois responded.

But gradually Jeanne's mood shifted, and she thought it might be kind of nice if Sal took to the Paradise. She took extra care with her makeup and hair that evening and pulled her favorite dress out of the closet, a wine-colored number that buttoned up the front and had a skirt that flared. It was a hand-me-down from Lois, and she was happy to have it. It had only needed the hem to be taken up a bit.

"You look beautiful," Sal said with an appreciative glance.

She twirled around in front of him, giving him the full effect.

He smiled. "Very nice." He pulled her into his embrace and gave her a lingering kiss, like he used to do when they were first married. This surprised her.

Maybe they would have a good time. Maybe Sal would love it as much as she did. This could be something they could do together.

She gave last-minute instructions to Terry, and on their way out the door, called out a good-night, adding, "and no *Three's Company*."

"Aw, Mom, I'm fifteen," Terry protested.

"I don't care," Jeanne said.

"Do what your mother tells you," Sal added.

The May evening was cool, and Jeanne pulled her thin shawl closer around her as they walked into the disco, sorry that she hadn't worn a heavier coat. She'd warm up as soon as she started dancing. As they wound their way to the entrance with Sal's hand on the small of her back, she spotted Lois's car parked in the fire lane and smiled to herself. Some things never changed.

Jeanne led the way to the coat check, thinking how different she was since arriving that first night with Lois a month ago. Dancing had given her a little bit of confidence. Sal took her shawl from her and handed it, along with his coat, to the young woman behind the counter. He threw a dollar into the small wicker basket on the counter.

Lois stood at a high table near the dance floor, talking to Keith and Steve. When Steve spotted Jeanne, he broke into a broad smile, but it soon disappeared when he spotted Sal beside her.

At the table, Jeanne kept her hand on Sal's arm, introducing him to everyone.

"I'll get drinks. Blue Hawaiian?" he asked Jeanne with a smile.

"You remembered."

"Of course, you're my wife, it's my job." Whistling, he walked off to the bar.

When he returned, he handed her her drink. They were alone at the table as Lois, Keith, and Steve had headed out to the dance floor.

"Do you want to try it?" she asked, holding her drink toward him.

"Just a taste to see what the big deal is," he teased. He took a tentative sip of her Blue Hawaiian and scowled. "Too sweet and too cold."

She indulged him with a smile.

"Aren't there any chairs to sit down?" he asked, looking around.

"We really don't sit here, we're too busy dancing," she explained.

Sal frowned. "I stand all day at my job. I don't want to stand all evening."

"The Hustle" blared out of the loudspeaker, and Jeanne set her drink down and reached for his hand. "Come on, honey, let's dance."

"Okay," he said, following her out to the dance floor.

They found a clear spot. He went to take her in his arms, but she pushed him away playfully. "No, Sal, we don't dance like that here."

He looked around. "Oh."

"Come on," she said with a laugh. "I'll teach you."

He was two left feet and couldn't get the hang of the steps, which she found hard to believe. He was usually such a beautiful dancer. When Randy announced he'd give a demo, Jeanne encouraged Sal to go up to the dance floor, but he resisted, saying, "I'm not a kid, Jeanne."

She pouted. "The first night I came here, I took the lesson."

But Sal wouldn't budge. He shook his head. "No thanks. I don't think this kind of thing is for me."

The way he said *this kind of thing* made it sound distasteful.

"Come on, Sal, give it a chance. We could have so much fun," Jeanne said enthusiastically, pulling his hands toward her.

"We can have fun in other ways," he said with a waggle of his eyebrows.

But that only made her angry. He wasn't making any effort to like it. She dropped his hands from hers and tried again. "Come on, let's dance."

But he pulled away. "You go ahead. I'll wait at the table."

"Suit yourself," she said with a shrug. On purpose, she spent the next thirty minutes on the dance floor. If her husband didn't want to dance, she wasn't going to force him. But inside, she seethed. Every time she looked over at him, he was standing there with a bored expression on his face, nursing his drink. Finally, she stopped looking in his direction, determined to have a great time. But after half an hour, she had to take a break. She was parched, and her bangs stuck to her forehead. She sailed off the dance floor, moving her hips to the music as she landed at the table and took a few sips of her drink.

Sal glanced at his watch. "Are you ready?"

She blinked rapidly. "You want to leave? I haven't even finished my first drink."

"Honey, it's almost eleven. I've got to get up in the morning and go to work."

Jeanne stood there, lips pressed together, arms folded across her chest.

"And the music is so loud in here I can barely hear myself think," he said. "We have to shout to each other to be heard."

Jeanne leveled a glare at him. "I don't come here to think or to talk. I come here to dance."

"Come on, let's go," he said.

She had no choice. She had to leave with her husband, but when he tried to put his hand on her elbow to guide her out, she pulled it sharply away.

The short ride home was tense, but she doubted Sal noticed. He whistled all the way home. At one point, he reached over and patted her knee. "I'll take you out to the lounge on Saturday night. Now that's music. Maybe we could go out to dinner beforehand."

"Hmm."

When they arrived home, Jeanne went upstairs and washed her face, pulled on her nightgown and quilted bathrobe, and returned downstairs. When Sal came out of the kitchen, she was already settled in on the corner of the couch, after turning on the news.

"Aren't you coming to bed?" he asked.

She shook her head. "Not tired. I'll stay up a little while."

"Aw, come on, Jeanne, come to bed."

She didn't look at him. She kicked off her slippers and put her feet up on the couch. "You go on up, Sal. I'll be up in a bit."

"Not too late."

She ignored him and picked up the *TV Guide*, looking to see what the late movie was for that night.

Chapter Nineteen

September 1975

Jeanne continued to go out dancing on Tuesday nights. Sal didn't like it and was vocal about it. But Jeanne didn't care. Things became tense between them, but she remained adamant that she was doing nothing wrong.

One Tuesday evening as she was getting ready, the phone rang, and she was able to grab it from the upstairs extension.

"Hi, Lois, I'm almost ready," she said, shaking her can of Aqua Net.

"That's why I was calling. I'm not going out tonight."

"Are you sick?" Jeanne asked.

Lois laughed. "Nope, just sick of going out."

Jeanne's heart sank and she bit her lip. If Lois stopped going out, what would become of her? Her Tuesday-night dancing would be over so fast her head would spin. She wasn't ready to give it up. It was the only thing that kept her sane.

"Maybe you only need a night off," she suggested.

"I don't know. Don't you ever wonder if there's more to life?" Lois asked.

No. Ironically, Jeanne wondered if there was more to life than being somebody's wife or somebody's mother. But now wasn't the time to get philosophical.

"Cheer up, and I'll see you next week." Jeanne hung up the phone. She sat on the side of the bed, thinking. She couldn't bear to sit in another night and watch television. Six nights a week was plenty for that. She'd been looking forward to tonight all week, like she did every week.

"Who was that?" Sal called up.

"It was Lois."

"What did she want?"

"She asked if I could drive tonight as she's having car trouble," she said easily. It scared her how smoothly that little lie rolled off her tongue.

"Oh." There was nothing more from Sal.

Jeanne summoned her courage and said good night to her boys and to Sal. The car was running in the driveway as Sal had started it for her to warm it up. She smiled at this. Someday, he'd get used to her going out and they could go back to being happy like they used to be.

She drove slowly to the disco, wrestling with her conscience. One voice told her she was doing nothing wrong, but another voice argued that it was how it looked: a married woman going out to a nightclub by herself. But the more she thought about it, the angrier she got. Why couldn't a married woman go out by herself without all sorts of rumors swirling around her? All she wanted to do was dance.

The parking lot at the disco was full. She didn't have the chutzpah Lois possessed to park in the fire lane, so she drove around until she spied a vacant spot at the back of the lot. She didn't care that she had to walk the distance to the front door. She only hoped she wouldn't back out. Maybe she didn't have Lois's pluck, but she had determination, and that was all she needed. She lifted her chin a bit higher and squared her shoulders, deciding she wasn't going to let what other people thought ruin her fun. Before she went inside, she promised herself she wouldn't stay late.

Keith and Steve stood at a table halfway between the bar and the dance floor. When she approached them, Steve moved over to the other side to make room for her. She flashed him a smile in thanks.

"Where's your partner in crime?" Keith asked, looking over her head to the door. It was no secret that Keith had a bit of a crush on Lois. He'd said she had a great pair of legs. But Lois wasn't interested.

"She's not coming tonight," Jeanne said, tapping her foot as she leaned against the table.

"Did you want a drink?" Steve asked.

She shook her head. "Not right now. I want to dance!"

Steve held his hand out and she gave him a smile as she placed her hand in his. "Let's do this."

The two of them moved as a unit, attuned to one another after a few months of dancing together. Easily they slipped into their rhythm, moving to the beat of the music. It felt natural, like they'd been doing it their entire lives. Months ago, she'd been impressed with his dance moves, but now she was confident that she was as good as he was.

All night they danced, never leaving one another's side. It was innocent and good fun, Jeanne thought. Meanwhile, Keith had worked his way through some of the single ladies in the club.

By midnight, she decided she should head home.

"Don't go," Steve protested, laying his hand gently on her arm. "We're having a great time."

"I have to. It's midnight and if I don't get home soon, I'm going to turn into a pumpkin."

He laughed. "When you put it that way, I guess you better go."

"I better."

"Sure. Come on, I'll walk you to your car."

"That's not necessary." She dug through her purse for her car keys.

"Yes, it is. Let's go." Steve escorted her out, holding the door open for her.

They talked about nothing in particular as they walked. She pointed and said, "I'm back there."

He took her car keys from her and unlocked her door, opening it for her.

"Thank you," she said. "I'll see you next week."

Before she slid into her seat, Steve reached for her, leaned in, and kissed her, his lips warm and insistent, his breath a mix of whiskey and mint. Stunned, Jeanne froze, then pulled away and whispered, "Don't."

She should get into the car and leave, she knew, but she was unable to move.

"I've wanted to kiss you for a long time," Steve admitted.

She didn't know what to say to that. She liked Steve. He was handsome, and she'd be lying if she said there weren't times she wished she wasn't married so she could date him, but that's all it had been: wishful thinking. Had she projected the wrong ideas and impressions to him? This was dangerous territory and she needed to be careful.

The door to the nightclub opened and people spilled out, laughing and talking. Hurriedly, Jeanne got into the car, but she couldn't close the door because Steve stood there, leaning in. Quickly, she looked around, hoping no one had spotted them. It was a small town; it wouldn't take long for rumors to spread.

"Jeanne? Tell me what you're thinking," Steve said.

She looked up at him. "Steve, I'm a married woman."

He shrugged. "Are you a happily married woman? Because I think if you were, you wouldn't be here every Tuesday night."

"It's just dancing. Nothing else." Why did it have to be anything else? There were no ulterior motives on her part.

"Is it?" Steve asked. He lingered for a moment before he said good night and closed her door. She waited until he was out of sight—he went back into the nightclub—before she started her car.

She turned the key in the ignition and leaned back and closed her eyes, needing to process what had just happened. Another man had kissed her. And as shocking as that was, what concerned her even more was that she had liked it, and hoped it would happen again. The car continued to idle as dangerous thoughts filled her head.

The following week, Lois canceled again at the last moment, which left unanswered questions for Jeanne. Not wanting to encourage Steve, she remained at home that night. Sal was both surprised and delighted. She parked herself in front of the television with the rest of her family, but her mind was on Steve and that delicious kiss he'd given her. If she had it to do all over again, she would never get married so young; she would work full time and date lots of men and go out dancing a few times a week. She only half paid attention to the evening's television line up, trying to stay focused on the parade of shows, but her mind constantly veering in another direction.

She took pride in her appearance, always made sure her hair looked nice and wore some makeup when leaving the house. She was appreciative of glances she received from the opposite sex. It was nice to be noticed, especially since she was a married woman. It meant that men still found her attractive. And it was supposed to be safe. The gold band that adorned the ring finger on her left hand was supposed to send a message that she was off-limits. But Steve had crossed a line the other night when he ignored that gold band on her hand and kissed her. Since then, her stomach had been in knots: anxious that Sal would hear about it from someone at his barbershop, and upset that she'd actually enjoyed it. But when the week went by and Sal had mentioned nothing, she breathed a sigh of relief, thinking she'd dodged a bullet.

The catchy jingle for Alka-Seltzer played on the television screen, and the boys sang along with it. She wondered who was at the nightclub that evening and what they were doing. More than once, her thoughts strayed to Steve. Was he dancing with someone else? Had he noticed her absence? Had he even *missed* her? She bit her lip. She felt like she was back at Hideaway Bay High School.

The boys were sprawled out on the shag carpet, laughing at every funny line as they watched one sitcom after another. As she sat curled up in the corner of the couch, her eyes glazed over, the canned laughter irritating. The shows weren't even that funny. Tears pricked her eyes from sheer boredom.

Sal stood and folded the newspaper, laid it aside, and walked to the kitchen.

Jeanne focused on her boys. The sight of them always softened her heart. There were only a few years left before they went off to college. Sal had his heart set on them going and had been saving for it since the day they were born. She, on the other hand, only wanted them to be happy. Life was hard enough without being miserable on top of it. And when the boys left, what would become of her and Sal? She winced at the thought of it.

Sal returned with a cup of tea in his hand and handed it to her. She looked up at him in surprise. He was old-school. It was her job to make the tea, the coffee, the breakfast, the lunches, and the dinners.

She accepted it from him, confused. "What's this?"

"It's nice to have you home on a Tuesday night for a change. I thought you might like a cup of tea."

"Thank you."

Her husband was a kind man, of that there was no doubt. And for that reason, it was not a good idea to go alone to the Paradise. Best to find someone else to go with.

It wasn't long before she came up with an idea.

Jeanne and Mary sat at Betty's kitchen table. They were getting their hair cut and colored. Betty did hair out of her kitchen as it was easier to keep an eye on her six kids, two of whom were currently racing through the kitchen, one chasing the other.

"Oh my goodness," Mary said with a laugh. "It's never dull around here, is it?"

"What I wouldn't give for half an hour of peace and quiet." Betty said, pulling a black plastic cape out of a bottom kitchen drawer. She tied it around Jeanne's neck. Jeanne had never dyed her hair before, but she wanted to frost it. "I can't even read an entire article in any magazine. It's a waste of money to buy them."

Betty laid her hand against her lower abdomen and winced. Jeanne narrowed her eyes at her. "You all right?" Betty looked pale, and Jeanne wondered if she was pregnant again. Her youngest was seven, but that didn't mean anything. Betty was still of childbearing age.

Betty waved her away. "I'm fine. Mary, I made a coffee cake, did you want a slice? I'll put the highlights on Jeanne's hair because they have to set, and then I'll cut yours."

"That's fine, Betty," Mary said. "Although I don't know where you find the time to bake."

At that moment, Betty's husband, Chuck, arrived. He kissed his wife on the cheek and set his metal lunchbox on the counter. With a grin he looked at the three women. "Beauty Salon central."

"I've got your dinner here, Chuck. Hold on a minute, Jeanne." Betty set the cap down on the table and pivoted toward the stove, where a large pot simmered. She removed the lid and ladled a generous portion of chicken and dumplings into a bowl, which she set down on a placemat at the far end of the table.

Chuck sat, looked at the bowl and pronounced, "Looks good, hon."

She nodded and filled a glass of water from the tap and put it in front of him.

"Kids already eat?" he asked.

"Yes."

He nodded, bent his head, and blew on the spoonful of food to cool it down.

One of the older kids ran into the kitchen and stood next to Chuck. Reluctantly, he looked up from his meal.

"Dad, can I get a new bike?"

"Ask your mother."

"Leave your father alone. Let him eat his dinner in peace," Betty chastised.

No sooner was he gone than Betty's second youngest, Lisa, all blond-haired and blue-eyed like her mother, arrived at her father's side, holding a Barbie doll in one hand and the Barbie's leg in the other. She leaned against her father.

Chuck set his spoon down and regarded her with a smile. "What's up, kiddo?"

"I can't get her leg back on."

"No problem. Leave it with me. She'll be as good as new. Her dancing days are not behind her, I promise you that. Go on now."

Giggling, Lisa ran from the room, and Chuck placed the Barbie doll and her leg on the table.

While he ate, Mary cut a slice of coffee cake for herself and the other two women. Chuck refused a slice when offered, explaining he'd have one later when he was watching television. Meanwhile, Betty pulled a cap over Jeanne's hair, using an instrument that looked suspiciously like a knitting needle to pull strands of hair through the cap.

"I think this is going to look great," Betty said enthusiastically. She looked over to Mary, who was washing down a mouthful of cake with a sip of coffee. "What about you, Mary? You want to frost your hair as well?"

Mary shook her head. "Nope. I don't want to get caught in that trap of the upkeep. I don't have that many gray hairs. I'm going to hold out as long as I can."

Mary had pretty hair she wore to her shoulder. She'd opted for the feathered look, whereas Jeanne's hair was all one length and fell just past her chin, like a bob.

"Can you cut my hair like Mary's?" Jeanne asked. She'd like something different. And a color and a different cut would scratch that itch.

Chuck finished his dinner and stood. "Betty, that was excellent as usual."

Betty blushed. "Thanks, honey."

Jeanne marveled at them. Six kids and married for more than fifteen years and they still acted like newlyweds around each other. What was their secret?

"I'll leave you ladies to it," Chuck said, and he put his plate in the sink.

"I put the newspaper on your chair," Betty said.

"Thanks, hon." And he disappeared from the kitchen.

Mary smirked. "You too seem pretty happy together."

Betty smiled and shrugged. "I don't know. I love him. He loves me. End of."

Jeanne wondered if it really was that simple.

When all the strands of hair that were to be frosted had been pulled through the cap, Betty painted the hair with dye.

"Gosh that stinks," Mary said, scrunching up her nose. She stood and opened the kitchen window.

"You've got to sit there for a while, so I'll cut Mary's hair now," Betty said. She pulled her timer off the stove and set it.

She leaned Mary over her kitchen sink and washed her hair. After she rinsed it, she wrapped it in a towel. Mary resumed her seat, looking regal with the toweled turban around her head. Jeanne had always thought she had fine bone structure.

As Betty cut Mary's hair, the three of them talked about their kids and what was new in their lives.

Mary leveled a glance over at Jeanne and asked, "Are you still going out dancing with Lois?"

"I am." She didn't mention that Lois had stopped going. She brightened up, as this was the opening she needed. "Why don't you two come with me? It's so much fun."

The scissors in Betty's hand paused mid-air. "Go out dancing? On a weeknight?"

"Yeah, sure, why not?" Jeanne's voice faltered.

"I'm not interested in that, Jeanne," Betty said. She added quickly, "I'm sorry, I know how much you love dancing, but I like staying home with Chuck and the kids."

"Really?" Jeanne found this hard to believe. "Aren't you ever bored?"

Betty shook her head. "No. Never. I don't have time to be bored." She laughed at this truth.

Jeanne turned to Mary. "Come on, Mary, it'll be fun."

Mary shook her head. "No thanks. Tuesday night is my busy night. I've got macramé at six and then my favorite shows, *Hawaii Five-O* and *Barnaby Jones*, are on."

Sensing an opening, Jeanne said, "All right. What about another night?"

Mary looked at Jeanne. "I have no interest in going out to a nightclub. Not without my husband. It doesn't seem right."

Jeanne bristled at this. "I can assure you, there's nothing wrong with going dancing." An image of Steve kissing her floated before her, and she realized the ground on which she stood was shaky.

She went quiet but Mary, always the outspoken of the three of them, filled the silence. "I'm surprised Sal is okay with you going out to the Paradise every week."

"He's not crazy about the idea, but I need to get out of the house," Jeanne griped.

"Aren't you afraid it's going to cause trouble in your marriage?" Mary challenged.

It was already causing trouble, but Jeanne wasn't about to admit that. "Sal and I have been married a long time. We're *fine*."

Mary and Betty fell silent, the only noise being the consistent *clip-clip* of the scissors.

Mary bent her head forward as Betty worked on her hair in the back. A couple of times, Betty's features contorted in a wince as she cut Mary's hair.

"Betty, is everything all right?" Jeanne asked again.

Mary lifted her head slightly and frowned.

"Yes, why?" Betty asked.

"You seem to be in pain at times."

"Just those damn cramps," Betty said.

Mary turned her head and looked over her shoulder. "That time of the month again?"

Betty shook her head. "No. I get cramps all the time."

Mary now twisted her body to get a better look at Betty. "You know that isn't normal, right?"

"It isn't?" Betty asked, her voice uncertain.

"No, it's not," Jeanne piped in, dancing forgotten as she was concerned about her friend. "I don't get cramps outside of my period, do you, Mary?"

Mary shook her head. "No." She peered at Betty. "Are you getting enough iron? You're pale."

"Sure," Betty said, maneuvering Mary's head so she could finish cutting it.

"Cream of wheat, spinach, and—oh, liver is good for that," Mary advised.

"Liver, yuck," Betty said with a laugh.

"Maybe go see the doctor," Jeanne suggested.

"Yeah, sure," Betty said.

Chapter Twenty

October 1975

Jeanne hadn't been to the Paradise in several weeks, and she called Lois to see if she might be ready for a night out, but Lois declined, citing other plans. Lois was seeing someone, and Jeanne was sure that was the reason she no longer went out dancing with her. She wondered why she didn't bring her boyfriend to the club.

"Are you mad at me?" Jeanne asked.

"No, of course not. Why would you think that?" Lois said.

"What am I supposed to think?" Jeanne couldn't hide the exasperation in her voice.

"Why don't you come over?" Lois suggested.

"Now?"

"Yes, why not? It's early. But I won't change my mind about going out dancing."

"All right."

Jeanne hung up the phone and turned to see Sal coming through the back door. He'd stopped at his mother's house after work to fix something.

"Everything all right?" she asked.

"Fine. The toilet was running non-stop. I fixed it."

"What did she give you to eat?" she asked, more out of habit than any actual interest.

He smiled. "Eggplant parmesan."

She knew he preferred his mother's cooking to her own, but she didn't care. It meant she didn't have to cook a big dinner, and she'd put down a bowl of tomato soup and grilled cheese sandwiches for herself and the boys.

Jeanne stood next to him and pulled her coat on.

"Going dancing tonight?" His voice was quiet, his expression clouded with disappointment. Things had been good between them, but despite this, Jeanne was restless.

"No, not tonight. I'm going to drive over to Lois's house."

"I heard she's getting married."

She knew she must have looked stunned. But she recovered as quickly as she could. How could Sal know, and she did not? Why hadn't Lois told her? She was more hurt than angry. She thought she and Lois were good friends.

"Judge Corcoran was in today for his haircut and shave," Sal said by way of explanation, and Jeanne wondered what Judge Corcoran would know about Lois getting married. But she remained silent, hoping Sal would enlighten her.

He accommodated her. "The judge told me that he popped the question and Lois said yes."

Judge Corcoran? That couldn't be right. He was almost twenty-five years older than Lois. Although Lois had mentioned she'd gone out with him a few times, Jeanne had figured it wasn't serious because of the age difference. She bit her tongue and murmured, "As long as she's happy."

If it was true that Lois was getting married, then that surely would be the end of her dancing days.

"I won't be late," Jeanne said.

"I'll wait up for you," Sal said, and he leaned in and kissed her goodbye.

The outside air smelled of wet earth and woodsmoke. She loved the smell of autumn. The last rainfall had brought down a lot of leaves, leaving most of the trees bare. Fallen leaves covered everything: lawns, sidewalks, driveways. Wet and slimy.

As she drove over to Lois's house over on Crescent Avenue, she couldn't help but feel hurt that Lois hadn't told her about her engagement. Some friend. But then she realized she had no idea what Lois did to fill her time aside from Tuesday nights. Other than work, she had no idea how Lois spent her evenings or her weekends. They'd never discussed it. The thing was, Jeanne didn't want to talk about her home life with Sal and the boys. She wanted a few hours free of thinking about the laundry that was piling up, or another way to cook chicken for their dinner. And as a result, maybe she wasn't interested in Lois's home life or dating. Maybe she wasn't such a great friend either.

As she pulled into the driveway behind Lois's car, she arrived at the sad realization that their friendship had become superficial. And she was as much to blame as Lois. That stung a bit. It wasn't like the friendship she had with Betty or Mary, where they knew all about the intimate details of their daily life and their families.

She slammed the car door and walked around to the back. Unlike most of the homes in Hideaway Bay, Lois's house had no front porch. The previous owner had walled it in, adding an extra front room to the house. They'd also put in a sliding glass door off the back, and a concrete pad. Jeanne thought it was more private and actually preferred it to a front porch.

Lois had been expecting her and was waiting at the side door as Jeanne approached. She held the door open, and Jeanne stepped inside, removing her coat as she followed Lois into her kitchen. Lois had purchased her home two years previously. The kitchen was done up in Harvest Gold appliances, orange countertops, and brown cabinets.

Lois invited her to sit on one of the brown vinyl kitchen chairs. She filled the kettle with water and set it on the stove to boil. She opened a cabinet and asked, "Coffee or tea?"

"How about a Blue Hawaiian?" Jeanne asked. She missed those. She had a blender tucked away in the cabinet above the refrigerator and she was going to drag it out, find the recipe, and drink herself silly over the winter.

"Ha! I wish!"

"Make it coffee."

"Is instant all right? I don't have a percolator. The glass knob broke and I haven't gotten around to replacing it yet."

"Instant is fine."

Jeanne pulled out the chair and sat sideways on it so she could face Lois. She crossed her legs and spied a pack of Virginia Slims on the table next to a beanbag ashtray and was sorely tempted to ask for one.

Lois wore bell-bottom jeans and a blouse with pointy collars.

She spooned instant coffee into two mugs, poured boiling water over them, and carried them over. There was a sugar bowl in the middle of the table, and she reached for it and pulled it closer to Jeanne.

"Cremora or milk?"

"Cremora is fine."

Lois sat down and reached for a cigarette, offering one to Jeanne, who refused.

Jeanne didn't waste any time. "A little bird told me you're engaged to Judge Corcoran."

Lois smiled and nodded. "That's why I invited you over. I wanted to tell you myself. But I guess good news travels fast." She sighed and took a long drag on her cigarette.

"Lois, I knew you had gone out with him a few times, but I didn't know it was serious. You never said." She tried to keep the accusatory tone out of her voice.

Lois shrugged. "We never talk about our personal lives anymore, do we?"

That much was true.

"Why?" Jeanne asked.

"Why what?"

"Why did you say yes?" Jeanne asked.

Lois held her cigarette and tapped her thumb against her bottom lip. She seemed to regard her with curiosity before speaking. "Because I love him."

"But he's quite a bit older than you." She couldn't help but point out the obvious to her friend. Maybe she wasn't thinking straight. Marriage was difficult enough without an age gap, something that was going to cause a host of problems.

"He's exactly twenty-one years older than I am," Lois said almost proudly.

"It doesn't bother you?" Jeanne asked.

"Of course not," Lois said. "I love him."

Jeanne had a hard time wrapping her head around this. There were so many men out there who'd be more suitable. "Wouldn't you prefer someone closer to your age?"

Lois laughed. "You mean like one of the many guys we see out dancing on Tuesday nights?"

"Well, yes," Jeanne said. They'd certainly be more exciting. Keith came to mind, and she thought he was more well-suited to Lois than Judge Corcoran.

Lois looked off in the distance to some unknown spot on the wall behind Jeanne, appearing pensive. She took a long drag of her cigarette, blue smoke floating up in front of her. "I'm sick and tired of going out every week. I'm sick of the endless dates with guys that go nowhere. I'm sick of guys only looking for one thing." She pursed her lips. "You don't know how lucky you are. You've got a nice husband and two beautiful sons. I'd give my right arm for your situation."

Jeanne snorted. "It's not all it's cracked up to be."

"I'm sure it isn't. But I'm alone in my house every night with no one to talk to, no one to take care of. But not anymore."

"But aren't you worried about becoming his nursemaid?"

Lois shook her head. "I'll take whatever good years I can get with him."

"Really?"

"Yes, really. We've been dating on and off for a couple of years but in the last year, we've been seeing each other more regularly. When we go out dancing on Tuesday nights, I always wish I were with him instead."

"Oh." A frisson of guilt stabbed Jeanne. On Tuesday nights, she never wished she was home with Sal. In fact, she hardly thought about him or the boys when she was on the dance floor.

"I don't want to spend the rest of my life alone. I want to share my life with someone," Lois said quietly. "And I want to share it with George."

The elongated ash on Lois's cigarette threatened to fall, and she leaned over and stubbed the rest of it out in the ashtray.

They sat there for a few minutes in silence. Jeanne wanted to be happy for her friend, but all she could think about was how it affected her. Did that make her a bad person? She plastered a smile on her face and asked Lois about her wedding plans. All brides liked to talk about that, as she herself had all those years ago when Sal had asked her to marry him.

When discussing her upcoming nuptials, Lois became animated, and Jeanne realized that her friend was truly excited to be marrying this man. Although it seemed like a lifetime, it wasn't so long ago that she, too, had been excited to get married. She'd been a different person back then.

It was dark by the time she left Lois's house. As Lois walked her out, Jeanne acted on impulse and threw her arms around her friend. "I'm really happy for you," she whispered.

"Thanks."

Chapter Twenty-One

"I think I'll go dancing tomorrow night," Jeanne said casually to Sal as they went to bed.

"Tomorrow night? Is Lois going?" he asked. There was displeasure in his voice.

She'd been prepared for this. There was no way Sal would let her go by herself.

"No, she has other plans."

"You're going by yourself?" he asked, a scowl disfiguring his features.

"Of course not, silly," she said, taking her bathrobe off and laying it on the foot of the bed. "I'm going with friends."

"What friends?"

"You don't know them. I met them at the Paradise. Rita and Kathy. They're hairdressers at Hair-Do Heaven."

There was some truth in what she said. She'd been introduced to both women months ago and they were friendly; they always said hello to each other and made small talk for a few moments. But to say she was going out expressly to meet the two of them was a bit of a stretch.

"I thought you got that out of your system," he said sullenly.

"No, Sal. You know how I feel about dancing."

"All right."

She kissed him on the lips. "Good night, honey."

The following evening as she walked toward the entrance of the nightclub, excitement filled her. It felt good to be back. She could already hear the music, and she couldn't wait to get out onto the dance floor. Right before she'd left the house, she and Sal had a terrible fight. They weren't usually fighters in their marriage; they were the types to retreat to their corners, licking their wounds.

"Jeanne?" called out a voice from behind her.

She turned and spotted Steve trotting toward her.

"I'm so glad to see you! I thought I'd never see you again," he said, grinning.

"Well, here I am," she said nervously.

He studied her for a moment and pronounced, "You look beautiful."

She blushed, lowered her head, and said quietly, "Thank you."

Without warning, he pulled her into a big bear hug. "God, I've missed you. No one dances like you."

When they pulled apart, he planted a quick kiss on her lips, wrapped his arm around her shoulder, and walked her into the Paradise.

"Now, let's go dancing!"

For the next four hours, she danced only with Steve, forgetting all about her earlier fight with Sal. And the Blue Hawaiians kept coming. By the fifth one, she was no longer counting, figuring all the dancing would work it off, or at least dull the effects. She couldn't stop smiling. Her cheeks hurt from it. But she was happy.

"Let me walk you to your car," Steve said at the end of the night.

"Sure," she said, losing her footing and falling against him.

Placing his hand firmly around her arm, he righted her and said, "Whoa, easy does it."

He held her coat out for her and she slid her arms into it. "Thank you." Not for the first time, she wished she had a short rabbit fur jacket like Lois. She wondered if Lois would ever let her borrow it.

Guiding her by the elbow, Steve walked Jeanne through the parking lot. She was glad she'd come out despite Lois not being there. In fact, she'd had the best time ever.

Her car was at the back of the parking lot, which was all but deserted at this time of night.

As they approached her car, Steve noted, "Look, I'm parked right in front of you. It's like it's destiny or something."

She thought that was a bit of a stretch but smiled, deciding he was too cute to argue. Obligingly, she stopped at his car, a brand-new white 1975 Buick Riviera, which Steve kept spotless. After dancing, Steve's passion was his car and the maintenance of it. It was all he talked about at times. But she was usually capable of getting him off the subject. Her station wagon behind his car looked, well, lacking.

Steve reached out and took hold of her hand. She was surprised at this gesture but didn't think it had reached her facial expression, but that could have been due to the alcohol. Her heart rate picked up a fraction, but she wasn't so drunk that she didn't notice it.

Still clasping her hand, he pulled her to him, his scent a mixture of his faint cologne and his maleness. Jeanne drew in a deep breath. As his face inched closer to hers, his eyes closing, Jeanne stared at his lips, her mouth slightly parted, wondering if he would kiss her again. Her arms felt tremulous. When Steve pressed his lips against hers, Jeanne didn't protest or push him away.

His mustache both tickled and scratched. He kept kissing her and kissing her, and soon her body became languid with heat and desire. She slid her arms up around him, her hands meeting at the back of his neck. Her knees wobbled, and she leaned against the side of the car for support as Steve pressed his body against hers, everything about him insistent.

He was so different from Sal.

He broke off the kiss, and a moan escaped from Jeanne's lips. She wanted more of that kissing. She pulled him closer to her.

Steve placed his hands on her arms. "I want you, Jeanne," he whispered. "I have for a long time."

She nodded, her head foggy from drink and desire.

Steve opened the car door and reached down and pushed the front seat forward so Jeanne could climb into the back seat. He followed, landing in her open, waiting arms.

A short time later, Jeanne drove home, her hands gripping the steering wheel. She leaned forward, barely blinking. What had transpired in the last half hour had sobered her up.

She had slept with another man. Had cheated on her husband. Had become, in her mother's words, a floozy. She swallowed hard. She'd had sex with a man other than her husband in the back seat of a car in a parking lot, like she was some hormonal teenager at the drive-in.

She groaned out loud.

What had she done?

When she pulled into the driveway, she didn't immediately get out of the car. She laid her head on the steering wheel and groaned again. How could she have been so stupid? So reckless?

The sound of a train whistle blew in the distance, startling her. It sounded as mournful as she felt.

As quietly as possible, she opened the front door and removed her shoes, tiptoeing through the downstairs. She went through to the kitchen to get a glass of water and some aspirin for the hangover headache that was sure to come. There was no pill for remorse.

Carrying her shoes, she headed upstairs and made the bathroom her first stop. She gave her face and teeth a good scrub, determined to remove any traces of Steve.

Would Sal know? Would he instinctively know? Would her betrayal be written all over her face?

As she crawled into bed, Sal whispered to her in the dark, "You said you'd be home early." And he rolled over and put his back to her.

The breakfast dishes were piled high in the sink, the grease in the frying pan now congealed. A basket of laundry that needed folding and ironing sat at Jeanne's feet. The coffee in her cup had gone cold but Jeanne remained unaware, still sipping away at it.

Sleep had been evasive. She'd tossed and turned. By the time the alarm went off, she felt shaky, and her head pounded from lack of sleep and too much alcohol.

As she made Sal's breakfast, she purposely kept her back to him, afraid he'd be able to read her betrayal on her face. Fortunately, on Wednesday mornings after she'd been out, Sal was usually sullen. This Wednesday proved to be no different. It would take him a week to warm up and he'd be fine by the following Tuesday, only for it to start all over again. This week, she was counting on his remoteness. She *needed* it. If only to process what she had done.

She sipped her cold coffee and squeezed her eyes shut. The images of what had happened in the back seat of Steve's car were not far from the forefront of her mind. At that moment, in the heat of it, she'd felt alive again, young and passionate.

But now all she felt was painful regret.

By noon, still with nothing done, she decided she'd reached the end of her dancing days. No one ever had to know what had happened. Granted, she couldn't guarantee that Steve wouldn't tell people, but she hoped he wouldn't. She promised herself that she would make it up to Sal, become a good wife again. Focus all her attention on him and the boys. Even though Sal had been cool toward her, she needed that now. Space and distance were required for her to get through her transgression. If Sal had been attentive or loving, she didn't think she'd be able to keep her secret. Guilt would drive her to admit it.

It had been a mistake, and she could make up for it.

No one would ever need to know that she had been unfaithful, especially Sal.

Chapter Twenty-Two

February 1976

It was time to tell Sal her news. She dreaded it like nothing she had ever dreaded in her life. But she had no choice. That morning, she hadn't been able to button the waistband on her pants. She figured she was about four months along. She supposed she should go to the doctor, but she wasn't ready yet. She was still in a bit of denial over the whole thing. This baby would be living proof to her and Sal that she had been an unfaithful wife. The thought of it made her swallow hard, but she had no saliva. She wondered if he'd divorce her. That particular thought made her sick.

"You're pregnant? That's wonderful," Sal said. "How far along?"

"Four months, I think." She could not look away. Could not pull her gaze from his face, like waiting for a train wreck she knew was about to happen. After she stopped going out dancing, they'd resumed marital relations after a while, but it hadn't been until after Thanksgiving.

It took only a quick moment for him to realize that the math didn't add up. His expression crumpled.

Jeanne hung her head. She couldn't look at him. Didn't want to see the pain that she had caused. Her shame was complete. She stared at her lap, unable to lift her head.

"It's not my child," he said finally.

"No." Her voice was barely above a whisper.

"When is it due?"

"It should be sometime in July." It was only five months away. Unlike her other pregnancies, time was hurtling past her with this one.

"How did this happen?" he demanded.

She shrugged, her eyes filling up with tears. "I don't know."

"You just fell into bed with him," Sal said, raising his voice. "Your clothes just fell off."

"Don't be vulgar, Sal," she said angrily.

He snorted. "That's rich coming from you, pregnant with another man's child."

She stared at the floor, unable to look at him.

"Do you want a divorce?" he asked.

"No."

"Does the other man want to marry you?"

"He doesn't know." And although she had imagined being with Steve, in the cold, harsh light of day, she did not want to give up Sal or the boys. She couldn't. Those dreams about Steve were only escapist fantasies.

"Why haven't you told him?"

She shrugged. Tears pricked her eyes, but she bit her lip to tamp them down. As much as it killed her to swallow her pride, she said quietly, "I don't love him. And I don't want him to know."

Sal's laugh was bitter. "Jeanne, do you love anyone besides yourself?"

She ignored his question. "I've given this a lot of thought."

"It's a shame you didn't give having an affair a lot of thought before you went headfirst into it."

"It wasn't an affair," she corrected him. "It was one night only." And that was dumb luck for her. One night with a man she didn't really know, and she was pregnant. Meanwhile, she and Sal had done nothing to prevent pregnancy, used no contraception all those years and still no baby. Fate had been cruel.

She didn't say anything. There wasn't much to say.

"Why don't you want a divorce?" he asked.

"It would be a mistake to break up our marriage." That she truly believed. But it had taken her a long time to figure it out.

"I'd say you've made a doozy of a mistake," Sal said. "But you haven't asked me what I want. If I want a divorce."

Finally, she lifted her head, half terrified of the answer but hoping the Sal she'd married, the one she'd known—the man who put family above all else—would shine through.

"You've cheated on me, Jeanne. I don't know how we can come back from that."

The silence loomed heavy, threatening, and suffocating.

"I know, I'm sorry." Her voice was a whisper. How she wished she could go back and change it all. Not go out that night with Lois for the first time. She wished she had stayed home and found another hobby: playing bridge with other women, macramé or ceramics. Anything but this would have been safer and without the devastating consequences.

"You're sorry now, but I doubt you were sorry while you were fooling around with another man," he said plainly.

Overwhelmed with guilt and sorrow, Jeanne began to sob, the tears falling freely.

"I need time to think about this," Sal said. "I'm not sure yet what I want to do." He slipped out of the room and left her to her despair. But she wasn't left alone with her thoughts for long as the phone started ringing.

"Hello?"

"Jeanne?" asked a male voice. It sounded familiar and for a brief, panicky moment, she feared it was Steve.

Her voice faltered. "Yes?"

"It's Chuck."

Relief flooded her, followed by concern. Why was Chuck calling her?

"Is everything all right?" she asked.

"No. It's Betty, she's in the hospital," he said, his voice breaking.

"What happened?" Jeanne asked, frantic.

"She started bleeding last night. Lots of blood."

"Where are you now?"

"At the hospital."

"I'll be right there," Jeanne said. She hung up the phone and pulled a coat out of the back closet.

Sal walked back into the kitchen. "Where are you going?"

"The hospital. Betty went in last night. Chuck just called." Her coat hung on her, unbuttoned, and she held her pocketbook in her hands.

"I'll drive you over," he said quietly, and grabbed his jacket before heading out the door.

They found Chuck in the third-floor waiting room at the local community hospital. He leaned forward in his chair, head in his hands, and both Jeanne and Sal froze in their tracks when they saw his back shaking and realized he was crying.

Oh no.

Jeanne swallowed the big lump in her throat and forced her feet forward.

"Chuck?" she asked, her voice barely above a whisper. She laid a hand on his trembling back.

He lifted his head, his face ruddy and his red-rimmed eyes full of tears.

Jeanne collapsed in the seat next to him. "Oh my God, what is it? Is Betty all right?"

He shook his head. "No, she's not. They say she's got a large mass in her uterus and that it's spread everywhere."

"What?" Jeanne said, her voice incredulous. How could this be? Betty was the same age as she: thirty-five. "I don't understand."

Chuck continued to blubber, wiping his nose with his sleeve. "They're saying it's too late and there's nothing more they can do."

"What?" Jeanne said again, unable to find any other words. This couldn't be happening. These types of things happened to other people, not to those she loved. Not to a good, kind woman with six young children at home. She looked at Sal, her mouth hanging open, and read on his face the shock that was surely apparent on hers. It was as if they were in an alternate reality, where all these things were happening that shouldn't be happening.

"What about Roswell Park up in Buffalo?" Sal asked, referring to the renowned cancer institute. He stood there, arms crossed over his chest, his expression grave.

Chuck shook his head. "My sister suggested Roswell, but the doctors said there's nothing more that can be done."

He leaned forward, put his head down and sobbed. Jeanne rubbed his back.

"I can't do it without my Betty. She's my heart," he said, his voice shaky.

"Does she know?" Jeanne asked. Her own voice was low, and quivered.

He nodded. "Yes, she does. She suspected as much."

Jeanne felt all the energy drain from her. She wondered if she'd be able to stand. "Can I see her?"

"Yes, yes. She'd like that. Mary's on her way up."

"Good." Jeanne stood but wobbled, losing her balance. At the same time she grabbed the arm of the chair for support, Sal reached out to steady her.

The three of them walked quietly down the corridor. Jeanne and Sal flanked Chuck. All the while, Jeanne kept thinking that this wasn't happening, that there must be some mistake. It was as if she were in the middle of a nightmare, and she'd wake up any minute and they'd all go back to normal. She wouldn't be pregnant, and Betty would be home, herding her six kids.

Betty's room was the last one along the corridor, farthest away from the nurses' station. Chuck led the way, and Jeanne didn't hesitate to enter the room. She was anxious to see her friend.

Her friend of almost thirty years looked shrunken in the hospital bed. Tubing from an intravenous drip snaked from a glass bottle to the crook of her arm.

Jeanne was alarmed at how much weight her friend had lost. She was as pale as a ghost. But when she spotted Jeanne and Sal, she broke into a smile.

"Jeanne! I knew you'd come!"

Jeanne rushed over to her, leaning down to kiss her forehead. "Of course. Where else would I be?"

A nervous giggle escaped Betty. "The news isn't good, Jeanne."

"We'll beat it, honey," Chuck said. He stood at the foot of the bed, his hands on the footrail. Sal hung back in the corner. He looked as shocked at Betty's appearance as Jeanne felt.

Mary pushed through the door, her pocketbook dangling from the crook of her arm. "I came as soon as I could." She rushed over to Betty and stood on the other side of the bed, across from Jeanne.

"Betty, what is going on?"

"They're saying I have cancer and it's everywhere," Betty said quietly.

"They must be wrong," Mary said firmly. As if saying it with conviction would change the circumstances.

Everyone went quiet.

"What's the plan? Chemotherapy? Surgery? Radiation?" Mary's questions were rapid-fire.

Betty spoke. "They say it's too late for any of that." Her eyes filled with tears. This triggered an outpouring of tears from Chuck. Betty reached her hand out to her husband. "It'll be okay, you'll see."

"How can it be?" he wailed.

Sal stepped forward. "Come on, Chuck, let me buy you a cup of coffee."

Chuck hesitated, not wanting to leave his wife's side.

"Go on. Jeanne and Mary will be here, and you need a break." Betty turned toward Sal. "See if you can get him to eat something. He's not eating."

"I'll take care of him," Sal reassured her, and he led Chuck out of the room.

When her husband was out of earshot, Betty said, "I'm glad he's gone. He's not handling this well, and I need to talk to you both."

"We're here," Mary said.

"Chuck doesn't know this. Well, maybe he does, but I don't think it's sunk in."

"Your diagnosis?" Jeanne asked.

"No. Not that."

Jeanne and Mary exchanged a glance over the bed.

"I don't have a lot of time." Betty didn't look at them, choosing to stare at the wall ahead of her. "The doctors say I only have a few weeks. I might get two months."

Jeanne blinked and felt the blood drain from her face. She felt dizzy and like she might throw up. This wasn't happening.

"That can't be right," Mary said, vocalizing Jeanne's thoughts.

"It's true. And you know, I can feel it, things winding down for me."

"Don't say that," Jeanne cried. "You've got to fight it, Betty."

"Jeanne's right," Mary said. "You've got to come out swinging!"

Betty laughed. "Mary, you know that's not my style." She held out her hands on either side of her. Her friends each grasped a hand.

"I want you to do one thing for me," Betty whispered.

"Anything," Jeanne said.

"I want to go home and die," Betty said. "I don't want to die in the hospital." Tears swam in her eyes. "I want to go home, but it'll be too much for Chuck to do by himself."

Jeanne nodded. "Of course. We can help take care of you."

"And the kids," Mary said.

Betty squeezed her eyes shut at the mention of her kids. "They're too young to lose their mother."

Jeanne bit her lip. She didn't want to cry in front of her friend and cause her further distress. A quick glance at Mary showed she was struggling to maintain her composure as well.

"Whatever time I have left, I want to spend it with my kids. Or at least be near them," Betty said.

"We'll do whatever we can."

"Chuck will be the biggest obstacle. He's a good man, but taking care of a dying wife will be beyond him," Betty said. "He wants me to stay in the hospital." She pulled her hands away from her friends' grasp and fiddled with the edge of the bedsheet. "He's hoping for a miracle."

All three went quiet. And the quiet grew and grew with all the images of what the short future held for their friend, until it became suffocating. When she didn't think she could take it anymore, Jeanne asked, "What can we do? To get you home?"

"Do we need to talk to the doctors?" Mary asked.

"I've spoken with them, but Chuck was here, and he wasn't that excited about the idea."

If her friend wanted to go home to die, Jeanne was going to make sure Betty's wishes were honored.

At lunchtime the following day, she was sorting out laundry at the kitchen table, a million things going through her mind, and she jumped when Sal walked in. He'd never come home for lunch. She placed her splayed hand across her chest and said, "You startled me." She kept her head bent, focusing on the laundry in the basket at her feet that needed to be folded. Since she'd told him of her pregnancy, they had not spoken about it. Earlier, she'd had an intense crying jag, and her eyes were still red-rimmed and her nose puffy.

"I'm sorry." He looked around. "Have you had lunch?"

"Yes. I had a sandwich about half an hour ago."

He pulled the chair out from across the table and sat down. "I suppose we should talk."

"Yes. I'd like to know where I stand." She wondered if she'd be packing a suitcase and moving out later that day. Her heart beat faster in anticipation of disastrous news. Sal held all the power. He and he alone would determine her fate and the fate of the child within her.

"I will raise the child as my own."

Relief flooded through her, and she grabbed the back of the chair and slumped onto it.

"But I have a few conditions," Sal said evenly.

Jeanne held her breath, wondering what they would be.

"No more going out dancing by yourself. No more going to a bar or nightclub by yourself. Even after the baby is born." For each point, he thumped the table with his forefinger.

She didn't think she'd ever go out again. Right now, she felt like she wanted to hide in the house for the rest of her life.

"Whoever the father is, you're to stop seeing him immediately. He's not to have any contact with the baby. None whatsoever. It's the only way it's going to work. And if I ever find out that you're seeing him again or taking the baby to see him, I will do everything I can to have you declared an unfit mother. And I will take all three kids with me."

Jeanne could only nod; Sal didn't make idle threats.

"He doesn't know, and I have no plans to tell him."

"Good." His voice had a sharp edge to it. "I'll go over after work and tell my mother. And tonight, after dinner, we'll tell the boys."

"How will we explain it? I mean, there's such an age difference between the boys and this baby."

"Many couples have a late-in-life baby. This won't raise an eyebrow." His face crumpled. "I would have been so overjoyed if it were my child." He pulled his hankie from his back pocket and blew his nose.

"I'm so sorry, Sal. I wish I had it to do all over again," she whispered. She'd caused him so much pain. Staring at her hands in her lap, she said, "Thank you for agreeing to raise the child as your own."

"There's no reason an innocent child should suffer because of your . . . adultery."

She winced. Despair filled her that this might be the new normal of her marriage. That this was how it would be between them in their house for the rest of their lives. Would she ever be happy again? She almost wondered if maybe they should get divorced. Why should they be stuck with each other, miserable? But momentary panic set in as she thought about how she would survive as a divorced, single parent. She had no employable job skills.

Sal bumped the edge of the table as he stood up to leave, and the vibration jarred her from her depressing thoughts.

"I'll see you at dinner" was all Sal said as he exited the house.

When she heard the car door slam and the engine start, she burst into tears and sobbed so hard that her body shook.

Chapter Twenty-Three

Betty was coming home to her house full of kids. It hadn't been difficult to convince Chuck that these were her wishes. As Jeanne and Mary spoke to him, promising they'd help and be there every day, Chuck nodded, pausing to either wipe his eyes or blow his nose with a crumpled handkerchief.

Jeanne and Mary stood on the front porch of Betty's home, waiting for the ambulance to transport her from the hospital to her front door. Jeanne pushed away her anxiety about caring for her dying friend.

Rain slammed down and the March wind howled, lifting their hair up from their coat collars.

"Gosh, did it have to rain and be breezy the day Betty came home?" Mary griped.

Jeanne and Mary spoke every day, sometimes as many as two to three times. They were trying to coordinate their schedules to take care of Betty, look after Chuck and the kids, and tend to their own families. It was going to require multi-tasking at an expert level.

The ambulance arrived and backed into the narrow driveway, and the attendants in their white coats and pants jumped out of the front and headed around to the back of the vehicle. Jeanne wouldn't have thought it was possible, but Betty appeared even more frail than she had a few days ago. It was as if she was fading fast. The ambulance attendants carried the stretcher up the porch steps, jostling Betty to the point that she cried out in pain.

"Take it easy," Jeanne said in a huff.

Mary held open the front door, and Betty was carried in. One of the twin beds from the boys' room upstairs had been brought down and put in the corner of the parlor. It had been Betty's choice; she wanted to be where all the activity was. Her children were currently at school and had not seen their mother since she'd gone into the hospital. Chuck had decided not to tell the kids of her poor prognosis.

Once they got Betty settled, with pillows propping her up, Mary said goodbye and left, as they'd agreed that Jeanne would keep Betty company for the afternoon and Mary would return for the evening with dinner for Chuck and the kids.

After Mary left, Jeanne made Betty a cup of tea and a slice of buttered toast, but Betty frowned at it and shook her head. "I can't. I have no appetite." She did take a few sips of the tea, and Jeanne set aside the plate of toast.

"Jeanne, are you pregnant?" Betty asked. Even her voice was fading.

Jeanne's head snapped up. "What?"

"After six kids, I can spot a pregnancy miles away," Betty said with a small smile.

"Yes, I am," Jeanne confirmed. She had not told anyone outside of her family that she was expecting a baby. And she certainly did not want to unburden herself to her dying friend about the circumstances regarding the pregnancy. One thing was for certain: she was going to make sure Betty died in peace. "Baby's due in July."

Betty grimaced. "I won't be here then." Before Jeanne could protest and make some false reassurance, Betty said, "Sal must be over the moon."

"He is," Jeanne lied.

Later in the afternoon, they were interrupted by the arrival of fifteen-year-old Mark, the oldest of the six kids, coming in early from school.

"Mom, where's my baseball jersey?"

Betty, groggy, said, "I don't know."

Jeanne stood up. "There are a few piles of clothes on top of the dryer. Let me help you find it." Over her shoulder, she said to Betty, "I'll be right back."

"I might take a snooze. I feel sleepy," Betty said, and her eyes were closed before Jeanne left the room. The doctor had said that was to be expected.

Jeanne went through the piles of folded clothes. "Mark, would you help me sort these? I don't know who they belong to." She'd managed to sort the boys' stuff from the girls' articles of clothing, but that was as far as she'd got. Three girls and three boys close in age made her think of *The Brady Bunch*.

"Mom will do that. She does the laundry and then puts it in our rooms," Mark said easily.

Jeanne stared at him for a moment. Softly, she said, "Mark, you realize your mother is very sick."

"I know, but when she gets better, things will go back to the way they used to be." He seemed so confident in this future with his mother that it made Jeanne's heart ache.

"How much has your father told you?"

Mark shrugged, lifting folded clothes off the dryer in search of his baseball shirt. "I dunno. Said she was really sick and that you and Mary would help take care of her."

Jeanne was torn. It was not her place to drop Betty's prognosis like a bomb on this young kid. But at the same time, she didn't want him believing in some airy-fairy idea that his mother might rise out of the bed in the parlor and start looking after them all.

"Your mother is very ill," Jeanne said again. "She has cancer."

"I know," he said, not looking at her. "Here it is!" He pulled his baseball shirt out of the pile, leaving the rest of it strewn all over the dryer. "I've got to meet the guys. I'll see you later."

"Dinner's at six."

"What are we having?"

Jeanne laughed. "I don't know. Mary's bringing something over."

"Okay. Bye!" he said, and he was out the door.

Jeanne looked at the empty space he'd just inhabited, worrying about him, like she worried about all of Betty's kids.

On the third day, Jeanne was a little more depressed and tired than usual. Betty was sleeping a lot, and she and Mary had yet to get into their groove. Both of them had showed up that morning before Chuck left for work, and Jeanne had to remind Mary that she couldn't do the following day, because she had a doctor's appointment and the boys had their six-month cleaning at the dentist.

In the evening when Chuck came home, she couldn't stop yawning. She didn't know if it was from the pregnancy or from the stress of Betty's illness. As she was walking out the door, Lois was stepping up onto the porch.

"Lois!" Jeanne said, surprised.

"Hey, Jeanne, I heard Betty is sick and I'd like to see her. Do you think she would like a visit?"

"I'm sure she'd love to see you," Jeanne said. She was glad to see Lois. Even though they had drifted in and out of each other's lives, they'd all been friends since they were nine years old.

Lois wore a stylish belted coat, and Jeanne caught a glimpse of her wedding band and diamond engagement ring on her left hand.

"How's married life treating you?" she asked.

Lois broke into a smile. "I'm really happy. He's a good man."

That warmed Jeanne's heart. "I'm really happy for you." She pivoted and opened the door. "Come on, let me check." She stopped and did a half turn. "Just a heads-up. Betty sleeps a lot. And she'll probably drift off mid-sentence."

Lois nodded. "How's she doing?"

Jeanne's eyes filled quickly with tears. Words left her, and she shook her head. She pushed through the door and asked Lois to hang on while she checked on Betty.

Mark sat slouched in the chair next to his mother, his head buried in a comic strip, while the rest of the family ate dinner in the kitchen.

Betty opened her eyes. "You're back already?"

Jeanne leaned over the side of the bed. "Lois is here. Would you like to see her?"

Betty's eyes filled up. "Of course! Bring her in."

Jeanne led her into the room. Lois's face registered shock when she saw Betty in the bed, but she quickly recovered and plastered a smile on her face. She leaned over and gently hugged her friend.

"Mark," Jeanne said, "you can go eat your dinner while Lois visits with your mom."

He looked from his mother to Jeanne to Lois and back to his mother. "Are you sure?"

"Yes, honey, go eat," Jeanne said. When he left, she said to Lois, "He's a good kid. They all take turns sitting with Betty during dinnertime."

"I hit the jackpot with those kids," Betty said.

"Do you want me to stay?" Jeanne asked. She thought Lois might feel uncomfortable as she hadn't seen Betty in years.

"No, I'm okay as long as Betty doesn't mind."

"We have a lot of catching up to do," Betty chimed in softly from the bed.

"All right, see you tomorrow, Betty," Jeanne said.

Lois took the chair Mark had vacated.

"Thanks, Jeanne, for everything," Betty said. "And good night for a second time."

Jeanne laughed and kissed her friend on the forehead for the second time that evening.

She walked home. It had stopped raining, but everything was mucky. She preferred to walk the ten-minute walk home even though Sal had offered to pick her up. It gave her a chance to clear her head and let the events of the day settle around her. It was a good thing spring was coming, because she could barely close the buttons of her coat around her baby bump.

Sal was already home when she arrived. He was in the kitchen. His mother had sent over chicken parmigiana. Since Jeanne had been taking care of Betty, her mother-in-law had insisted on cooking dinner for them. And Jeanne had been too tired to argue. It was nice to come home to a dinner already made. Food tasted better when someone else cooked it.

Sal looked up from setting the table. "You're late." His words weren't unkind or accusatory, more born of concern.

"Lois showed up as I was leaving," she said. Sal stiffened at the mention of Lois's name. Weary, Jeanne ignored it. She only had so much energy to go around. She sank down into the chair.

"You look tired," he said. He removed a pan from the oven, set it on a hot plate, and removed the tin foil covering it.

"I am tired," she said.

"You need to look after yourself." As an afterthought, he added, "And the baby."

Briefly, she wondered what it would be like when the baby arrived. Would every time he looked at the child remind him of her infidelity? How could it not? But she couldn't go there now, she was too damn tired, and her plate was already full of things to worry about.

She was so tired she couldn't move from the chair. Quietly, Sal served up the chicken with a side of spaghetti, and she was grateful because she didn't even have the energy to do that. It looked and smelled so good she wanted to cry at the sight of it. Her stomach growled in response.

Sal looked at her. "Are you eating, Jeanne?"

She nodded. Tea and toast counted, didn't it?

She scarfed down the chicken parmigiana and accepted the second helping that Sal put on her plate. She was happy to sit back and listen to the boys and all the concerns and topics of conversation of teenagers. From time to time, she smiled. At one point, she reached behind and rubbed the small of her back. It had ached all day long.

They were just finishing when the doorbell rang.

"Terry, answer the door," Sal said.

Terry jumped up, his own second helping half eaten, and headed to the front door.

Sal looked over at Joey. "Tomorrow after school, go over to Nonna's and give her a hand. She wants to clean out some of the closets."

Joey sagged in his chair. "Okay."

Jeanne smiled to herself. As much as Joey complained, she suspected he secretly liked going over to Nonna's, where his grandmother doted on him and there was always something good to eat.

Terry landed back in the kitchen. "Mom, it's for you."

Jeanne stood, pushed her plate back, and went to investigate. She was surprised to see Junie Reynolds and Thelma Schumacher standing in her parlor, both of them holding disposable thirteen- by nine-inch pans in their hands.

"We did some baking for Chuck and the kids," Junie said.

"That's so sweet." Jeanne said. It wouldn't take long for six kids to go through the pans of baked goods. "Come on through to the kitchen so you can set those pans down."

"That would be great," Thelma said. She'd married Stan Schumacher, the owner of the Old Red Top, the previous July. Jeanne and Sal took the boys there regularly, especially when Jeanne didn't feel like cooking. She was quite fond of the Texas red hots.

She led them back to the kitchen, where the boys had taken their plates to the sink and Sal was wrapping up the leftover chicken. He said hello to Junie and Thelma.

The women set the pans on the table, and Jeanne invited them to sit down.

"I made a Watergate cake," Junie said. The light pistachio-flavored cake was a favorite of Jeanne's.

"And I made chocolate," Thelma added.

Jeanne didn't know where Thelma found the time. It seemed she was always at the restaurant with Stan.

"Betty will really appreciate this."

"We didn't want to drop in on her unannounced, that's why we came here," Junie said.

"There's a lot going on, and she probably doesn't want us gracing her doorstep," Thelma chimed in.

"She probably wouldn't mind a short visit," Jeanne said truthfully, especially since they'd gone to all this trouble.

"Okay, maybe. But we wanted to talk to you about something else," Junie said.

"I'll be in the parlor if you need me," Sal said to Jeanne, getting ready to escape to the front room with the newspaper. "Nice to see you ladies again."

"We heard that you and Mary are taking care of Betty," Junie started. "My Nancy is friends with Betty's daughter Dena."

"Betty wanted to be at home," Jeanne said.

"Of course," Thelma agreed. "There's no place like home."

"Anyway, Thelma and I would like to help," Junie said. "You and Mary, I'm sure, are pretty busy taking care of Betty and her kids. Plus, you have your own families to look after. We'd like to do the cooking and baking for Chuck and the kids."

"You can't do everything," Thelma said to Jeanne.

Jeanne was speechless. "I don't know what to say. That is so generous."

"My mother died when I was young. It was awful," Thelma said, her voice quiet and laced with a hidden sorrow.

"And my sister was killed in a car accident before she was thirty," Junie added. "We do understand heartache."

Overcome with emotion, Jeanne bent her head to hide her tears, but a big hiccough escaped and then the dam burst, and she shook with uncontrollable crying. Junie jumped up out of her chair and reached for her, pulling her into an embrace, and Thelma wrapped her arms around both of them. Pretty soon, all three were crying.

And so it was decided: Junie and Thelma would do the cooking daily for the Nugents. Lois offered to sit with Betty in the evenings after work so Betty's family could eat their dinner together. And Jeanne and Mary continued to take care of their dying friend.

Chapter Twenty-Four

Over the course of six weeks, Betty continued to fade. In April, her decline picked up speed, which alarmed everyone. Suddenly, she was unable even to stand with assistance, and she'd stopped eating.

On the Easter weekend, she developed terrible pain and some difficulty breathing.

"Maybe we should call an ambulance," Chuck said, running his hand through his hair.

"I'm not leaving the house," Betty said weakly.

"Honey, you're in a lot of pain and it's hard for you to breathe," Chuck said nervously. He began to pace.

"Let me call the doctor's office," Jeanne suggested. As it was the weekend, her call was taken by the answering service, who promised to pass on the message to the covering physician.

Within half an hour, their call was returned. The covering doctor, someone Jeanne had never heard of, was short and snappish. She explained the situation.

"Why is a young woman dying of cancer at home and not in the hospital?" he barked.

"Because she wants to be with her family," Jeanne replied. She couldn't understand why the doctor was so angry. She described Betty's difficulty with pain and breathing.

"Send her to the hospital and I'll treat her there," was his reply.

Jeanne's sigh was one born of frustration and exasperation.

"She won't go to the hospital."

"Then I can't help her."

She pressed on. "Can't you give her anything to ease her pain?"

"Not at home I can't. Send her in," he said, and he hung up.

She replaced the receiver, then turned to find Chuck and Sal staring at her. Betty's eyes were closed, but there were deep furrows along her forehead, and from time to time a moan escaped her lips.

"He says she has to go to the hospital."

"No," Betty moaned.

"The doctor wants you to go to the hospital," Chuck said.

"No." She shook her head but the effort cost her, and a low moan escaped her lips.

"Maybe we could ask Dr. Walsh to stop by," Sal volunteered. "He was in for a haircut yesterday, said they were down from Buffalo for the weekend."

They all looked at him like he'd just ridden in on a white horse.

Everyone knew who Dr. Walsh was; he and his family had been coming to Hideaway Bay for the summer for years.

Hopeful to the point it was painful to witness, Chuck asked, "Sal, do you think he'll come over? And help my Betty?"

"Let me go and see if he's home," Sal said.

Jeanne was so grateful to him.

Sal returned shortly with Dr. Walsh in tow. Although his appearance and manner were serious, there was a warmth and kindness that emanated from him.

He was introduced to everyone and sat in a chair next to Betty's bed. He spoke to her in low, hushed tones, and she gave him one-word answers, fighting to keep her eyes open. Jeanne and Sal left the room to give Betty and Chuck some privacy with the doctor. Jeanne decided to tackle the laundry, and Sal offered to take the younger children outside and walk them around the block.

Jeanne carried the basket full of clean clothes to the kitchen table. When she sat, she closed her eyes, relishing the quiet, something that was rare in a house full of six children.

It wasn't long before Betty's oldest, Mark, strolled through the back door, balancing a basketball on his hand, twirling it.

Mark frowned. "Where is everyone?"

Jeanne folded a kitchen towel. "Sal took the younger kids for a walk. Greg is over at a friend's house. And the doctor is in with your mother and father."

He nodded, his gaze pinned to the basketball.

"Do you want me to fix you something to eat?" she asked, looking up from her growing pile of folded laundry.

"Nah. Thanks though." He stopped twirling the ball, palmed it, and set it out in the back hall. He stood at the other end of the table, his hands on the back of the chair. "Jeanne, can I ask you a question?"

"Sure, honey, go ahead."

"Is my mother going to die?"

Jeanne froze, a white T-shirt dangling from her hand.

Mark looked at her beseechingly. "I'm old enough to know the truth."

As painful as it was, she couldn't lie to him.

"Yes."

Mark bent his head and nodded. "Thanks." He disappeared from the room.

No sooner had he left than Sal returned with the younger children, who immediately ran upstairs and turned on a television.

Chuck appeared with Dr. Walsh and closed the kitchen door against the noise of the blaring television set coming from a room upstairs.

Dr. Walsh nodded in their direction and then spoke to Chuck. "I know Mrs. Nugent's doctor quite well. I'll call him when I get home and tell him what's going on."

"Thank you, Dr. Walsh," Chuck said with a nod, his voice full of relief.

The doctor hoisted his black bag up onto the table and pulled out a little brown bottle.

"This is morphine. I've given her a dose now to help relieve her pain." He looked around the room and asked, "Who will be administering this?"

"Mary and I are here during the day, and Chuck is here overnight," Jeanne told him.

The doctor nodded and proceeded to give instructions on dosage and administration, scribbling them down on a sheet of paper.

He tore off another piece of paper and scribbled a phone number on it. "I'll be here until Monday morning. Call me any time if there's any problems."

The relief was palpable and rolled off all of them.

With a deep frown, he closed his doctor's bag and pushed his eyeglasses up on his nose. "I believe in being honest here. Mrs. Nugent doesn't have a lot of time left."

Chuck appeared to deflate.

"You need to prepare yourself," Dr. Walsh continued. "Is everyone comfortable with Mrs. Nugent remaining at home?"

Jeanne spoke up immediately. "Yes. We'll take care of her."

"Very well," he said. "That's all I can do for now. Keep her as comfortable as possible."

"Doctor, she's not eating," Chuck said as Dr. Walsh turned to leave.

The doctor stood grim-faced in the doorway, the bag at his side. "No, she won't eat much now, if she eats anything at all. This is what happens."

"Oh." Chin quivering, Chuck was unable to say anything more.

Betty died four days later, in the middle of the night. All her children were snug in their beds upstairs. Jeanne and Mary were home in their own beds, out cold from sheer emotional exhaustion. And Betty's husband was sound asleep in the chair next to her bed, her hand in his. She'd slipped away peacefully, not wanting or making a fuss.

Chapter Twenty-Five

There was only one word to describe how Jeanne felt after the death of her friend Betty.

Raw.

It was as if her skin had been torn off and every nerve ending, every muscle and bit of flesh, was exposed, making her sensitive to everything.

As her belly grew, Sal became more distant, and Jeanne had never felt more alone in her life. If she had thought she was isolated before when she'd been lonely and bored at home, she truly was now. Betty was gone, Mary went home to her own family, and Lois had gone back to her newly married life. She and Sal barely spoke. Her grief overwhelmed her at times. She was glad she was home alone during the day, so she could break down and weep without any witnesses.

How life had played a cruel trick on all of them. Six children without a mother. She and Mary spoke on the phone every day, working out how to keep Chuck and his kids in the loop. Jeanne's boys were off with their friends most of the time. Terry, now sixteen, was embarrassed by his mother's pregnancy. She and Sal had to ignore his discomfort, because how could they also admit that they were embarrassed by the circumstances that had led to a new baby coming into their life? The fact was, they couldn't.

Her unease with her future, with this baby, with her marriage, continued to plague her.

In the second week of May, she was in the middle of a meltdown when the doorbell rang. Hurriedly, she wiped her eyes with the first thing she grabbed, a dish towel, making a note to toss it into the hamper. She blew her nose with a paper towel and threw it into the garbage bin beneath the sink as the doorbell continued to ring.

"Coming," she called as she navigated her way to the front door, her hand on her blooming belly. She couldn't remember her belly being this big with the boys. But then that was a long time ago. Maybe she was misremembering.

She was surprised to see Junie Reynolds on her porch. As she opened the door, a broad smile broke out on Junie's face. Jeanne would never forget how Junie and Thelma had pitched in and helped during Betty's sickness.

Jeanne held the door open for her visitor, nodding her head. "Come on in, Junie."

"Thank you." Junie stepped in, looked at Jeanne and halted. "Is this a bad time?"

Jeanne laughed and said, "I'm fine, really." All the earlier crying had made her nose sound stuffed.

"I remember those crying jags during and after pregnancy." Junie sighed. "Sometimes it isn't easy being a woman."

"Truer words were never spoken." Jeanne walked back to the kitchen and said over her shoulder, "I've got coffee, or tea if you'd prefer."

"Coffee's fine. I won't keep you long."

"It's nice to have some company," Jeanne said truthfully.

"It's a long day when everyone is out of the house at work and school."

"It sure is."

In the kitchen, Junie sat at the table while Jeanne poured two cups of coffee from the stovetop percolator. She set the mugs on the table and pulled a carton of creamer from the refrigerator and put it in the middle of the table next to the sugar. She pulled down a jar of Cremora from a cabinet and set that on the table too.

Both the women fixed their coffee.

"Pretty soon you'll have a new baby to keep you busy," Junie said.

"Six more weeks." In a way Jeanne dreaded it, and there was a part of her that never wanted to have it.

Would the baby serve as a constant reminder of her shame and to Sal, of her infidelity? Once the baby was here, would things further deteriorate between them? She couldn't see how they could avoid it.

Junie sipped her coffee. She was an attractive woman; she had always reminded Jeanne of the actress Suzanne Pleshette with all that dark hair and her blue eyes and dark eyebrows. Even with the beginning of fine lines around her face, her eyes, she was still striking.

"We're organizing the Fourth of July festival this year," Junie said. "And we're hoping it's going to be a big one with it being the bicentennial year and all."

Jeanne nodded. Throughout the town, people were taking the two-hundredth anniversary of the Declaration of Independence seriously. Mr. Lime over at the five-and-dime had ordered boxes of silver bells, which he was selling at a discount so everyone in town could ring their bell at two p.m. And some people were already talking about painting their mailboxes or tree trunks red, white, and blue. When Joey excitedly suggested that they paint something to get into the spirit of things, Sal had said that he was ahead of the game with his barber's pole, and that was the end of that. Patriotic spirit was severely lacking in their house. Their minds were occupied with other, more serious things.

As if reading her mind, Junie laughed and said, "Have you seen the Masterson house? They've already painted it in red, white, and blue stripes."

Even Jeanne had to chuckle at that.

"I know you're due with a baby that week, and I would never ask you to help out then, but would you be willing to join our committee now? To help with some of the organizational tasks?"

"I don't have any experience with that sort of stuff," Jeanne said honestly.

Junie waved her away. "No one does. You run a house though, don't you? Organize everything for Sal and the boys? It'll be along the same lines, but for the festival."

"What would I have to do?" Jeanne said. She could hear the wariness in her voice and wondered if Junie had picked up on it too.

"Nothing too difficult. If I give you a copy of the master list, maybe you could keep track of everything. I'm embarrassed to say that I'm a little overwhelmed." Junie stirred more sugar and creamer into her coffee. "I'm in charge." She laughed as if it were a ridiculous idea. "I'm trying to source things, organize events, and raise funds, among other things. I'm running around like a chicken with its head cut off."

Jeanne hesitated, still unsure.

"If you could make the phone calls, that would help. I realize this is a big ask, so feel free to say no. It was Thelma who suggested that I ask you."

"Oh, all right."

"And if you should feel unwell, it goes without saying, call me and let me know," Junie said kindly.

"I'll give it a try." Jeanne ignored the wobble in her voice. The distraction might be good for her. Take her mind off of Betty's death, her disintegrating marriage with Sal, and a baby that was coming whether she wanted it to or not.

Junie reached forward and laid her hand on the table near Jeanne. "Are you all right, Jeanne? I know it's been a rough year for you. Betty's death must seem unfathomable to you."

Jeanne lowered her head and nodded, her chin quivering. The mention of Betty's name made her want to wail.

"I've heard that you and Mary are helping out as much as you can with Chuck and the kids."

More nodding, still unable to speak.

"Is there anything I can do? To help out?"

Jeanne found her voice. "That's so kind of you, Junie. But we're managing. Mary and I are trying to keep Chuck and the kids from falling below the waterline."

"You two are very good friends."

Jeanne's gaze drifted, seeing the past, the four of them, she and Lois and Mary and Betty standing on some corner in Hideaway Bay, Betty clutching her two dolls, Natalie and Margaret. "We were all friends since childhood."

"I understand. Old friends are the best friends."

The urge to unburden herself to this kind woman overwhelmed her and for the second time that day, she wanted to cry. She was looking for something, maybe forgiveness, or maybe someone to say that she wasn't a bad person even though she had done a bad thing. And maybe to reassure her that Betty's death wasn't some form of punishment for her mistakes.

Jeanne drew in a deep breath and smiled, more for herself than Junie. "Now, let's go over the Fourth of July plans."

The month of June was the worst of all. Days flew by, and Jeanne's due date neared with alarming velocity. It was also a hot month, and she was big and bulky and uncomfortable.

She kept busy with organizing things for Junie for the Fourth of July festival. It was easy as she was able to do everything from home. She'd created folders to keep track of everything from vendors to entertainment to what kind of fireworks would be used. Once a week,

Junie stopped by and they went over the plans. By the last week in June, she'd handed all her files over to Junie, who was appreciative.

The days leading up to the birth were not happy, easy ones. Everything irritated her. Sal and his silence. The boys and their screaming and shouting as they ran in and out of the house and up and down the stairs with friends in tow. She was tired, she was cranky, and she was fed up with Sal's silence. She didn't want to cook or clean or change bedsheets or anything. Her ankles were swollen, and she was usually breathless by the time she reached the top of the stairs.

They never spoke about the baby. They never spoke about the pregnancy. If the baby kicked or she felt unwell, she kept it to herself. And Sal never asked. He kept his questions general, along the lines of "how was your day?" Nothing so specific that he would have to confront anything to do with the baby that was coming shortly.

Jeanne didn't know if she could take it anymore. Since Betty's death, she felt adrift. There had been no comfort forthcoming from Sal. She didn't know if he was punishing her or simply withdrawing from their marriage in the way she had the previous year.

It was not an ideal situation.

The boys' summer vacation had begun, and they had taken off right after breakfast to go be with their friends.

They stopped in briefly for lunch and after they ate two sandwiches apiece, took off again and promised to be back in time for dinner.

Jeanne made her way upstairs, thinking a cool bath might do the trick. She pushed wet bangs off her forehead, her skin damp and sweaty.

She sat in the cool water for a few minutes and started crying. A soft knock on the bathroom door startled her and she sat up quickly, water sloshing over the side of the tub.

"Jeanne? Are you all right?"

Sal.

"What are you doing here?" She was unable to mask the irritation in her voice.

"Came to check on you," he said.

"I'm fine." She sighed and pulled herself out of the tub. "I'll be down in a minute."

She pulled the stopper from the drain to let the water out. After drying off with a towel, she got dressed and went downstairs.

When she reached the kitchen, she found Sal sitting at the table eating a salami sandwich. She was glad he'd made it himself.

He said nothing to her.

"Are you ever going to speak to me again?" she asked.

He lifted his head quickly, looking at her. "What do you mean? I talk to you."

She snorted. "You speak more to your customers than you do to me."

He didn't have a reply, and she was surprised he hadn't trotted out his usual "there are consequences to actions." If he had, she might have lunged for him.

"I don't know what to say to you." It was probably one of the most honest statements he'd ever made to her.

Despite the bath, she was hot again. Uncomfortable. She sank into the chair across from him. His sandwich was left forgotten on the plate.

The torrent of tears appeared out of nowhere, and she buried her head in her hands. Now that she had started crying, she couldn't seem to stop. She hated herself for crying in front of him. It made her feel weak. Like it shored up his idea of females being the weaker sex.

Sal held a handkerchief in front of her, just like he had all those years ago when they first met. "Here, Jeanne, you can use my handkerchief."

She wiped her eyes and blew her nose. When she'd settled down and there was no further threat of tears emerging, she spoke. "I can't go on like this, Sal."

"Like what?"

"Like this!" She waved her hand in front of her for emphasis. "We don't talk. We co-exist. And I realize I've ruined everything but if we can't fix it, if this is how our marriage is going to be, I want out."

She had to know where she stood. She didn't want to spend the rest of her life trapped. Maybe she'd be better off if she struck out on her own, even if she had to go on welfare.

A horrified expression transformed Sal's face.

"I don't want a divorce," he said quietly.

"But you're okay with our marriage as it is."

He shrugged, looking down at the table, not meeting her eyes. "We're going through a rough patch."

"Sal, I cheated on you. I don't know if we can come back from that. Especially with this baby as a constant reminder." She was tired. She wanted to deliver this baby and most of all she wanted to move on with her life, whatever new version that might be. With or without him.

"Are you saying you want a divorce?" he asked, his voice incredulous.

She scowled. "Not really, no. But I can't live like this." She stared at him. "And you certainly can't want to live like this."

"It's not ideal," was all he was able to offer.

"If you don't want a divorce, what do you want?"

"I don't know how to move on from your cheating," he said quietly. He looked at her now and his eyes were full of pain.

"Sal, thousands of times, I've wished I could go back and change things."

"Me too."

She frowned, not understanding. "What do you mean?"

He looked away, focusing his gaze on the cabinets as if gathering his thoughts. "You always told me you wanted a job outside the home, and I never listened. Sometimes I wonder, if you had gotten a part-time job somewhere, if your need to go out dancing every week would even have occurred."

Jeanne sighed. She didn't want him feeling guilty; her guilt was enough for both of them.

"I don't know," she said honestly. "I was so bored and frustrated, feeling my life was sailing past me and I was making no contribution to the world. I was fed up."

"I can see that now." He shifted uncomfortably in his seat. "And I can see that I was wrong not to agree to you getting a job. I have a certain idea of how our home life and our family should look, but I never took your opinion into consideration."

It was good to hear Sal take some responsibility for her unhappiness, but it changed nothing. A part of her wondered if it was too late.

"I don't know how to get past this, but I want to try," he said.

"The problem is, I don't know how to get past it either," she admitted. "Can you ever forgive me?"

He shrugged. "Honestly, I don't know."

She appreciated that he was being truthful. "Even if this is something we can fix, I don't think either of us knows where to start." How she wished it was something she could solve. Instead, they were left to stumble in the silent, dark space between them.

"Do you have any suggestions?" he asked.

"I have one." She eyed him. "And I ask that you keep an open mind."

"I'll try."

"I think after the baby is born, we should see a marriage counselor."

Sal blanched beneath his tan. "Tell our marital problems to a stranger?"

Jeanne sighed. She'd half expected this to be his response. "I know it goes against everything you believe in, but if we're serious about putting this behind us, I think we need outside, professional help. It may be the only way."

He blew out a deep breath. "I don't know. I wouldn't feel comfortable sharing the intimate details of our life with a stranger."

"I understand."

"I'm not saying no, but I do need to think about it."

"Sure," she said with a nod.

Sal stood, the legs of the chair scraping against the linoleum. "I need to get back to work."

Jeanne nodded.

As he passed her, he laid his hand on her shoulder, and Jeanne reached up to lay her hand over his, grateful for his touch.

"I promise you, I will think about it," he said.

"Okay." She nodded, feeling weary from it all. As hard and awkward as it had been, this had been a good conversation. And if Sal had said he would think about it, she didn't doubt that. Her husband had always been a man of his word.

Chapter Twenty-Six

September 1976

Jeanne stood at the kitchen sink, washing the dishes. September was her favorite month of the year. And this year it was no different. They were enjoying record-breaking temperatures as summer lasted a little longer than usual. All the windows of the house were kept open all day and all night.

She spied Sal in the backyard, watering his tomato plants. Parked next to him was the buggy where the baby slept. When he was home, he was all about the baby. She couldn't fault him; he treated Della as if she were his own. No one knew except for the two of them that Della wasn't Sal's child.

In spectacular fashion, Della Elizabeth Rossi had arrived on the Fourth of July of the bicentennial year.

A cry burst forth from the buggy, and Jeanne pulled off her yellow gloves and draped them over the side the sink. She went about the task of heating up a bottle.

When it was ready, she squirted a small bit on her inner arm to make sure it wasn't too hot. She carried it outside, listening to the lazy drone of a bumblebee as it went from flower to flower along the back of the house.

The garden hose had been abandoned, and Sal sat in a lawn chair, cradling the baby. With a big smile on his face, he spoke in Italian to Della. Ten weeks old, she regarded him with wide open eyes, mesmerized. This made Sal laugh, and he continued to speak in Italian to her. He'd done that with the boys. There was a stab to Jeanne's heart. Sal had always wanted a daughter.

He lifted his head as she approached, bottle in her hand. As soon as he saw her, he smiled. True to his word, he had thought about going to marriage counseling and they had their first appointment the following week.

She'd intended to take the baby from him, but he held out his hand for the bottle. She handed it to him and watched as he nestled Della in the crook of his arm and gave her the bottle.

Jeanne sat down on the orange and yellow webbed lawn chair on the other side of him. Since the birth of Della, they were trying to pick up the pieces. But it wasn't easy, because in the beginning they didn't know where each piece belonged.

To start, they tiptoed into normal, everyday conversation. Mundane was safe. *There's a wind warning. Did you see the fruit and veg stand has corn for sale? Mr. Lime's father fell and broke his hip. What a shame.*

Sal looked off into the distance, the baby sucking contentedly at her bottle. "When Della's a little older, I think we should take her to Disneyworld. I always wanted to go to Florida. All that beautiful, sunny weather." He looked over to Jeanne and said, "Would you like that?"

She nodded. "I would."

The air was still. It was remarkable how nothing moved. A tiny seed of faith took root and for the first time in a long time, Jeanne felt hopeful.

Chapter Twenty-Seven

October

Something woke Jeanne in the middle of the night. She turned and watched as Sal sat up on his side of the bed and began pulling his trousers on.

"What's wrong?" she asked.

The window was open a couple of inches, and a cool breeze blew through it. It felt good after all the heat of the summer. Jeanne pulled the blanket up around her shoulders.

"I can't sleep. I'm going for a walk."

"Okay."

"I won't be long," he said. He shuffled out of the bedroom.

For their entire marriage, up until the point he'd learned about her affair and subsequent pregnancy, Sal had always been a terrific sleeper. Since then, he was often up in the middle of the night, going downstairs to make himself a sandwich or if the weather wasn't too bad, going for a long walk. In a rare bit of conversation, she'd asked him once if it was safe walking around Hideaway Bay at that hour. He had laughed and said, "It's so peaceful. The whole town is asleep, and no one is around. I feel like I have the whole place to myself. It allows me to think."

From downstairs came the sound of a door opening and closing as Sal left the house. Jeanne closed her eyes and fell back to sleep. Hours later, the wail of a siren woke her. Pre-dawn light filtered into the room through the curtains. Beside her, Sal slept, snoring lightly. Leaning forward, she peeked into the bassinet parked next to her side of the bed. Della slept peacefully, looking angelic, which made Jeanne smile. She leaned back, yawned, stretched, stood, and shuffled over to the bedroom window, which faced in the direction of the lake.

A large plume of black smoke rose on the horizon to the southwest. She gasped.

"Sal!" she called, and went to the bed to shake him awake.

He opened his eyes. "What is it? Is something wrong with Della?"

"No, she's fine. There's something on fire. I think it's on Main Street."

"What?"

"Yes, come and see. What if it's the barbershop?"

He sat up, flipping the sheet back, and didn't bother with his slippers, heading straight to the window.

Jeanne stood next to him and together they peered out at the thick, black smoke. "At first, I thought a ship was in trouble out on the lake," she said.

Sal shook his head. "No, it's too close." He continued to stare out the window. "I don't think it's the barbershop, though."

"How can you tell?" she asked. Smoke billowed into the sky, and there was enough of it that Jeanne couldn't be sure it was only one building. "Don't you want to go check it out?"

He walked over to the bed, sat on the edge of it, and pulled on his trousers and his socks and slippers. He didn't bother with a shirt as he was wearing a short-sleeved white T-shirt.

"I won't be long," he said. His face full of sleep, he took a look into the bassinet at Della, smiled, and left.

Jeanne listened as he made his way down, his slippers padding along the staircase. She didn't think she'd be able to go back to sleep, so she pulled her bathrobe around her, tying the belt at her waist, and went downstairs. While she waited for Sal to return, she made a pot of coffee and placed it on the stove. As the percolator brewed, she unlocked the front door, opened it, and stepped out onto the porch.

Crossing her arms over her chest, she noticed she wasn't the only neighbor outside this early in the morning. Marge Kandefer from across the street stood on the sidewalk in front of her house, wearing a peach-colored robe and a pair of slippers, her head covered in pink rollers. She was deep in conversation with her next-door neighbor, Ellen Whitaker, who was similarly attired. Jeanne stepped off the porch and made her way across the street.

"What's going on?" she asked.

Marge shrugged. "I don't know. I elbowed Ralph to go and check it out but all I got was 'What do you want me to do? I'm not a fireman.'" Marge said this in a funny deep voice, and Jeanne and Ellen laughed. Marge rolled her eyes.

"Sal walked up," Jeanne said. "He wanted to make sure it wasn't the shop."

"Of course," Ellen said. "Hopefully not."

"How's the baby?" Marge asked, the fire forgotten. Between them, they had nine children.

Jeanne launched into a tale of Della's routine and how for the most part she was an easy baby.

"You can already see that she's going to be a daddy's girl," Marge said knowingly. "Sal always has her out in the buggy."

Jeanne smiled but didn't know what to say. She was at a loss as to why Sal was so devoted to Della, but she certainly wouldn't complain about it. It was more than she could ask for.

"It's wonderful to see a father so involved with the children, isn't it, Marge?" Ellen asked.

With a roll of her eyes and a shake of her head, Marge said, "Ralph didn't know we had kids until they started eating us out of house and home."

Sal came into sight as he rounded the corner and walked toward them. As soon as he was near them, they barraged him with all sorts of questions.

"What's going on? It's not the shop, is it?" Jeanne asked.

"Is it more than one building?" Marge asked.

Sal looked at Jeanne. "It's the Paradise nightclub. It's burned down. There's nothing left of it."

Jeanne blinked several times, her heart thudding.

"No loss there," Marge pronounced. "The people who live near it say the noise level at night is ghastly."

"Was anyone hurt?" Ellen asked.

"As far as they know, no. It appears to have started in the early hours of the morning, after the place closed."

"Thank God for that," Ellen said. "Are you all right, Jeanne? You're white as a ghost."

Jeanne placed her hands on her cheeks. "Am I?"

"She's got a newborn at home. She's exhausted," Marge said to Ellen.

"I left the coffeepot on, I better get home," Jeanne said, dazed. "I'll talk to you later."

She left the three of them standing there and headed back home. Sal remained with the neighborhood women, the three of them speculating on the blaze.

Shaking, Jeanne made her way to the house and went in through the front door. The smell of fresh-brewed coffee filled the air, and she ran back to the kitchen to turn it off before she burned down her own house.

In her kitchen, she went through the motions of starting the day, all the while listening for any sounds of the baby. She poured herself a cup of coffee, loaded it up with creamer and sugar, and sat at the table. She was dying for a cigarette.

The Paradise was gone. She sighed and stared unseeing at the wall in front of her. Her feelings about its destruction were mixed. It had been the most liberating time of her life and yet with the most devastating consequences. She hoped no one was inside when it caught fire. She prayed that everyone was safe. She thought of the regulars: Keith and Steve, Randy, Jed, Rita, Kathy, and even the coat check girl. Lois wouldn't have been there, of course; after marrying the judge, she'd moved with him to a bigger house on Star Shine Drive, directly across from the lake. Jeanne had no idea what had become of Steve and Keith. They were probably still going disco dancing every Tuesday night. She wondered, as she did from time to time, if Steve knew he had a daughter. When she was low and feeling full of despair, especially on those days when Sal hardly spoke to her, she imagined what life would have been like had she divorced Sal and gone off with Steve. But the practical, now grounded-in-reality Jeanne thought that scenario would have had its own set of problems. The boys certainly would have suffered. And in the end, she supposed it was best that she bore the brunt of the suffering. It had been her mistake, after all. There were consequences to actions.

The noise of the side door opening jarred her from her reverie. She jumped up and rinsed out her half-drunk coffee cup in the sink and laid it on the drainboard. When Sal appeared in the doorway, she asked, "Would you like bacon and eggs for breakfast?"

"That would be nice," he said. "I'll go up and check on the baby."

She nodded and opened the refrigerator and pulled out the carton of eggs and a slab of bacon, setting them on the countertop next to the stove. She retrieved the cast iron skillet from the oven where she stored it, set it on the stove and lit the pilot light. She put on a small pan of water to heat Della's bottle; she'd be waking up soon.

Like she did every day, she went about preparing Sal's breakfast in a robotic manner. Going through the motions, on autopilot, no thought involved, which was probably just as well, as she didn't want to examine her feelings too closely.

By the time she was setting down his plate loaded with three eggs, sunny-side up; three strips of bacon, extra crisp; and two pieces of toasted Italian bread slathered in butter, Sal reappeared. As he sat down, she poured orange juice into his glass, emptying the pitcher.

"Thanks."

"Hmmm."

"The baby is still sleeping."

She rinsed out the orange juice pitcher and took a can of Minute Maid concentrate from the freezer, popping the lid off and using a knife to loosen the frozen mass.

"I can't say I'm sorry to hear that the Paradise has burnt to the ground," Sal said.

Jeanne froze, the block of orange juice sliding out of the can and into the pitcher. She was surprised he said anything. She filled the empty can with water from the tap and added it to the pitcher, repeating the motion two more times.

When she didn't respond, he added, "You must be upset."

She stirred the orange juice with a large wooden spoon and turned to him. "Not really." And she said no more. She didn't know what he wanted from her. Did he expect there to be wailing and gnashing of teeth? A part of her wished it had burned down before she ever stepped foot inside of it. Another part of her realized that the landmark that represented her own personal undoing no longer existed. The only reminder she had to prove that it was ever a part of her life was the baby upstairs in the bassinet.

There was a cry from Della upstairs and Jeanne had never been so grateful. She grabbed the bottle she'd been warming and headed upstairs. "See you tonight," she said to Sal on her way out of the room. "Don't forget to come home early. We have counseling."

"I remember."

They'd gone three times to the counselor. It had been both enlightening and exhausting. Jeanne came home after each hour-long session needing to lie on the couch. But they were committed to continuing with it.

After lunch, she put the baby in the buggy after she fell asleep drinking a bottle, packing another one to take with her just in case. She didn't plan to be gone long. She had to see for herself that the Paradise had burned down.

She wheeled the buggy down the driveway, to the end of the street, turned on Erie, and headed west, in the direction of Main Street. It was perfect fall weather: still warm, but the leaves were beginning to turn and sported the early hues of gold and orange.

She waved to people as she passed, some stopping to admire the sleeping baby. But she was sure-footed in her destination. As she turned onto Main Street and headed south, she could see smoldering smoke in the distance, where the Paradise was located. As she got closer, the air smelled acrid and thin tendrils of smoke rose from the black, charred rubble of what was left of the Paradise.

Jeanne stood in front of the ruins, rocking the buggy as Della began to fuss. She stared at the pile, thinking she'd spent a lot of time there. Nothing was recognizable. She looked for anything that was familiar from the interior, but nothing was identifiable. It was hard to believe.

"They're saying it's arson," said a voice behind her, causing Jeanne to jump.

"Junie, you scared me," Jeanne said with a nervous laugh, placing her hand across her chest.

"I'm sorry, I didn't mean to. I thought you heard me approach."

"What did you say about it being arson?" Jeanne asked in disbelief. She must have heard her wrong.

"That's what I heard from my neighbor. That the fire was deliberately set," Junie informed her.

Jeanne swept her gaze back to the smoldering ruins in front of her. "How awful. No one was hurt though, right?"

Junie shook her head. "No. It happened after hours, so thank goodness for that."

"Thank goodness is right," Jeanne muttered. She eyed Junie. "What time did you say it happened?"

"In the middle of the night. I don't know." Junie said.

Jeanne nodded and thought about Sal going for a walk in the middle of the night. There was no way he could have done something like that, could he? No, it had to be a coincidence that Sal had gone for a walk around the same time someone had set fire to the Paradise.

Feeling uneasy, Jeanne took the brake off the buggy. "I better get home."

"It was nice to see you again, Jeanne, and congratulations on your new baby," Junie said, waving her off.

"Thanks." Jeanne turned the buggy around and walked quickly in the direction of home. She refused to believe that Sal had anything to do with this.

During dinner, it was all the boys could talk about. They had walked by the burnt-out shell of the nightclub on their way home from school, lingering a little too long as Jeanne could still smell smoke on their clothes when they arrived home.

Chapter Twenty-Eight

1981

Jeanne clutched Della's hand and made her way down Main Street. In her other hand, she carried a bag full of brand-new clothing. Della was starting kindergarten the following month.

"Let's surprise Daddy and stop in and see him," Jeanne suggested. She knew Sal liked it when she brought Della around to the barbershop.

It was a bright day at the end of August. But you could feel autumn in the air. The air was softer, cooler, and not as brutal as the summer sun that beat down on your scalp, the back of your neck, and your face.

Della nodded, her face tilted upward, squinting against the sunshine. She skipped along as they made their way to Sal's barbershop.

If it wasn't for the barber's pole, you'd walk right by Sal's shop. It was the narrowest shop on the street, which suited Sal's needs fine. A slim orange

Italianate building, it was tucked neatly between the five-and-dime and the pharmacy. The helical stripes of red, white, and blue stood out on Main Street amidst all the different-colored awnings. The barbershop was one of the few shops that had no awning. Sal refused to put one up, saying it would only darken the narrow space.

As soon as they reached the barbershop, Della let go of Jeanne's hand and ran for the front door, eager to see her father.

"There's my girl!" Sal said as Jeanne followed Della inside. He lifted the little girl up and held her, planting a kiss on her cheek.

The only other people in the shop were a couple of elderly residents who sat along the vinyl window seats, reading the newspapers and magazines Sal kept on hand. They lowered their papers briefly to say hello. One of them handed Della a quarter with a laugh.

When Jeanne reached Sal, he set Della down, and she ran around the shop, ending up in the barber's chair. He stood there with his hands on his hips.

"How did you make out?" he asked.

Jeanne nodded. "Good. She's got lots of new clothes and a new pair of shoes. She's all ready for kindergarten."

"Good. Last one starting school," he said proudly.

This made Jeanne a little nostalgic. Terry had gotten an apprenticeship with the electricians' union thanks to Junie Reynolds's husband, Paul. Terry had moved up to Buffalo and was sharing an apartment with a few other guys, working full time and making a good wage. Although Sal had been disappointed that Terry didn't want to go to college, he made peace with the fact that Terry liked what he was doing and earned a good living. Joey was in his first year at college; he wanted to be a teacher. Jeanne and Sal were very proud of their boys. She was grateful that Della was only just starting school, as she wasn't ready to give up those childhood years yet. It had gone by too fast.

Things had settled down between her and Sal. Eighteen months of marriage counseling had been exhausting emotionally, but productive. Things hadn't gone back to the way they used to be and probably never would. Things were definitely different, and they were building from there.

The subject of Jeanne getting a job had been explored in counseling, with Sal admitting that he needed to get used to the idea. Once Della started school, Jeanne knew she'd be bored. Again.

And the disco music she'd loved had faded and died as all fads did. She didn't miss it. It had turned out that it wasn't an arsonist that had burned the Paradise to the ground, but faulty wiring. Relief had filled her to know that it wasn't Sal that had set the fire. But that had been replaced by guilt that she had ever doubted

Sal in the first place. She knew her husband better than that, but maybe some part of her yearned for Sal to make a mistake if only to level the playing field. Sometimes when she heard an old song on the radio, she thought back to that time when for a little bit she felt young, pretty, and carefree. But life moved on.

Sal glanced at his watch. "Why don't we go to the Old Red Top for lunch?"

It was so unlike Sal to make a spontaneous suggestion like this during his workday that Jeanne frowned. "Now?"

He smiled. "It is lunchtime." He spoke to Della. "How about going with your old man for some lunch?"

The girl was enthusiastic and clapped her hands, her face full of glee.

Sal nodded toward the two old men reading the newspapers. "Gene, Doug, can you keep an eye on things for half an hour?"

"Sure."

"If anyone comes in, tell them I went to lunch and will be back soon," he said.

"Lunch sounds nice," Gene said longingly.

Sal laughed. "I'll bring you each back a footlong with Texas sauce."

"Sounds good," Gene said.

"We'll hold down the fort," said Doug.

The three of them walked to the Red Top, Della walking in the middle, holding on to their hands. Sal said, "One, two, three, lift," and in unison, he and Jeanne lifted Della off her feet. She squealed in delight.

They stepped off the curb, Sal holding his hand out in front of them, indicating they should wait for a break in the traffic. As they waited, Jeanne's gaze was distracted by a couple across the street, walking along hand in hand beneath the awnings.

Steve.

Her breath hitched in her throat. She hadn't seen him since that night in the back seat of his car. He'd never known she'd gotten pregnant from their encounter. She'd heard from Lois that he had gotten married. The woman whose hand he held was heavily pregnant.

He must have realized she was staring because he turned his head in her direction. They made eye contact, and shock registered on his face. Then his gaze traveled away from Jeanne and landed on Della. For a few moments he stared, and then turned his head and walked on.

That was it. No acknowledgement. Jeanne swallowed hard and blinked.

"Okay now," Sal said.

"What?" Jeanne asked, momentarily confused.

Sal began to cross the street, practically dragging Della and Jeanne with him. As she stepped up onto the opposite curb, she looked over her shoulder toward Steve. But he never looked back.

It was ironic how inconsequential it was. She'd thought about it from time to time, how it might be if they ran into each other, what they might say to one another if she introduced him to Della, ascribing some imaginary meaning to it. But the actuality of it was they'd regarded each other as no more than a stranger.

And maybe that was for the best.

After Thelma took their order, Jeanne sat back in the booth. She was anxious to bring something up with Sal. Next to her, Della was busy with crayons and paper. Every time Sal looked at Della, he smiled.

Jeanne figured now was as good a time as any to broach the subject of going back to school herself. Opening her purse, she pulled the newspaper clipping from an inside pocket. It was an ad for the local hospital's nursing school. She'd cut it out weeks ago, but school started soon, and she had to get Sal on board. She slid it across the table to him.

"What's this?" he asked, pulling his glasses out of his shirt pocket. After he scanned the clipping, he looked up at her, surprise evident on his face. "Nursing school? Are you serious?"

Slightly embarrassed, Jeanne felt her cheeks redden. "Yes. Very." As soon as she read the advertisement, she knew it was something she wanted to do. *Had* to do.

"I'm not trying to be smart, but aren't you a little old to be going back to school?" Sal asked.

She knew her husband well enough to know he wasn't trying to be offensive, only practical.

"I'm forty-one, Sal. With plenty of years of working left in me," she said. "Besides, I think I'd make a pretty good nurse."

"How long have you been thinking about this?"

"Honestly?" She looked straight at him. "Since I took care of Betty."

That time spent with Betty had given her purpose and a sense that there was something out there that was greater than herself.

They both went quiet at the mention of Betty's name. That was the problem with death. There was no solution, no coming back from it. No happy ending. Chuck and the kids were lost without her, and their new normal—constantly struggling, the palpable heartache—was painful to watch. But they remained involved in their lives. She and Mary made sure the kids had their birthday and graduation parties and took turns hosting Thanksgiving, Christmas, and Fourth of July parties for them. Chuck seemed overwhelmed, even now, years later. It was a big black hole that could never be filled. They were left to go on around it.

Sal tucked the clipping into his shirt pocket and reached over and patted her hand. "Let's talk more about it tonight after dinner."

She felt hopeful.

Chapter Twenty-Nine

Sal came home in a good mood after work. He teased Della, who giggled with abandon, and relayed funny stories about his customers, which even had Jeanne laughing. She tried not to read too much into it, but she was hopeful. As she cleared the dishes, Della ran off to play, and Sal made no move to get up and go into the parlor to read the paper.

When the last dish was washed, Jeanne pulled off her yellow gloves and hung them over the edge of the sink, leaving the dishes to dry in the rack. She wiped her hands on her apron and leaned against the counter.

He'd set the newspaper clipping on the middle of the table. Since she'd cut it out, she'd rehearsed all her replies to the inevitable arguments and protests Sal would have. Even though she felt a little shaky, she was ready to stand her ground.

Sal didn't say anything for a few moments. He continued to stare at the article until finally he looked up at Jeanne.

"You really want to do this? It'll be two years of your life."

The words came quickly. "Very much so." When he didn't say anything, she added, "Nurses make good money."

"I make enough money to support us," he said. It was his eternal argument.

"I didn't say you didn't." She wanted to avoid having this turn into a circular argument as had happened so many times in the past when she brought up the idea of working outside the home.

"But what about Della?" he asked.

Years ago, it had been "what about the boys?" But now they were grown and gone. Jeanne leaned against the countertop, the edge of the Formica blunt against her back. She crossed her arms over her chest. "Della will be starting kindergarten next month. The nursing school offers an evening course, so I'd still be here all day to take her to school and pick her up and get the dinner ready."

He nodded, considering. It was encouraging that he hadn't objected yet.

She continued. "I'll be upfront and tell you that the tuition is steep, but I can pay you back when I start working."

Sal blanched at that. "You're my wife, Jeanne, you don't have to pay me back."

She shrugged and tilted her head, conceding his point.

"And this is important to you?" he asked.

"Yes," she practically gushed. "I feel I have more to offer than cleaning house and raising children."

"Childrearing is the most important thing, above all else," he said.

"I'm not saying it isn't. And haven't I been a good mother?" she demanded. She hoped she didn't sound too shrill.

"Yes," he said quietly. What was left hanging in the air was the question of "haven't I been a good wife?"

"All my life, my own wants and needs have been sidelined because someone else's were more important. And because I'm female, it's expected. I feel like I'm at the mercy of my husband and society."

Sal fingered the clipping, said nothing.

"For the past twenty years," Jeanne said, "I've wanted something more. If I die tomorrow"—Sal's head shot up— "What will it all have been for? If Betty's death taught me anything, it's that everyone needs a purpose, a way to contribute. I still have a lot to offer." She grumbled, "If someone would let me. If someone would give me a chance."

"You must feel like I've boxed you in," Sal said quietly.

She blew out a heavy sigh of exasperation. "You made all the decisions, Sal. And I felt like I had no say, even when it came to my own life. Do you have any idea how it feels to be powerless like that? That your life and your fate are in someone else's hands?"

"I suppose I haven't been the most supportive spouse," he conceded. "I'm trying to work on that."

Jeanne relaxed. "Sal, you're a good man, there's no doubt. And you will never know the regret I have that I hurt you so deeply," she said. "But your ideas about a woman's place in society are vastly different from mine."

"I was raised differently."

"It wasn't a criticism."

For a moment, neither said a word. It was Sal who spoke first.

"There's an open house at the nursing school next week. We could go together if you like."

Jeanne stared at him, speechless. In the past, she would have rushed him, excited, wanting to kiss him and hug him, but they weren't that couple anymore.

September

Della loved kindergarten, and Jeanne loved going to night classes. It was amazing to be in a classroom again and if someone had told her back in high school that she'd love being in school again, she would have scoffed at the very idea. As a teenager, she couldn't wait to get high school behind her.

There were fifteen women in the class, coming from various backgrounds and family situations. Five of the women, including Jeanne, were married, four with children at home, and the rest were single women, some fresh out of high school and a few in their twenties and thirties, who wanted to do something other than work minimum-wage jobs.

After dinner, she quickly did the wash-up, and dried and put the dishes away, her eye always on the clock. She liked to arrive fifteen minutes before the start of class to get in her seat, get organized, and chat with some of the other students. She combed her hair and put on light makeup and a casual pantsuit.

Downstairs, Sal and Della were in the kitchen. Sal was teaching five-year-old Della how to make pasta, which would find its way to the dinner table the following night. In the past few years, Sal had taken up cooking, more specifically, making sauce and pasta. It had been explored in marriage counseling; he'd admitted to always wanting to do it but had dismissed it as a "woman's job."

He had everything set out: flour, water, egg, a wooden board, and a dowel for rolling out the pasta. Since she was three years old, Della had showed an interest in "helping" Sal when he cooked. Her constant refrain was

"I wanna do it, Daddy, let me do it." Sal seemed to have the patience of a saint.

He looked up at Jeanne as she entered the kitchen, his hand clutching the dowel. "Are you all set?"

"I am," she said with a smile. "What are we making tonight?"

"Gnocchi," Sal said proudly.

"Come on, Daddy, make the well!" Della commanded.

"Oops, sorry." Sal pushed the pile of flour around on the wooden board until there was a pit in the center of it.

Jeanne walked over to them, "Good night, firecracker! Be good for Dad."

Della wrapped her arms around her mother's waist, and Jeanne leaned down and laid a kiss on the top of her head, inhaling the scent of fresh shampoo.

Della disengaged herself and returned her attention to the well of flour. Jeanne leaned up to Sal and kissed him on his cheek. She whispered, "I'll be home right after class."

"We'll be here."

As she headed out the door, she heard Sal say, "Now Della, crack the egg just like I showed you."

With a smile on her face, Jeanne closed the front door behind her.

Chapter Thirty

March 1984

Jeanne and Sal walked over to the school. A fundraiser had been organized by the PTA to raise much-needed funds for uniforms and sports equipment for the various teams. There was a huge bake sale, and the town's librarian, Carol Rimmer, had organized a drive to sell used books.

The gymnasium was crowded, and the floor had been polished to a gleam by the janitor, Morty. Jeanne winced every time she saw a puddle or a drip of water on the shiny floor. March had been damp and rainy; the beach looked depressing, and people's front lawns were nothing more than piles of mud.

Jeanne carried a Texas sheet cake in a disposable tin. Sal carried a container full of Italian wedding cookies and another one of cannoli. These were their contributions to the bake sale.

"It looks like a good turnout," Sal remarked. He'd donated free haircuts for the raffle that would be held at the end of the afternoon.

"It sure does."

They walked around until they landed at the table with the baked goods. It was covered from one end to another with all kinds of sweets and cakes and desserts. As they set their containers down on the table and made small talk with the organizer, a stroller pulled up beside them. Jeanne glanced up to see Junie Reynolds pushing her granddaughter, Isabelle Monroe, in the canvas stroller. The child didn't look to be more than a year old.

Junie's daughter had gotten pregnant by that wild Monroe boy. He'd done the right thing and married her, but Jeanne couldn't see it lasting. There was something about the boy that suggested he didn't have staying power.

"Hi, Jeanne. Hi, Sal," Junie said.

Sal nodded.

"How are you, Junie?" Jeanne asked.

"I'm well, thanks for asking," Junie said. She seemed a little harried.

"How's the little one?" Sal asked, hands in his pockets, with a nod toward Isabelle.

"She's a wonderful little girl," Junie said.

"She's beautiful," Jeanne said honestly. The girl had very dark hair and blue eyes, resembling her grandmother.

"Children are the balm of life," Sal added.

Jeanne smiled at him. His devotion to Terry, Joey, and Della backed up his pronouncement.

"It didn't start out too well for Nancy, and she's certainly paying the piper now," Junie admitted. "She's trying to balance motherhood and a low-wage job."

"But Dave is there," Jeanne said.

"He is, but he's also working a minimum-wage job," Junie said.

"That's too bad," Sal said.

"It is, but this little one is certainly a ray of sunshine."

"No matter the circumstances, babies are always welcome," Sal said.

"Hopefully, when the baby gets a little bit older, Nancy will be able to go back to school," Jeanne said assuredly. "I did." She loved her job at the hospital. It was hard work, but she'd learned so much, she loved taking care of people, and she felt like she was making a difference.

"Well, that's what we're hoping for."

Jeanne and Sal remained silent, but Junie continued talking. "Nancy's a good girl who made a mistake. And why should she be punished for that for the rest of her life?"

Jeanne swallowed hard and could not look at Sal.

"I'm sure she'll get her life back on track," Sal said.

The baby began to fuss in the stroller. "I better drop off these chocolate chip cookies and get Izzy home for her nap," Junie said.

"It was good seeing you again, Junie," Jeanne said.

Junie wheeled the stroller around. "You too."

Jeanne stared after her for a moment, contemplating the other woman's words.

"Come on, Jeanne, let's walk around and see what else they have," Sal suggested.

"Okay."

As they walked on, inspecting all the tables with their wares on offer, Sal did something he hadn't done in years. He reached over and took her hand and held it while they walked. And it was all Jeanne could do to not start crying.

Chapter Thirty-One

2010

"We don't have to stay long," Jeanne said to Sal. She had his arm tucked into hers as they walked slowly toward Della's shop.

Today was the grand opening. With help from her parents, Della had purchased the old Milchmann's grocery store. It had been vacant for years but Mrs. Milchmann, getting on in years herself, had decided it was time to sell up.

The shop's front was decorated with a burgundy awning.

Sal stopped to look up at the sign.

"Hideaway Bay Olive Oil Company," he read out loud, his voice frail. His smile was broad. He shook his head, became unsteady on his feet when he pulled a handkerchief from his pocket and dabbed at his eyes. "I wish Papa and Mamma could see this. They'd be so proud."

Jeanne gave him a reassuring pat on his arm. "On some level, they can see what's going on." She believed that.

Sal smiled at her. "I suppose you're right."

"I usually am," she teased.

Now he patted her arm. "Yes."

Sal had not been to the shop since Della had purchased it months ago. He'd gone with her to help with negotiating the terms of the sale. But since the closing, his health had been deteriorating, and he'd said simply that he'd wait and save his energy for the grand opening as he wanted to be surprised.

As they stood on the sidewalk, they were approached by their sons, Terry and Joey. Both hugged their parents.

"Dad, how are you feeling today?" Terry asked, his expression clouded with concern.

"I made it!" Sal said with a laugh. "It's a great day."

Jeanne agreed. "That it is."

Sal glanced at his wife. "Besides, I've got the best nurse!"

What Sal didn't know was how Della had agonized about whether she should move up the grand opening to accommodate his failing health, but there was no way the shop could be ready any sooner. There was simply too much to do. Jeanne suspected Sal had hung on this long through sheer force of will.

Joey held the front door of the shop open for them. "Come on, Dad. Della's anxious for you to see everything."

Sal nodded and took a couple of slow steps, still hanging on to Jeanne's arm. Terry had gotten on the other side of him, and linked his arm through his father's for extra support.

"Take your time, Dad, there's no rush," Terry said.

Sal laughed. "I hope I make it inside before it closes."

The four of them crossed the threshold, and the door closed behind them. Joey stood behind the three of them as Sal and Jeanne surveyed the scene. Renovations had removed any trace or reminders of Milchmann's grocery store, which Jeanne thought was a good thing.

"Would you look at this place!" Sal's voice was a whisper.

"It's amazing, isn't it?" Joey asked.

"It sure is."

"Dad!" Della called out from the other side of the shop. "You made it." She rushed them but as she neared her father, she slowed down and wrapped him in a gentle hug. "I'm so happy you're here."

"I wouldn't have missed this for anything."

When they pulled apart, both Sal and Della had tears in their eyes.

"Come on, Mom and Dad, I want to show you everything."

Della led her parents over to a side wall lined with stainless steel tanks on legs. Next to each tank was a label indicating a different type of olive oil.

Sal withdrew his reading glasses from the front pocket of his shirt, slid them on, and leaned forward, scrunching up his nose to read them. There were all sorts of flavors: basil, cilantro and lime, bacon, blood orange, garlic, lemon. Jeanne couldn't read the others as they were too far away.

"I didn't know olive oil came in all these flavors. I didn't know you could grow a bacon olive tree," he teased.

Della laughed.

"And look at all these tanks," Jeanne said. They were really cute. Each had a spigot, and small plastic cups next to it for taste testing.

"They're called *fustis*," Della said.

"Fustis?" Jeanne scrunched up her nose. "You'd think they could have come up with a better name."

Before Della or Sal could respond, they were approached by an elderly woman pushing a walker in front of her.

The woman's pearl-white hair was cut short with a bit of a wave. She wore diamond stud earrings and a plain gold band on the ring finger of her left hand. On the collar of her coat was an attractive peacock brooch. But it was her eyes—they reminded Jeanne of a hawk's:

narrow and never missing a thing. Immediately she recognized Elvira Milchmann, the former grocery store owner. She had to be close to one hundred years old. Jeanne would have thought she'd be long dead by now. Mr. Milchmann had died decades ago.

"Is this the young woman who bought my grocery store?" she croaked, her voice still shrill after all these years.

"Hello, Mrs. Milchmann," Della said, thrusting her hand forward in greeting.

Mrs. Milchmann scowled and did not shake her hand. Della quickly withdrew hers. Despite her advanced years and frail appearance, the former grocery store owner appeared sharp and still formidable.

"Elvira," Sal said.

"Sal Rossi? You don't look so good," Elvira said brusquely.

"I've been better." He paused, leaning on his son's arm. "What brings you back to Hideaway Bay?"

Elvira turned her attention to the store, her gaze scrutinizing the interior of Hideaway Bay's brand-new olive oil shop. "I had to come see for myself what was being done with my store." She narrowed her eyes. "The grocery store was much bigger."

"When we renovated, we made the back room larger," Della explained.

Elvira Milchmann scowled. "But that leaves less space for your product." She sniffed and added, "Though I suppose there's only so much olive oil you can display and sell."

"She'll be selling things other than olive oil, Elvira," Jeanne chimed in. That this woman had to come back to Hideaway Bay today of all days grated on her nerves.

"You should take a look around, Mrs. Milchmann," Joey suggested.

"No thank you," she said. "I've seen everything I want to see. I can't see how you'll be able to make a living off of selling olive oil, but then what do I know—I only ran a grocery store business with my late husband for over thirty years."

"It was nice of you to stop by," Jeanne said, determined to get the other woman on her way and out of Della's shop.

But Elvira wasn't finished yet. She leveled her gaze on Della. "I get it, though. A young woman like yourself who hasn't found a husband needs something to do. But olive oil?" She paused and took a breath. "In my day, women didn't own businesses. Don't get me wrong, I was a full partner in the store with Mr. Milchmann once I married him. And I contributed. I worked right by his side every day."

"Well, Elvira, things change over time." Jeanne said. She stole a glance at her daughter, who remained speechless.

Elvira sniffed. "Not always for the better. These days, women aren't content with being a wife and mother. They want to have it all."

Jeanne didn't add that Mrs. Milchmann had had no children herself so was hardly one to comment. Or the fact that she was mean and miserable, which hardly constituted contentedness, though Jeanne suspected it was due more to a personality flaw than to any of her life circumstances. The Milchmanns had become wealthy with their store. It used to be said that Elvira could get blood out of a rock.

The elderly woman continued to talk, leaving the rest of them frozen in place, unable to move. "These women these days want to have it all. Why they couldn't be satisfied with being a wife and mother is beyond me."

Sal spoke up. "Why should being a housewife and a mother be enough? I'm not saying it isn't important, but women have the right, like men, to pursue careers and outside interests. To have a sense of purpose in their lives."

That little speech had cost him, for suddenly he paled and a small tremor rippled through his body.

Jeanne spoke quickly. "It was good to see you again, Elvira." To Sal, she said, "We should find someplace to sit." Without waiting for the other woman to respond, Jeanne took Sal by the arm and guided him away.

"Dad, there's a chair over here," Della said. The Rossi family focused all their attention on Sal, anxious to get him seated. They huddled around him and led him away.

Elvira, no longer the center of attention, huffed and turned her walker, heading toward the exit.

Some things never change, Jeanne thought. Time hadn't tempered Mrs. Milchmann's demeanor at all.

When Sal was seated in a chair at the back of the shop and away from the public, Della said, "Dad, I'll get you some bread and olive oil to taste."

"That would be wonderful." As she turned to step away, he reached for her hand. Clasping it, he said, "I'm so proud of you, Della, and all that you've accomplished here. You have no idea how proud I am to be your father."

Della's smile was broad and generous. She leaned in and kissed him on his forehead. "Thanks, Dad. I love you."

He nodded, his eyes filling up with tears.

Part Three

Present Day

Chapter Thirty-Two

Della

There had been no meaningful conversations between Della and her mother in the weeks since the discovery of her dubious parentage. She went to work, stayed as late as possible, and waited until dark before heading home, not wanting to spend one more minute in the house with her mother, who insisted on pretending that everything was all right even though it wasn't. Jeanne Rossi might have been content to live that way, but Della could barely stand it.

Finally unable to tolerate the situation anymore, she confronted her mother.

"Just tell me," Della demanded. "Did Dad know he was not my real father?"

Her mother swallowed hard. When she spoke, there was a tremor in her voice. "Yes."

Della collapsed onto a chair at the kitchen table and buried her head in her hands. She let out one long sob of relief.

Her father had known, and he'd loved her anyway. Treated her like she was his own flesh and blood. Never, during her entire life while he was alive, had he ever let on that he wasn't her father. She'd never felt that he didn't love her. And she had never suspected. It made her cry harder.

When she stood up, she pushed the chair in and didn't look at her mother. She couldn't.

"I'm sorry, Della," her mother whispered.

Della nodded. "Mom, I'm going to move out. I'm a grown woman. It's time I got a place of my own."

"You don't have to do that. We'll get over this little hump."

"We will with time. But I need some space to figure things out."

"What will I do without you?" Jeanne asked.

"Mom, you'll be fine," Della said firmly.

This much was true. As long as Della could remember, her mother had always been the strong, independent type. Had been a nurse for over twenty-five years.

But Della's mind was made up. It was actually kind of exciting to think about setting up her own place. She might even get a cat, like Sue Ann.

"Can you ever forgive me?" her mother asked.

Della didn't hesitate. "Yes. This all happened before I was born." Although her loyalty was to her father, she imagined her mother might have been punished enough for her transgression. She sighed. "But I need to be by myself."

"Okay."

Her mother suddenly looked frail and elderly. The events of the past few weeks had aged her. She supposed that's what happened when you were carrying around a secret for decades and then it blew up in your face.

Della was able to arrange the rental of an apartment from Thelma Schumacher fairly quickly. It was only temporary, she told herself, until she could find a house to purchase.

After work one day, she took a drive over to Lavender Bay. Less than an hour away from Hideaway Bay, it was situated along the Lake Erie shore closer to the Pennsylvania border. Unlike Hideaway Bay, Lavender Bay had not started out as a resort community for the wealthy of the previous century, being too far away from the city for the drive. It was a much older community than Hideaway Bay, its residents permanent. There was a vague general recollection of the founding father being French. Della had no idea why it was called Lavender Bay, as there wasn't a sprig of lavender in sight.

But there were grapes everywhere. It was a large grape-growing region, much larger than Hideaway Bay. The Gibson's Grape Jelly factory had been there since before World War II and was still operational. Growing up, there'd been a phase where Della would eat nothing else but peanut butter sandwiches with Gibson's grape jelly. She'd lived on them in grade school.

Earlier that morning, she'd dashed off a text to Sam, asking him to meet her here. If they'd gone to the beach at Hideaway Bay, they were bound to run into someone they knew. A friend. A customer. A patient. For right now, she preferred to be alone with him. She wanted to give him her undivided attention and an explanation for their missed date. At the very least, he deserved that.

She hadn't thought to bring a beach towel or chair to sit on, but she didn't mind. She got comfortable in the sand, crossing her arms over her knees and staring out at the water. The sky was mesmerizing. It was a deep lavender with a splash of pink near the horizon. Maybe that was where the town got its name. It seemed reasonable. The water was so dark it was almost navy.

While she waited for his arrival, her thoughts drifted to her father. Once she'd purchased her own home, there would be things she'd do to honor him in her new place. There'd be a garden where she'd grow tomatoes and zucchini and eggplant. She'd learn how to can tomatoes; her nonna's recipe was tucked neatly in her cookbook, which she'd taken with her when she moved out. She was going to start taking Italian lessons. And maybe someday, she'd take that trip to Italy. She didn't mind going alone. Besides, it was about time she took a vacation.

"Della."

She looked up at Sam and smiled. "Hey there."

"Fancy meeting you here," he said.

His face had some color. It was the first time they'd spoken since she'd forgotten their date. Sadly, he hadn't been in the shop since. She supposed she couldn't blame him.

"Hi, Sam." Her nerve endings tingled as he joined her on the sand, sitting next to her.

When he sat, he displaced a pile of sand in her direction. He looked at her sheepishly and said, "Sorry." She couldn't help but laugh. His cologne was heavenly and despite the heat, goose bumps broke out along her arm. She inhaled the scent of him and briefly closed her eyes.

"I'm sorry I'm late, we were busy today," he said.

He wasn't that late. Only ten minutes.

"No problem."

Sam looked around. "Good idea to come here instead of our beach. I love being the doctor in Hideaway Bay, but sometimes when I run into people, they treat it like an office visit."

"I can imagine," she said. "That's why I asked you to meet me here. I wanted to talk to you privately, without any interruptions."

"Are you all right? You look tired and you've lost some weight."

She smiled at him. "I didn't know you held office hours on the beach."

"Only emergency ones," he said with a grin. His grin was beautiful to behold. It was almost uplifting. She missed their banter from when he used to come into the shop. Her heart ached over his recent absence.

A couple walked by with a black lab. The man tossed the stick, and the dog, Scout, ran to fetch it and returned, and then they'd start all over again. The dog seemed tireless.

She twisted her upper body slightly to look at him and smiled. His kindness reminded her so much of her father. There was warmth in those brown eyes of his. And he had that gorgeous hair. It was slightly shorter than usual, indicating a recent haircut.

"Do you remember that night I forgot our date?" she said.

"Do I remember?" he teased, placing clasped hands over his chest. "It broke my heart!"

She grimaced. "I am sorry about that."

"I'm sure you had a good reason for ditching me." Even though he grinned, she still felt bad about it.

She protested feebly. "I didn't ditch you. I forgot."

He made a mock grimace. "That's worse. That means I'm forgettable."

"I can assure you, you're anything but." She smiled and refolded her arms around her bent knees, turning to stare out at the horizon. Where did one start? She'd like to share it with him. He had a great bedside manner. And more than that ... she also liked to think of him as a friend.

"I had just received some shocking news."

He watched her, waiting patiently.

She drew in a deep breath and poured out her story. She couldn't look at him as she told him the truth about her parentage. There was a part of the whole ordeal that seemed sordid to her.

When she finished, he said, "I'm sorry for your troubles."

She shrugged and smirked. "Everyone has trouble in their life."

"True. Can I say that your father sounds like he was a remarkable man?"

Della was quick to agree with him. "More than ever before, I realize now what a great man he truly was. Even now, after all this time, I miss him."

"Of course."

"I prided myself on my Italian heritage, and it turns out I don't have any," she said. This idea, that the identity she'd assumed about herself was no longer the truth, made her sick to her stomach.

"You may not have a biological connection, but your father's part in your upbringing is still your heritage."

"Maybe."

"You can't easily dismiss how you feel about your background. You can claim it because of who brought you up. Not necessarily because of who fathered you." He paused. "You were raised as an Italian American."

She didn't know if she agreed, but it was something to consider.

"I've moved out of my mother's house," she confessed.

"Are things tense between the two of you?"

"Yes. To me, there's something so seedy about my mother having an affair or a one-night stand that I can't help but be disappointed. For most of us, I think we tend to hold our mothers to a standard."

Sam sighed. "If there's one thing I've learned in my career, it's that human beings are complicated creatures. And sometimes they make mistakes. Big ones. Even mothers are human beings."

An easy silence descended between them. The sun seemed to be racing toward the horizon, which meant it would be dark soon and they would have to leave. She didn't want to part from him. It was the best she'd felt in a very long time, and she'd forgotten that she could feel good again. And not distracted by the curveball life had thrown her.

Sam appeared to be gathering his thoughts.

"How is your mother handling all of this?" he asked.

"She's in a bit of denial. She thought we'd go back to living the way we used to before I found out. I can forgive her for what happened—although I realize it isn't for me to forgive—but I am loyal to my father. He must have been so hurt by it all. It was a magnanimous gesture on his part to offer to raise another man's child."

"Infidelity can be a dealbreaker."

"Things are still a little hazy. My mother isn't really forthcoming with the information. Sometimes, she refuses to talk about it."

"It might be painful for her as well. She may be ashamed of it."

Della said nothing. She hadn't thought of that. "My parents did stay married; they never split up or divorced, so maybe on some level, Dad did forgive her. I guess I'll never know."

"I think we tend to paint others with the brush of their mistakes and ignore any redemptive qualities."

Della thought about this, embarrassed that in her anger and hurt, she'd ignored all her mother's good qualities, choosing instead to focus on one colossal mistake.

"Do you think your mother ever had another extramarital affair?"

Della shook her head. "My gut tells me no."

"Eighty plus years times three hundred and sixty-five days is a lot of days. It's a shame that all the days are seen through the filter of one misguided one."

"You're very wise, Sam Morrison."

He chuckled. "Experience makes you wise." He was quiet for a minute. Reflective. "My grandfather was not a nice man."

Della waited, patient.

"He was mean to his wife and to his children. They did not like him at all, and I think when he died, there were a lot of mixed emotions, but mostly relief. But with my brother and me, he was a totally different person. Every major event in my life, he was present, all spruced up in his suit." He smiled at the memory of it. "He was there for me. But it was more than that. It was how he made me feel when I was with him. Like I was . . . something special. When he died, I was grief-stricken. Do I judge him by the way he treated them, or do I judge him by the way he treated me? We should all be so lucky to have that one person who makes us feel like that." He seemed lost in the memory of it. "And for me, that is redemptive."

Della was glad that Sam had had someone in his life like that. Like her father had been to her.

"Your mother's elderly, and sometimes it's a kind thing to let go of the past," Sam said. "Maybe not be too harsh because of one terrible mistake."

"Maybe."

He looked at her, his grin lazy and his eyes full of mischief. "Besides, if she hadn't made that mistake, you wouldn't be here. And how awful would that be for me."

She felt herself blush and looked away. That thought had never occurred to her. She looked up and the lavender sky had turned a dusky blue, the sun a small slice of orange lying on the horizon. "It's getting late, I should probably get going." She bounced up and brushed sand off her bottom and the back of her legs. Sam walked by her side as they made their way across the beach toward the parking lot.

"Did you want to go for a drink or a bite to eat?"

"I didn't eat dinner, so a bite to eat would be great," she replied. She looked over at him. "What other nuggets of wisdom have you learned?"

He stared at the sand. "That sometimes life can break your heart, but that you can heal."

They walked in silence for a while as Della thought about this, wondering if he'd had his own heart broken.

"Della?"

"Yes?"

"Would you be interested in going to Alice and Jack's wedding with me?"

She didn't have to think about it. "I would love to!"

And she'd tattoo the date and time on the back of her hand so she wouldn't forget this time.

Chapter Thirty-Three

Alice

Alice was in a good place. It had taken almost all summer to get there, but she'd arrived. And just in the nick of time, as her wedding was only two weeks away.

It was going to be perfect, she decided as she sat at the dining room table, going over her checklist and making sure nothing was forgotten. In fact, she couldn't wait for the day. The ceremony and reception would take place on the beach, in view of their house, and the *Farmers' Almanac* called for great weather for September. They'd hired a supply company for marquees and tables, and a local catering company would be providing the food. She and Jack had sampled some of their offerings and picked out a menu for the day. They were expecting over two hundred guests.

Her mind drifted to Paris. They'd booked their honeymoon in the most romantic city in the world. And as she had never been there before, to say she was excited would be an understatement.

"Alice?" called Isabelle from the front porch.

The old wooden screen door creaked as Alice pushed it open. They really had to replace that, but Isabelle said she liked the sound of it as it reminded her of when they were young.

Isabelle wore a pair of jean shorts and a T-shirt. She was tanned from spending the summer with Joe's kids around the pool or at the beach. Her abundant dark hair was pulled back in a ponytail and tied with a silk scarf. Alice always thought Isabelle made her fashion choices look so easy, uncomplicated, and sublime. If Alice tried to pull off a similar look, she'd land on the worst-dressed list. Besides, Lily always said Alice was a Laura Ashley kind of girl.

Isabelle looked up with a scowl on her face. "There you are. Have you seen this?" She waved a note card in front of her.

"It's my wedding invitation," Alice said with a smirk. "I may have seen it once or twice in the past six months."

Isabelle jumped up from her chair and handed it to her.

Confused, Alice took it from her, read it, and looked back at her sister. "What? What's wrong?" Her laugh was nervous; she hoped she hadn't missed something, because it was too late now.

"Look at the date," Isabelle prompted.

"September seventeenth," Alice said. "That's right. That's the date we're getting married."

"No," Isabelle said, "read the day and the date."

Out loud, Alice read, "Saturday, September seventeenth." Her brain caught up. "Wait. What?"

"Yes. How did we miss that? It should read Sunday, September seventeenth, not Saturday."

"Does it matter?" Alice asked, knowing full well it mattered very much. She sank into the white wicker chair across from her sister, her brain going full speed, trying to figure out how to sort this out.

"As long as everyone realizes the date is more important than the day."

Granted, it was unusual to get married on a Sunday as most weddings took place on Saturdays, but surely her guests had figured that out, right?

The potential for disaster started to make headway with Alice and she whimpered, "Oh no."

"Let's not panic," Isabelle advised.

Jack pulled up and parked his car in front of the house. When he emerged, he was smiling, but his smile disappeared when he landed on the porch and saw the sober expressions of Alice and Isabelle.

He leaned over and kissed Alice. Distracted, she half-heartedly returned the kiss.

"Is everything all right?" He rested his hand on Alice's shoulder.

"We've got a little problem." Alice hoped it was minor. She and Isabelle explained about the date and day being wrong on the invitation.

"It's odd that no one picked up on it and called us," Jack said.

"It's a good thing we caught it," Isabelle said.

"No, it's a good thing *you* caught it," Alice said. "We've got to call everyone and make sure they have the correct date."

"But that's over one hundred couples," Jack said.

"With three of us, it's only about thirty calls each," Isabelle pointed out.

"Let's get started," Alice said with a sigh.

"I'll put on some coffee." Isabelle unfolded her legs and hopped off the two-seater and headed into the kitchen, the screen door slamming behind her.

Jack pulled Alice up from the chair and took her in his arms. Instantly, she closed her eyes and breathed in his smell: a mixture of fading cologne and laundry detergent. He rested the side of his face against her ear. "Don't worry. Everything will be all right."

Not wanting to give voice to her fears, she nodded. She didn't want to worry but she couldn't help it.

By the time Lily and Simon arrived, the three of them had each made one phone call and were sipping coffee.

"What are you doing here?" Alice asked.

"Isabelle called. Said there was a bit of a glitch with the wedding."

Alice snorted. "A little more than a glitch."

"What's going on? Isabelle said there was a problem with the date."

Simon and Lily stood together as Alice gave them the bullet points of the problem.

When Alice's voice gave a little wobble, Lily pulled her into a hug and whispered against her ear, "Don't worry, Sparrow, everything will be all right, you'll see."

"That's what I told her," Isabelle said, emerging from the kitchen. "You guys got here fast."

"We don't live far."

"Coffee will be ready soon. We should get started so we can make as many phone calls as possible before it gets too late."

Alice agreed. The only way to fix this was to deal with it head on.

Three hours later as it was nearing ten o'clock, the five of them decided that it was now too late to be calling any more people and they'd finish their task the following day.

The coffeepot empty, Isabelle pulled out a bottle of wine and poured each one of them a glass. Alice and

Jack sank back into the cushions of the two-seater on the porch, and Isabelle sat in the rocker. Lily and Simon declined the offer of wine, deciding to call it a night and hugged everyone goodbye.

Lily offered to return the next day, but Alice told her it wasn't necessary. Between her and Isabelle, they'd be able to contact the rest of the guests and determine a final, albeit smaller, number of attendees.

"So where are we?" Isabelle asked, pulling up one leg and resting her foot on the cushion of the chair.

Alice leaned forward, set her glass of wine down on the table, and picked up the sheets of paper that had been assigned to each one of them. As they were making their calls, they'd ticked off the responses and put a final number at the end of each page and circled it.

Her expression was a moue of disappointment. "First, we managed to reach two-thirds of the guests. Of that two-thirds, no one had picked up on the typo, and all, *all*, if you can believe it, assumed the wedding was scheduled for Saturday. Of those that we reached, who now know the wedding is actually taking place on Sunday, more than half can't make it because of previous plans." Alice set the list down, her eyes filling with tears.

Jack immediately reached for her, wrapping his arm around her shoulders, and kissed the side of her head. "Hey, it'll be all right." He looked at her and smiled.

"I'm a definite. I'll be there." And through her tears, Alice leaned into him and smiled.

"It'll be all right, Sparrow," Isabelle said reassuringly. "Whether there's only a handful of people or a crowd, it's going to be a perfect day."

Alice smiled at her sister. She appreciated Isabelle's efforts to make her feel better. With only two weeks until the wedding, suddenly there was a lot more to do.

"I can finish up notifying the rest of the guests tomorrow," Alice said. "And then I'll have to call the caterer, the baker, and Val Fisher to adjust the numbers."

"Do you want me to help? I can call all those people for you tomorrow. Especially if you're busy at work," Isabelle offered.

"I have court tomorrow, but I was planning on doing it when I got home," Alice said.

"Let me do it. I have nothing urgent with work tomorrow," Isabelle said.

Grateful for the help and one less thing to do, Alice relented and handed over the guest list and their notes. "I really appreciate this, Isabelle."

Isabelle gave a dismissive wave of her hand. "Don't worry about it. Glad I can help."

Alice walked with Jack, hand in hand, to his car. Before he left, he embraced her again, rubbing her back, and they fell into a long, lingering kiss.

"Everything is going to work out, don't worry," he said.

Alice frowned. A lot of planning went into a wedding. Now she half wished she and Jack had eloped like Lily and Simon.

When she didn't respond, he cupped her face and placed a light kiss on her lips. "Look, as long as you and I are there, that's all that counts for me. It's our day. It's about us."

Alice nodded and closed her eyes, leaning forward and resting her forehead against his chin. "You're right, of course."

She waved Jack off as he left, and re-joined Isabelle on the porch.

They talked about generalities, and Alice realized that there wouldn't be too many more conversations between them on the porch, watching the sun set. It was already different now that Lily had left. Her eyes were once again brimming with tears.

"Hey, hey, what's the matter?" Isabelle said, her face a mask of concern.

Alice shook her head, wiping the tears away with the back of her hand. "After years of barely speaking to one another, we end up living together, and it's been one of the happiest times of my life."

"Mine too," Isabelle said softly.

"And now we're all leaving and going off on our own," Alice said sadly. "And we'll never have this again."

"If I've learned anything in life, it's that nothing lasts forever. Good times, bad times, nothing lasts. But at least we had this. The three of us were given a second chance. And maybe because we solidified our relationships with each other, it strengthened us and helped us to find ourselves and our other halves."

"I never thought of it that way," Alice said. She took a sip of her wine and eyed her sister. "You never struck me as the philosophical sort."

Isabelle grinned. "I'm full of surprises."

With a smile, Alice raised her wine glass in a salute to her sister. She was contemplative for a bit. "It's bittersweet, really. I love Jack, there's no doubt about that, but I loved what we had here."

"No matter where we live, whether together or separate, we'll always have that. But we've all got our own lives now."

Alice felt a little better. Things had turned out well for all of them.

They were each lost in their own thoughts until Isabelle broke the silence. "I suppose at some point the three of us will have to sit down and discuss what needs to be done with the house."

Alice nodded. "I was thinking we should hire a contractor and have the outside painted next spring. You know, spruce it up a bit. And maybe get a new screen door."

Isabelle looked at her, her expression blank. "No, I meant we should talk about selling it."

"What?" Selling Gram's house? How could they? It was simply not an option for Alice.

"Lily doesn't live here anymore," Isabelle continued, "and you'll be leaving soon, and that just leaves me. And I may be leaving as well."

Alice momentarily put aside the topic of selling the house and jumped on that last sentence of Isabelle's. "Is there going to be another wedding in the family?"

Isabelle laughed. "We're talking about it."

Alice clapped her hands and crowed with delight. "I'm so happy for you. Joe's a great guy."

"Yes, he is."

"You and Joe and the kids could move in here. There's plenty of room, and this is a house that should be filled with people."

"I'm sorry, Sparrow, but that wouldn't happen. Joe's house is perfect for all of us. Plus, he has the pool for the kids."

"You don't mind moving into another woman's house?" Alice asked. She certainly didn't want to cause trouble between Isabelle and Joe, but she wanted to make sure this was what her sister wanted. Lily had not minded moving into Simon's house and was in the midst of redecorating the place to suit both their tastes. And she and Jack had decided to build a new house on a piece of property they'd purchased off of Erie Street.

"No, that doesn't bother me at all. It was so hard for Joe's kids when their mother died, and the home is their last connection to her. Someday, when the kids are grown and gone, we might like to get one of those patio homes or something, but for right now, the house on Moonbeam suits us fine."

"I'd like to keep Gram's house in the family, though," Alice said.

"I'd hate to see it empty if we all move out," Isabelle countered. She looked around the place.

Alice couldn't agree more with that statement.

"Maybe it's time to let another family live in it. The Reynolds family have had it for almost sixty years."

From her own research, Alice knew that no other family had lived in the house on Star Shine Drive as long as her family had. It was a wondrous thing.

"Boy, that's a long time if you think about it."

"It is. After the wedding, the three of us should sit down together and talk about it."

Alice did not look forward to that conversation at all.

Chapter Thirty-Four

Della

Della hummed as she unpacked a box of bottled olive oil. Sue Ann stood at the register, checking out customers. Outside, the sun shone brightly. Alice's wedding was coming up, and she was really looking forward to it.

"Della?"

She popped her head up to see Mark Nugent standing there.

"Hi, Mark, how are you enjoying retirement?" she asked.

"I love it. All these newfound hobbies."

"Mom said you stopped in to see her."

"I did. I visited Mary as well, and I'm taking them both out to lunch next week. I owe your mom and Mary a lot," he said.

She frowned, puzzled, and looked at him. "What do you mean?"

"You know she took care of my mother when she was dying."

Della must have looked like an idiot, because she had no idea what he was talking about.

"Your mother and Mary took care of my mother at our house when she was terminally ill. Jeanne was pregnant with you at the time. Mom was home for six weeks before she died," he said.

"I'm so sorry," Della said. Mark couldn't have been more than a teenager. She couldn't imagine losing a parent at that young an age. She knew of her mother's friend, Betty Nugent, dying young, but her mother had never mentioned taking care of her.

"She and Mary came over every day while my father was at work."

"She never said." *The stinker.*

"Well, you should know. Your mom was amazing. So was Mary. They were such good friends to my mother." He paused and said quietly, "My brothers and sisters and I are very grateful."

Chapter Thirty-Five

Alice

Alice whipped up some salted caramel brownies, and once they were cool enough in the pan, she covered them with a clean dish towel and walked them over to Thelma's house, several blocks away.

Thelma was sitting on her porch, dressed in yellow: yellow capri pants and a short-sleeved yellow floral top. On her feet were a pair of yellow cotton socks and brown sandals. She immediately smiled when she spotted Alice approaching, and threw up her hand in a wave.

Alice loved to visit and spend time with Thelma, and she was always delighted when she ran into her in town. Thelma was the last link to Gram; she and Gram had known each other since they were children, so it was like she was the last keeper of Gram's lifelong secrets.

Thelma started to stand up, but Alice thrust her hand out. "Don't get up, Thelma."

"It's good to see you, Alice," Thelma said, settling back into her chair and crossing one leg over the other. At her side, on the little table, sat a half-finished glass of iced tea and the evening newspaper. She lifted her head and indicated the pan in Alice's hands. "What did you bring me?"

"Salted caramel brownies," Alice said, whipping off the kitchen towel.

"Nice. Would you mind putting that on my kitchen counter? And get yourself something to drink while you're inside."

"I will, thanks," Alice said.

"I have your pie plate inside on the counter. That lemon meringue pie was delicious. I ate it in two days." Thelma beamed. "Don't forget to take it with you when you leave."

Alice nodded, stepped into Thelma's house, set the brownies down in the kitchen, and helped herself to a glass of iced tea. She carried the pie plate and the glass back out and joined Thelma on the porch, setting the two items down on the table.

"How are things coming along with the wedding?" Thelma asked.

Alice nodded. "Good."

"I still can't believe Lily ran off and got married. Surprises, surprises. But they seem like a good match.

Your grandmother would be delighted with all the weddings." Thelma smiled as she rubbed her upper arm.

"Isabelle and Lily think it might be time to sell the house."

That hung in the air for a moment as Thelma digested it.

"That must be difficult for you," Thelma said. "There are a lot of memories in that house."

"The thought of other people living there makes me sick."

Thelma chuckled. "I can understand that. I felt the same way about the restaurant. And this house, as well. I'll stay here until I die as it was the first house Stan and I lived in after we were married. And although we weren't married for a long time—we didn't even make twenty years—by God, we were happy." She shook her head, smiling at the memory of it. "But I couldn't let go of the restaurant. I held on to it because it felt like selling it would be a betrayal of Stan."

Alice nodded, feeling the same way. Like letting go of the house would mean betraying her grandparents and her mother. It felt like abandonment of the past and the people they'd left behind in previous years as they all moved forward without them. She knew this was ridiculous thinking, but it was how she felt. And certainly, she was entitled to her feelings.

Thelma picked up her glass of iced tea, took a sip, and set it back down. "And then I began to think that I was denying someone else an opportunity. The restaurant was only sitting there, becoming more of an eyesore with every passing year. If there was one thing my Stan loved, it was an opportunity." She smiled.

"Selling the restaurant to Val Fisher was one of the best decisions I've made, aside from marrying Stanley, of course. She's done a lot with that space. And a chocolate shop right on Main Street in this town is perfect!"

They sat there in comfortable silence for a bit. Alice felt a bit unsettled, still not keen on the idea of selling the home that had been in her family for almost sixty years.

"Can you and Jack buy out your sisters and live there?" Thelma asked. "I mean, if you're that dead set against selling."

Alice folded her arms across her chest and shook her head. "I thought briefly of that. But the staircase would be tricky for Jack, and I couldn't ask that of him." Though if she did ask him, he'd think nothing of his bad leg and say yes. They were having a bungalow built on the property they'd purchased, and she was excited about that, which left her torn.

Thelma appeared pensive and eventually spoke. "You have to be careful looking over your shoulder, because you don't want to go stumbling and tripping into your future."

When Alice said nothing, Thelma said quietly, "Alice, by all means, keep your memories tucked in your heart, but don't drag the past with you into your future." Thelma paused, folded her hands in her lap, and looked off into the distance. "If you sell the house, it doesn't mean that you are being disloyal to your grandparents."

When Alice stepped off the porch a short time later with her empty pie plate in hand, promising to bring another lemon meringue pie back soon, she felt better. The feeling of being burdened was lessened. And as she walked home, Thelma's sentiments rattled around in her head. She had been right, of course. Alice switched gears and thought about her future life with Jack, and that put a smile on her face.

She got home and cleaned up the kitchen quickly, loading the few dishes into the dishwasher and reminding herself to turn it on before she went to bed.

She turned off the kitchen light and headed to the dining room, throwing on the wall switch. The overhead light fixture immediately illuminated the room, and she made a note to herself to get lower-wattage bulbs for the chandelier. It was time to put away all the paperwork from her research into the past owners of the home.

With music playing in the background, she took a big black garbage bag and began to sort through everything spread out on the table. She saved only those photocopies of articles and photos that pertained to the house. Everything else could be recycled. She'd stopped at 1960, knowing that the house had stood empty until her grandparents had bought it in 1976.

After an hour of fighting the urge to get sucked back into the past and look through all these old newspapers again, Alice had cleared off the dining room table and had enough paper to fill the recycling bin for that week alone. She took the items she'd put aside, photocopies of the previous deed owners and the photos of the Bernards, and carried them into the front room to put away.

Gram had a small box of old, loose photos that she'd kept in a box in the cabinet next to the fireplace. Alice and her sisters had gone through it shortly after Gram's death, but she'd not looked at it since.

She pulled the box out, sank down onto the floral rug, and got comfortable with the box in front of her. The box always brought a smile to her face as she knew what its contents were. She removed the lid and set it aside. But she couldn't resist the urge to look through the photos and clippings one more time. It was almost impossible not to. She wondered if it happened to other people as well. If it required Herculean effort on everyone's part not to sift through the past.

Right on top of the pile was an old newspaper clipping from 1976. Alice picked it up, pulled it closer, and examined it.

In the yellowed clipping was a photo from the Fourth of July, the bicentennial year. It showed Grandad with his arm around Gram. Next to them were Thelma and Stan, holding small American flags. On their other side was Barb, holding Sue Ann.

Alice sank a bit, holding the clipping and not taking her eyes off of it. All of them were laughing, even the baby. She could feel the happiness in the photo. It was funny to see all of them before they went gray, before their faces became lined with time.

It wasn't long before she lost all track of time and forgot the reason she'd pulled out the box in the first place.

As the sun dimmed and the shadows lengthened, she continued to dig through the box, pulling out each individual item. There were Polaroid photos with their white borders and the month and year stamped in black. She studied them as if there were going to be a test in the morning. There were lots of photos of her grandparents and her mother on the front porch, relaxing in the heat of the summer, or down at the beach. Her favorites were the ones of her mother at her birthdays: her face illuminated by the candles, the shape of her mouth distorted as she went to blow out the candles, and Junie and Paul behind her, smiling, clapping, encouraging.

There had been sadness, of course. No life was immune to it. Her mother and her grandparents were gone. But there had been so much living in this house over the past sixty years. All that living and breathing and laughter and crying. It certainly had kept the dust out of the corners.

After she put aside a couple of photographs that she'd like to display in frames in her new house, she tucked everything neatly back into the box and put it away in the cabinet.

This house was meant for people and for love and for laughter.

And Alice realized that Isabelle was right. It might be time to move on.

Chapter Thirty-Six

Della

Della stood on the sidewalk in front of her childhood home. The place that had been her home until recently suddenly looked different. Prior to moving out, she might have eyed it with sentiment and nostalgia. But now, returning as a former occupant, she cast a critical eye over it, deciding it was holding up but needed some work. At some point in the future, when the dust settled, she would have this conversation with her mother. The concrete driveway was cracked, and one slab lifted near the garage, making it dangerous. She knew her father always preferred concrete, but maybe asphalt or paved brick might be a better option. Her mother could trip if she wasn't careful. Funny how you accommodated the quirks of a home, just as you accommodated the eccentricities of the people you loved. You knew which step on the staircase creaked, so you tended to avoid it in the middle of the night. You threw a small throw rug over a stain on the carpet. You listened for the sump pump every time it rained. There was the door that always warped in the heat and humidity, requiring a gentle tug to either close it or open it.

After making a mental list of some overdue exterior improvements, she made her way up to the front porch. She paused at the screen door, unsure of the protocol for someone who used to live there but didn't any longer. Did she just walk in? Knock first? In the end, she decided to rap on the door a few times and then walk in.

"Mom?" she called out, half expecting to find her mother at the dining room table, leaning over some craft she was working on. But the dining room was not only empty, the table was clear, indicating that Mrs. Rossi wasn't working on anything at the moment. This was strange to Della, because her mother liked to keep active, and she could never remember a time when the table wasn't covered in some kind of arts and crafts.

Walking through the house, she found it strangely quiet. It felt off. Was this what it was like when you returned after you left? Did the place you'd lived in for so long exist for you only as far as your departure date, even though you went on without it?

She found her mother out back, sitting on the porch Sal had added in later years. It was a small rectangular room with a blue felt rug and cheap-and-cheerful, functional furniture. Her father used to like to watch television out there on a hot summer night, with his vegetable garden for his view.

The screened windows looked out on the back lawn, her father's vegetable garden long gone. Her mother had no interest, and Della had not had the time. But she'd make time for it in the future at her new place.

Her mother sat idle in the chair, staring motionless out the screened windows. She wasn't one known for sitting and staring. As Della thought about it, she could never remember her mother sitting around and doing nothing. Her hands were always busy, whether doing crafts or crosswords, anything to keep engaged physically and mentally. It occurred to Della that maybe her mother did all these things as more of a distraction than anything. She couldn't imagine being burdened with the type of secret her mother had carried.

"What are you doing out here?" Della asked, taking the chair next to her mother.

"Just thinking," Jeanne answered, staring but not seeing.

A frown burrowed between Della's eyebrows. "Mom, are you all right?" For a moment, she wondered if her mother had had a stroke. She looked pale and tired, reminding Della that despite her mother's active life, she was getting on in years.

"I don't know," she said quietly. She removed her gaze from the windows and stared at her hands.

Now worried, Della asked, "What is it?"

Her mother sighed. "I never wanted you to find out, and neither did your father. I thought it was all behind us."

"I'm sorry you're upset."

"And I'm sorry this information has caused you pain." She continued to stare at her hands like an infant who had discovered them for the first time.

Della was at a loss for words. She couldn't deny that the information that had come to light regarding her parentage had indeed caused her pain.

"I suppose you want to know who your real father is," her mother said.

"Did he know he had a child?"

Her mother bent her head and shook it.

It would be a lie to say she hadn't wondered about her biological father, whether he was in town or not. Whether he had family. But what would it serve to go looking for him? The thought of embarking on that search left a small pit of nausea in her stomach, left her feeling as if she were being disloyal to her own father.

Della sighed. "Right now, no, I don't want to know his name. I had a dad. A wonderful dad. I don't need to look for another one."

"What good is my life?" her mother asked.

Alarmed, Della sprang out of her chair and knelt in front of her mother, taking her hands in hers. "Mom, don't say that!"

"But it's true!" Jeanne said. Della hadn't been gone long, but she could see that her mother had aged since she'd left. "I made a terrible mistake, and I can't forgive myself for it."

Della lowered her voice. "Dad forgave you, didn't he?"

"He did, though it took him a long time."

Della had nothing to offer to that. Adultery was such a dealbreaker in most marriages. But she knew of some marriages that carried on. Apparently, her parents' was one of them.

"Was that the only time you cheated on Dad?" She hated to ask, but she had to know.

Her mother lifted her head and in her eyes was a lot of pain. "Yes. After that, I never put a foot wrong."

If her father, who'd been the wronged party, could forgive her mother, then she would have to learn to as well.

"Mom, come on, I'll get us some ice cream," Della said in an effort to cheer her mother up. "Come on, don't cry."

"I feel as if all is lost. If Terry and Joey find out, they'll never forgive me," Jeanne said.

"They're not going to find out," Della reassured her. She hated seeing her mother this upset. "I'm not going to tell them, and I've canceled my genealogy account. It's no one's business."

"But you've moved out," Jeanne cried.

"It was time. For Pete's sake, I'm almost fifty years old. It's time I branched out on my own," Della explained. As much as she'd loved living with her parents, it was time to grow up and get out and get on with her life. Maybe the whole scandal had pushed her in the right direction.

"You won't come back?" her mother asked, her eyes searching Della's face.

Della smiled gently and shook her head. "No. This is for the best. For both of us. You don't want your adult daughter living with you forever."

"I didn't mind. I thought we got along quite well."

"Of course we did."

"If you'd never found out about your father, you'd still be here, living here with me," her mother said, choking up.

"Probably, and you know what? It wouldn't be the best thing for me."

That was true. She'd discovered she liked finding out who she was other than the owner of the Hideaway Bay Olive Oil Company or someone's daughter or friend. It was an avenue she was eagerly willing to explore. Who was she, by herself? In the silence of her home?

Chapter Thirty-Seven

Alice

The morning of her wedding, Alice stood at the window of her bedroom.

"Does the sky look dark to you?" she asked, looking out over Lake Erie. Off in the distance, toward Canada, the sky looked ominous. She hoped she was imagining it.

Lily and Isabelle joined her at the window, one sister on each side of her.

"It's a little dark, but I don't think there's anything to worry about," Isabelle said reassuringly.

"At least it's not raining," Lily added.

They were expected to leave shortly. The woman from the town's salon had been by earlier to do their hair and makeup. Alice had made blueberry scones and a coffee cake, and they took bites of these and drank tea—even Isabelle had forgone coffee—while their hair was being transformed into updos.

The photographer had taken some preliminary photos but had given them a few minutes to be alone. And now the three of them stared out the window, worried about that dark cloud off in the distance but trying to remain cheerful.

Earlier, Alice's sisters, dressed in delicate, wispy, ankle-length sage green dresses, had helped Alice into her own gown. It was an "Alice dress," Isabelle had mused as they gently pulled it down over her head. It was a "romance dress," Lily had said.

Alice's wedding gown was gorgeously feminine, an Edwardian-inspired A-line, scoop-neck dress of chiffon with a full lace overlay and scalloped lace sleeves, accented with small, beaded details and an ivory satin belt.

Alice bit her lip, frowning, not reassured about that black cloud out there, looming on the horizon.

"Don't bite your lip, you'll get lipstick on your teeth," Lily chided.

"We need to get going," Isabelle prompted. With a quick smile, she said, "You don't want to keep Jack waiting."

The three sisters stopped and stood there, looking at each other.

"We can't hug because we'll crush our dresses," Alice said.

"No, but we can hold hands." Lily took Alice's hand in her right hand and Isabelle's in her left. Isabelle and

Alice joined their other hands, and the three of them stood in their small circle for a moment.

"Jack is a true gem," Isabelle said. "And I'm sure Lily agrees with me when I say we couldn't be happier for you."

Alice nodded in full agreement with her sisters' assessment of Jack. With a quaver in her voice, she said, "I wish Mom and Gram and Grandad were here."

Isabelle nodded, her own eyes filling with tears. Lily sniffed. "It's difficult. I know. It makes the day bittersweet."

Alice's eyes brimmed with tears and threatened to spill over.

"No crying," Lily teased. "You'll ruin your makeup."

Alice nodded quickly, sniffed, and swiped at one runaway tear.

"Be happy, Alice, no matter what."

"We'll always be close, right?"

Isabelle smiled, and it was like the sun on a hot sunny day: big and bright. "Always."

"Always," Lily added.

Alice squeezed their hands. "Come on, it's time to get married!"

It was a short walk to the beach across the street. Set up on the sand was the canopy with its flowing white fabric and garlands of sage and lavender flowers draping along the top and corners. Chairs were set up in neat rows with big, gauzy ribbons and matching flowers tied to the back of them.

Nearly all the chairs were occupied, and Alice breathed a sigh of relief that so many of their guests had shown up. The things you worried about. Jack waited beneath the canopy, talking to the minister and leaning on his cane. Her expression softened at the sight of him. She had not once worried that he might not show up. What was the word Gram used to use? Dapper. He looked dapper in his navy suit and white shirt and tie. In the buttonhole was a small white rosebud. And even though that black cloud appeared bigger on the horizon, Alice ignored it. It was off in the distance, not something to be fretted over now.

As she stepped onto the beach, her heels sinking in the sand, her sisters linked arms with her and hurried her to the small platform with the white runner she'd walk down, leading her to Jack and her future.

As they stepped up onto the platform, Lily asked, "Are you ready?"

Alice nodded. She took one last look over her shoulder at the house on Star Shine Drive. As her sisters walked her down the aisle, the wind picked up a bit, lifting the hems of their dresses and attempting to wreak havoc with their hairstyles. But their hairdresser had secured everything with a battalion of bobby pins and lots of hairspray.

It surprised Alice that she wasn't emotional as her sisters walked her down the aisle. They cried openly. But one look at Jack waiting at the end, and all Alice could do was beam. Every step in her life had led her here: to marrying the man of her dreams.

When they reached the canopy, her sisters kissed her goodbye, their eyes filled with tears, and handed her off to Jack.

As she linked her arm through his, he said with a voice laced with emotion, "You're the most beautiful bride I've ever seen. How lucky am I?"

Now she blushed and lowered her head.

"Shall we get started?" asked the minister.

The ceremony was short and sweet, and they'd arrived at the part where the minister said, "You may kiss the bride."

"Happily," Jack said with a laugh. As he took Alice in his arms and kissed her passionately, there were whoops from some of the guests.

When they pulled apart, one of the guests said, "Is that a waterspout out on the lake?" This was followed by a boom of thunder.

The scene before her resembled a disaster. Actually, it *was* a disaster.

Fortunately, the waterspout had stayed out on the lake. But the wind had arrived on the beach, the sky had darkened further, and it was clear that rain was imminent. Unoccupied chairs were knocked over. The billowing canopy blew all over the place, some of the ends of the cream fabric lifting straight up like hair with static. A garland of flowers landed in the surf. The marquee collapsed, poles and all, its canvas landing across the tables. There was the sound of glass breaking as the table settings were destroyed beneath the heavy canvas.

It was turning into an epic wedding day catastrophe. All of Alice's dreams of a fairy-tale wedding had turned into her worst nightmare. The wind pulled strands of her hair from her updo, and mist lay over her wedding dress like fine gossamer threads.

Her sisters were busy shepherding guests off the beach, their lovely sage green dresses being whipped violently around them. Isabelle's matching shawl was missing, and Lily's hair hung straight around her face, the hairclips loose in her tangle of hair.

Alice supposed she should cry. She wanted to.

From behind her, Thelma Schumacher, all decked out in lavender, looked up at the black sky and said, "It looks bad, I know, but rain on your wedding day is actually good luck."

"Really?" Alice said.

Thelma laughed and patted Alice's arm. "Everything is going to be fine."

Ahead of her, Jack leaned on his cane. A furrow deepened along Alice's forehead as she watched him. She knew that look on his face. It was familiar. It was his tell. He was in pain. It had been a long day from the beginning. A long week. She thought they'd never get here.

Her face softened as she watched him. He was talking to several people at once, trying to fix things. Trying to salvage the whole day. Trying to get it right. For her. Because that was what Jack did, always helping people. Always trying to make things better.

It was one of the many reasons she loved him. And despite the mist and that big black cloud overhead, Alice smiled.

Everything was going to be all right.

Everything *was* all right. Just as it was.

She had Jack, and what more could she ask for?

But she had an idea. It made her take charge. With both hands, she hiked up the hem of her wedding dress and made her way as quickly as she could to Jack. The flowers in her bouquet, still clutched in her hand, were beginning to wilt.

He smiled when he saw her, reached for her hand, and pulled her closer to him. "We're working on things. Are you all right?"

She smiled at him, loving him more in that moment than she ever had. "I'm fine. I have an idea."

"I'm all ears."

She leaned over and whispered in his ear and pulled back to watch his reaction.

"Are you sure?" he asked, searching her face.

"I am."

He clasped her hand, giving it a gentle squeeze. "I think it's a great idea."

"I'll let Isabelle and Lily know."

"And I'll start organizing moving everything. And everyone."

"We're only going to need the chairs and the food."

Jack nodded. "Everyone can hold their plates in their lap."

As she made her way to her sisters, her mother and her grandparents came to mind. She knew they would approve of her plan.

Isabelle placed her hand on Alice's arm as she approached. "We're working on it, Sparrow. Everything is going to be all right. Don't worry." There was a smudge of mascara beneath Isabelle's left eye.

"I know."

"We're asking around to see where we can go for the reception."

"Let's bring everyone back to the house," Alice said.

"It's not big enough! Where will everyone sit?" Lily said.

"We've got the whole downstairs. All we need to do is lay the food out on the dining room table and bring the chairs with us."

Simon interrupted, placing his arm around Lily. "Are we all right?"

"Alice thinks we should have the reception at the house."

His eyes widened. "Are you sure? I was going to suggest that Lily and I could host the party at our house."

But Alice shook her head. Lily and Simon's large home was definitely more suited, but it was up on the bluffs overlooking the lake, and that would mean getting everyone up there. Although the house on Star Shine Drive was smaller, it was closer. All the guests had to do was walk across the street.

"No, I want my reception at Gram's house. It feels right." She nodded to herself, happy with her choice. It did feel right. It felt . . . perfect.

It was funny how things had worked out for the best. She'd bemoaned the fact that many of her wedding guests couldn't make it. That a mix-up on the wedding invitation had cut her guest list by more than half. But how would Alice have fit a couple of hundred guests into the house on Star Shine Drive? It would have been impossible. No, it had worked out perfectly. The hem of her dress was dirty, but she didn't care. She hitched it up and smiled happily as she and Jack walked across the street amidst all their guests. They were married now, and nothing else mattered.

As she walked hand in hand with Jack, adjusting her gait to accommodate his use of the cane, she spied Lily and Simon ahead of them, arm in arm, gazing at each other as they walked, laughing and smiling, lost in each other, oblivious to everything going on around them. Parallel to them were Isabelle, Joe, and the kids. Joe's oldest, Kyle, walked with his best friend, Mimi Duchene, and his younger son, Aiden, was at Isabelle's side. The youngest, Casey, walked between Isabelle and Joe. Isabelle's gaze swung back and forth between Joe and his kids, and at one point, she reached over to ruffle Aiden's hair with a laugh. And ahead of the whole gang: Charlie and Luther, dashing back to the house. And just in time as the fine mist falling around them became more persistent.

Alice's heart wanted to burst.

As she neared the house, it became the focus of her attention, especially with the crowd descending upon it. Isabelle and Lily were right. It was a house that was meant to be lived in. It would be wrong to let it sit there empty for her own selfish, sentimental reasons.

She sighed with the realization that she couldn't hang on to it. It was time to let it go.

"You're okay?" Jack asked beside her.

"I'm happy, Jack."

The resulting smile from her new husband was breathtaking for its beauty.

It was true. She was happy.

Isabelle and Joe and Lily and Simon were the first ones back at the house, throwing open the doors and turning on lights. Dylan Satler had gone home for his van and had backed it up to the beach so all the chairs could be loaded into it. Kyle and Aidan had circled back to help him load up the chairs. Martha Cotter sent Mimi home for her crystal punch bowl. Sue Ann, Jackie Arnold, and Ben Enright had managed to salvage the flowers from the canopy and the collapsed tents and were currently carrying them into the house. Della and Sam gathered up the ribbons that had bedecked the chairs so they wouldn't end up all over the beach.

By the time Alice and Jack stepped into the house, the place was beginning to look transformed. The caterers had set up in the kitchen and carried chafing dishes to the dining room table. When the lights started to flicker, candles were located and placed on every available surface.

Word quickly spread that the DJ was a no-show, and Mimi offered to pull up a wedding playlist from her

Spotify account to play on the Monroe sisters' sound system.

The last ones through the door were Sue Ann, Jackie, Ben, Della, and Sam, their arms full of flowers and ribbons. Sue Ann and Della began to set up the flowers throughout the house.

"Just in time," Jackie said, pushing her hair off her face. "It's raining."

The house was crowded, but Alice loved the fact that part of her wedding was being held in the family home, which made it all the more special. She and Jack were first in line to walk around the dining room table, availing of the buffet that was set out before them. The table was crowded with chafing dishes of hot food, dinnerware, and napkins. They helped themselves, though Alice's stomach was in knots and she couldn't eat much. Outside was the constant rumble of thunder and the pelting of rain against the house.

As they sat in chairs with their plates on their laps, various people stood up with their champagne flutes in hand to toast the new bride and groom. After all the plates were cleared, the caterers brought in the wedding cake from the kitchen. As they were coming down the hall, Charlie bolted by them, pushing into one of the caterers and causing her to lose both her balance and her grip on the cake. Down it went with a crash, to everyone's silent horror. Hands clapped over mouths as they all stared in disbelief.

"I don't believe this," Alice whispered, mesmerized by the sight of their beautiful wedding cake with its buttercream frosting and raspberry filling in a cracked, broken heap on the floor. Simon and Lily were trying to pull Charlie off the remnants as he gulped as much as he could. Isabelle and Joe were also trying to get a hold of the wily Luther, who had joined his friend and was proving to be much more slippery.

"Luther, come here!" yelled Isabelle as the dog slipped out of her grasp.

Simon grabbed hold of his collar and said to Lily, "I'll take him home."

"It's for the best," Lily said with a wince. She turned to Alice and clasped her hands as if in prayer against her face. "I am so sorry, Alice."

"It's all right, I guess we should have expected that with the way the day has been going."

Lily did not appear mollified.

"And don't take Charlie home. He's part of the family."

"I don't want him ruining anything else," Lily said. She pursed her lips and said to him, wagging a finger, "You're grounded, mister."

Charlie responded by licking his lips. He still had some frosting on his nose.

"Let's get him away from the cake," Lily said to Simon.

He called the dog and took him out the front door as the caterers, apologetic, went about cleaning up the mess. Joe followed him, holding Luther close as he squirmed in his grasp.

"I think it's time for the first dance, now that dessert has been taken care of," Thelma quipped.

Alice frowned and said, "The song we picked is with the DJ." It was an obscure song, but it resonated with her and Jack.

"Maybe someone has it."

Alice stood from her chair and mentioned the name of it, but the blank expressions seemed pretty uniform from the group.

Thelma beckoned Mimi over with a wave. Mimi bent down and she whispered in her ear.

Mimi stood, smiling, and announced, "Thelma has the perfect song for you. It was the song she and Stan danced to at their wedding." She quickly queued it up on her phone.

Those sitting in the living room pushed their chairs back as far as they could, and Joe and Dylan rolled up the area rug and leaned it against the wall in the far corner of the room.

As the strains to Etta James's "At Last" began to play, Jack stood in the middle of the floor and held out his hand for Alice. She joined him, and he wrapped his arm around her waist and leaned on his cane with his other hand. Standing in one spot, they swayed together in place. Alice closed her eyes and rested her head on his shoulder, thinking that it had been the best day of her life.

Epilogue

The Following Year

Della stepped out into the backyard of her new home, a beach cottage on Sunrise Street, which ran between Seashell Lane and Moonbeam Drive. It was nice to own her own home. It was another first for her in her life. She'd settled in quickly.

It wasn't the house that had drawn her. It was the land that came with it. Years ago, the cottage next door had burned down, and the previous owners of Della's house had purchased the vacant property to add to their own. As soon as Della had pulled up with the realtor, she knew she was going to buy it. She didn't care that the kitchen needed to be overhauled. Didn't care that the place needed a new roof. Once she saw the size of the lot, her head filled with images of a large vegetable garden. She could practically picture her father there, standing at the edge of a bed of zucchinis growing with abandon, watering them with a green garden hose.

She'd purchased the house at the end of winter and when she moved in back in the spring, she focused on the outside of the house instead of the interior. As much as she would have liked to do all the work herself, in the end she had to hire a landscape company to get the yard and the garden beds cleaned up and ready for planting. After all, she had a business to run. They'd created a large rectangular bed for her vegetable garden. When she'd moved out of the family home, she'd taken, with her mother's permission, the small metal box that contained all her father's pasta recipes, written on index cards that were now yellow with age.

Some people here in Hideaway Bay liked to watch the sun set over Lake Erie in the evenings. But not Della. She liked to sit out in her backyard and look at her blooming vegetable garden. There were rows of staked tomatoes, and as soon as they were ready, she'd give some away and can the rest. Dylan had already built a storeroom in her basement.

The twilight cast lavender shadows around her yard. She leaned over and lit the citronella candle on the table. There was no breeze, but she could still smell the roses from the back of the garden. There were beds that lined the border of her yard, filled with all sorts of flowers and ornamental decorations. But her gaze always swung back to the tomato plants, growing tall.

There were two chairs parked there and her mother sat in one of them, a cane resting next to her. On some evenings, Della would pick up her mother after work and bring her over. They'd sit outside in companionable silence, enjoying the dwindling evening.

Della carried two plates. She handed one to her mother.

"What is this?"

"First tomato of the season," Della said excitedly.

Each plate held a tomato sandwich, just like her father used to make: two pieces of white bread, one buttered; a nice, thick slice of beefsteak tomato; and a sprinkle of salt.

"Just like your father used to do," Jeanne said. Her eyes were bright as she smiled at the memory of it.

Della sat down in the other chair and took her first bite, and the homegrown tomato was juicy and flavorful. Between mouthfuls, she reminded her mother, "Don't forget to make a wish like Dad used to do."

"Already done," her mother said, taking another bite of her sandwich.

Sam had had to work late that evening, but Della was expecting him soon. As she was thinking about him, he rounded the corner of the house. He wore a shirt and tie, but his suitcoat was draped over his arm. The weather was too warm for it.

"Hello, Mrs. Rossi," he said with a nod.

"How are you, Sam?" Mrs. Rossi said. She and Sam got on well and, with her being a retired nurse, there was always something to talk about.

Della jumped up out of her seat and greeted him with a kiss.

When she pulled away, he asked. "How are the tomatoes coming along?"

"We're just having a tomato sandwich," she said. "Sit down, I'll make you one."

He pulled up a third chair, close to the other two.

"You look tired, Sam," Della said.

He smiled and the lines in the corners of his eyes crinkled up. "Not too bad."

"Beer or wine?"

"Do you have beer?" he asked, knowing she was not a beer drinker.

But she did. She knew he liked the odd one, and she made it a point to always keep some on hand.

With a grin and a lift of an eyebrow, she said, "Ice cold."

"Sold."

Two years later

The smell of smoky barbecue and the sounds of laughter, conversation, and waves crashing against the shore filled the air of Hideaway Bay Beach.

It was the second-year anniversary of Alice and Jack Sterling. And this year the weather was so different from the day they got married. Not giving a hoot about the weather—after all, they'd survived a wedding day disaster—they'd decided to throw a big party on the beach for the residents of Hideaway Bay.

The area from the boardwalk to the end of Star Shine Drive had been designated for the party. There was a large tent, its white canvas sides secured to the spikes in the sand, not moving, for there was very little breeze. It would provide shelter from the hot sun or the rain, if there was any. But the sky was blue and cloudless, and the sun blazed that September day. Three sides of the tent were open, to aerate the inside and give the occupants a view.

Those who had chosen the tent as an escape from the sun were Thelma Schumacher, Martha Cotter, Mr. Lime, and Ben Anderson. They were joined at the table by Jeanne Rossi and her friends Lois, Mary, and Rose. Thelma had brought a dice game called Left, Center, Right, and had corralled the rest into playing along with her. Baddie Moore passed by and stood between Ben and Martha, commenting on the game until eventually, he gave up and joined in.

A volleyball net had been set up at the opposite end of the beach to avoid anyone in the tent getting hit by an errant ball.

The Monroe sisters were busy setting up the long line of buffet tables, securing plastic tablecloths over them with duct tape. Disposable plates and silverware were the first stop. Every resident had made a dish to share, except for Thelma and Martha. Thelma had provided a few buckets of Buffalo-style chicken wings with an accompanying platter of celery, carrots, and blue cheese. Martha had contributed two pans of chicken lo mein from her favorite Chinese restaurant.

The tables began to fill up very quickly with all sorts of donated dishes.

Isabelle surveyed it and said, "If anyone walks away hungry, it's their own fault."

"That's for sure," piped in Alice, sorting the coolers full of soft drinks and beer, determined to keep an eye on the beer cooler in case anyone underage decided to try something tricky.

"Would you stop lifting, please?" Isabelle said to Lily for what had to be the hundredth time.

"Stop!" Lily said, setting down a pan of barbecued hamburgers and bags of buns. Her belly bumped the edge of the table. Lily was due with her first baby at the end of the following month. It was a happy time for her and Simon.

Alice had similar news but had decided not to share it yet. She was still in the first trimester. She loved the fact that only she and Jack knew.

Ben Enright, manning the long commercial barbecue grill covered in barbecued ribs and chicken, turned to them and said, "We'll be ready to serve these up in ten minutes."

"Great," Isabelle said, hands on her hips in a Wonder Woman pose. "Because I'm starving."

"Simon and Joe can round everyone up to eat," Lily suggested, looking adorable in her flowery maternity dress.

"But let's make sure Thelma, Martha, Ben, and the rest of the elderly get in line first," she said, eyeing all the teenagers and young people on the beach, in the water, and at the volleyball net. "Or there will be nothing left."

"Good call," Alice said.

Lily's face widened in a smile. "Look who's coming! It's the Wrights." She nodded in the direction of Gram's house as the new owners, Jim and Stacey Wright, walked across the street. Jim carried their nine-month-old, a little boy with dark hair, and Stacey had their four-year-old daughter, Savanna, by the hand. The dark-haired four-year-old skipped by her mother's side, dressed in a daisy motif: her dress and white sandals had daisies on them, and she wore matching daisy barrettes in her hair.

They had done so much with the house. A month previous, they'd invited Isabelle, Lily, and Alice to come take a tour. All three sisters had found it strange to return to a home that had been in their family for almost six decades. There were toys and baby equipment strewn all over the place. But all that could not hide the extensive work that had been done.

The screen door had been replaced. Gone was the wicker furniture from the porch, to be replaced with contemporary cedar-wood porch furniture with bright red cushions. The exterior of the house had been painted white, and all the shutters had been replaced with brand-new red ones. The new look had taken some time to get used to.

The old shed where Lily had created her beach glass projects had been turned into a man cave for Jim, although he confessed he was so busy with work, the kids, and the house projects that he rarely had time to relax in it. But he was hopeful.

The only thing that was different in the front room was the furniture. The color scheme remained the same, with those robin's-egg blue bookshelves flanking the fireplace. But Stacey excitedly told them of her plans to remodel the room and give it a more updated look.

All the rooms upstairs had been given a fresh coat of paint. Savanna's room was a super-cute explosion of pink and daisies, her favorite flower.

The nursery was done in various shades of blue, the furniture all white. It had made Alice wistful for a baby of her own, not knowing at the time that it would be only a matter of weeks before she discovered that she was expecting.

But the biggest changes had been the bathroom and the kitchen. The old clawfoot tub was gone, to be replaced by a modern tub and shower. Stacey had said it was easier.

The kitchen was unrecognizable. Isabelle, Lily, and Alice had stood there with their mouths hanging open. The new kitchen was bright and sleek—all white with gray granite countertops, the walls painted a light gray with white woodwork. The old linoleum had been ripped out and replaced with a gray hardwood-effect tile floor. The layout had been changed as well. The refrigerator was moved, and there was a small island in the middle of the room. Alice complained about it later to her sisters, but Isabelle and Lily had raved about the changes. As Isabelle said, "It's their home now and they're putting their stamp on it, just like Gram and Granddad did all those years ago."

Begrudgingly, Alice agreed, but it would take her a bit to come around and realize that the kitchen did look better. She remembered Thelma's words, to never look over your shoulder, always be looking ahead, and she repeated that mantra to herself daily.

But now today, a month after their viewing, Alice was genuinely happy to see them. After all, she and Jack had had their own house built, a sprawling ranch bungalow with a big, enviable kitchen where she could bake to her heart's content. She hoped someday her own children and grandchildren would look back on the family home with the same fondness she had for her grandparents' home.

There were hugs all around, like the Wrights were old friends, but Alice supposed their common bond was that wonderful house. They spoke for a few minutes, and the Wrights informed them that they were taking a break from renovating until the spring because remodeling was costly. The sisters understood.

"Oh, there's Mimi!" Stacey said and she smiled and waved.

Alice, Isabelle, and Lily turned to see Mimi approaching them. Although a later addition to Hideaway Bay, she looked like she'd lived there all her life. Currently, she was away at college but home for the weekend.

"You look like you're missing your other half," Isabelle said with a grin. Joe's son, Kyle, was Mimi's best friend and in the last year, their relationship had turned romantic. He, too, was away at college, but couldn't come down this weekend because he had a big project due and had decided to hole up in his dorm.

"I know, right?" she said with a bubbly laugh. "I keep going to say something to him but then I realize he isn't there. How nutty is that?" She made a funny face to the baby, who giggled, then bent down and said hello to Savanna.

"Are you home for just the weekend?" Alice asked.

"Yes, I'm going back tomorrow night."

"Your grandmother must miss you," Lily said.

"We miss each other, but I try to come home as much as I can. We've upgraded her phone, and now we text every day!" Mimi said.

Wonders never cease, thought Alice.

"Are you sure you don't mind babysitting tonight?" Stacey asked. "Wouldn't you rather go out with friends?"

Mimi shook her head. "Nope. I'm looking forward to it."

"Great, because Jim and I are looking forward to a date night," Stacey said.

Alice tucked that away for future reference. The thought of having children with Jack and going out on a date and having a babysitter come to the house filled her with a sense of anticipatory euphoria.

Their little group broke off, Mimi dashing off to say hello to some friends she spotted, and the Wrights moving on with their children to say hello to the other residents of Hideaway Bay.

"How are you feeling about everything, Sparrow?" Lily asked.

Alice smiled. "I'm feeling great. I realize now that we sold the house to the perfect family."

"I was thinking the same thing," Isabelle said, hands on her hips.

"It feels right," Lily said.

They all agreed.

"I think Gram and Grandad would be happy," Alice said.

"Our grandparents were pragmatic people. Sensible. Loving and kind. And sometimes, you just have to move on," Lily said.

"True," Alice said, wistful.

A lone gull cried overhead as the three sisters stood there under the sharp September sun, thinking of all the memories they had, seeing the past, their grandparents on the front porch sitting there with their mother. This didn't make them sad. It made them grateful for having had that. But they were also happy that a new family had moved in and was loving the house the same way they had. That more happy memories were going to be made there at 12465 Star Shine Drive.

Author's Note

I hope you've enjoyed the Hideaway Bay series and the lives of Isabelle, Lily, Alice, Junie, Thelma, and Barb. I loved writing this series. When my mother's lifelong friends flew in from all over the country to see her in her last months, she remarked, 'Old friend are the best friends.' And I have to agree.

To stay up to date with new releases and receive exclusive bonus material, sign up for my newsletter here.

COMING SOON

Be on the lookout for my new series, The Lavender Bay Chronicles, coming out in 2024. The first book in the series, The Inn at Lavender Bay, will be out in March 2024.

ALSO BY MICHELE BROUDER

Coming in 2024
The Lavender Bay Chronicles

The Inn at Lavender Bay

Hideaway Bay Series

Coming Home to Hideaway Bay

Meet Me at Sunrise

Moonlight and Promises

When We Were Young

One Last Thing Before I Go

The Chocolatier of Hideaway Bay

Now and Forever

Hideaway Bay Series Books 1-3

Escape to Ireland Series

A Match Made in Ireland

Her Fake Irish Husband

Her Irish Inheritance

A Match for the Matchmaker

Home, Sweet Irish Home

An Irish Christmas

Escape to Ireland Box Set: Books 1-3

Happy Holidays Series

A Whyte Christmas

This Christmas

A Wish for Christmas

One Kiss for Christmas

A Wedding for Christmas

The Happy Holidays Box Set: Books 1-3

Printed in Great Britain
by Amazon